FACING WEST

A FOREVER WILDE NOVEL

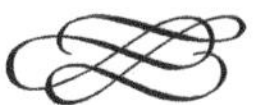

LUCY LENNOX

Cover Designer: Angstyg - www.AngstyG.com

Cover Photography: Wander Aguiar Photography - www.wanderaguiar.com

Editor: Anne Victory - www.VictoryEditing.com

Professional Beta Reading: Leslie Copeland (lcopelandwrites@gmail.com)

Sign up for Lucy's newsletter for exclusive content and to learn more about her latest books at www.LucyLennox.com!

❀ Created with Vellum

SERIES NOTE

The Forever Wilde series is set in the same world as the Made Marian series but features a different family and locations. It is not at all necessary to read the Made Marian novels to enjoy the Forever Wilde novels, and all Lucy Lennox books can be enjoyed on their own without reading the rest of the series.

Facing West, Forever Wilde book one, introduces the very large Wilde family from tiny, fictional Hobie, Texas. Each Forever Wilde novel will tell the story of a different Wilde child finding true love.

Happy reading!

Facing West is dedicated to those of you who know how unlikely a predominantly gay family is but happily allow me to create one anyway. Realistic or not, these families are a joy to create and get to know. I hope you enjoy meeting the Wilde family as much as I enjoy writing about them.

THE WILDE FAMILY

Grandpa (Weston) and **Doc** (William) Wilde (book #6)

Their children:

Bill, Gina, Brenda, and Jaqueline

Bill married Shelby. Their children are:

Hudson (book #4)

West (book #1)

MJ (subplot in book #5)

Saint (book #5)

Otto (book #3)

King (book #7)

Hallie

Winnie

Cal (book #8)

Sassy

Gina married Carmen. Their children are:

Quinn

Max

Jason

Brenda married Hollis. Their children are:

Kathryn-Anne (Katie)

William-Weston (Web)

Jackson-Wyatt (Jack)

Jacqueline's child:

Felix (book #2)

PROLOGUE

WEST - SIXTEEN YEARS AGO

"*Someone might hear us.*"

I honestly didn't care. I finally had a cute guy's hands on me and was having a hard time keeping my breathing under control. I was sixteen and horny as heck, so my biggest concern was trying not to come before there was even a hand on my dick.

"Right there, yes." I gasped as his hand finally fumbled awkwardly over my fly. Any shred of concern I'd had over making out in the movie theater of my small town had flown out the window the moment one of the hottest guys in school had leaned over during Spanish class and whispered those words into my ear.

"*Quiero chuparte.*" I want to suck you off.

What I'd originally thought was a joke had turned out to be an invitation.

I'd agreed to meet him at the movies the following night. I hadn't known the guy very well since he was fairly new in town, but I was flattered as all hell he'd picked me to ask out. We'd been on the same baseball team for half a season, and I'd only just noticed him checking out my ass in my uniform pants a few weeks before.

Oh, he was sly about it, but it was there. I'd tested my theory after a game one night when I made a show of leaning over to pick up some stray equipment right in front of him. I thought for sure he was going to stab someone with the wood he popped. When I'd caught him staring, he'd blushed crimson and spouted off a bunch of bullshit about my having something on the back of my uniform pants.

It had surprised me, to be honest. He was the kind of guy who cracked queer jokes and called everything he didn't like "gay." A typical sporty dude who fit the homophobe jock stereotype to a *T*. But once I realized he was into me, I assumed all that bluster was for show, done out of fear of being discovered as gay in small-town Texas.

I'd gotten up the nerve to throw him a wink, letting him know I was cool with it. After that, it was just a matter of dropping flirty hints here and there to see whether he'd flirt back or punch me in the face. Lucky for me, he'd flirted back. Well, maybe not flirted so much as whispered the hottest line of Spanish that had ever been spoken.

He fumbled for my zipper and finally got his hand into my pants. *Thank fucking god.*

"Yes," I hissed as his hand wrapped around my cock.

"Shut the hell up or someone's going to hear us," he growled.

Like I cared. I was so hot and turned on my head was beginning to buzz.

"Oh god" I couldn't help but gasp as his hand squeezed pressure up and down my raging hard-on. I remembered the giant wad of paper napkins I'd grabbed in the lobby and wanted to be ready so I didn't have to walk out of the theater with giant come stains all over my clothes.

"Shh," he snapped again. "Cut that shit out, or I'm stopping."

Jeez, what was his problem?

"Gonna come." I hissed through my teeth as quietly as I could. There was no telling why I even warned him. Maybe I had some fantastical notion he'd want to lurch forward and suck down my release like it was a gift from the gods or something. No such luck.

Regardless, my release hit in a blaze of fucking glory. I felt like the king of orgasms with come shooting everywhere. In my imagination, it spattered my chest, my face, my partner, the popcorn bucket, the seat in front of me, and the projector high above our last-row seats.

In reality, it barely covered the guy's fist.

Because, let's be real, I may or may not have already jacked off three times that day in anticipation of the hookup.

After tossing him some of the rough paper napkins from my pocket, I used others to wipe myself off before tucking everything away again.

Once we were cleaned up and facing front, I watched the group of actors preparing to rob a bank on the big screen. My movie partner mumbled something, and I turned to face him.

"What?"

"That's a little selfish, don't you think?"

The high I'd been riding came crashing down with his words.

He continued. "Seems to me, you owe me one," he said with a smirk, unbuckling his belt and opening his own pants.

It's not that I disagreed—for sure I wanted him to feel as good as I had, but I'd just kind of thought we'd go for round two after catching our breaths and then he could be on the receiving end.

Honestly, it didn't matter to me. I was horny enough to make out like that all night long. And with someone that sexy? Yes please. Sign me up. If things kept going that way, I'd have an actual boyfriend by the end of the night.

I threw up the armrest between us and lunged for his face with my own, crashing my lips down on his in what was probably an overeager kiss. He shoved me off, sputtering, and put his strong hands on my shoulders to push me down. Ah, okay. He wanted a blow job.

I was cool with that. It was for sure on the long list of sex acts I'd barely gotten a chance to begin checking off in my brief time on earth. Despite never having done it before, I had full confidence in my abilities to at least give it my full enthusiasm.

After quickly dropping to my knees on the nasty cement floor, I reached for his open fly and took him out.

Oh god I might come again just from touching it. It's a hard fucking penis. In my hands. And it's not mine. Jesus.

I lurched forward with little to no grace and put my mouth on it.

We both groaned, and I felt the chair at my back shift. Was someone sitting that close to us and we hadn't realized it?

Who the fuck cares—I have a cock in my mouth. An actual stiff cock.

I licked and sucked like a newborn calf, hungry for any positive reaction out of the guy above me. The sounds he made were like gold stars on a child's work sheet, and I tried diligently to earn more. It seemed to last forever but was probably only about ten point five seconds before he was yanking on my hair and coming all over my face.

Thank god for the supply of napkins I still had in my pocket.

After cleaning up the second time, I lay back in my chair, feeling triumphant. I was the king of sex. I was the motherfucking king of cocks and orgasms. Hopefully, someone had seen that display of manly perfection I'd just put on. I wanted to shout it from the rooftops.

I just gave Curtis Billingham head and rocked it.

Who was I going to tell first? For sure my brother Hudson. And maybe—

"Don't tell anyone what we did," he warned in a growly voice—the mean kind of growl, not the sexy kind.

I let out a breath. Fuck.

Fuck.

I should have realized he was one of those guys—happy in the closet and not about to tell anyone his "shameful secret." His antigay rhetoric hadn't been a front after all. It had been real.

My face felt numb. I couldn't decide if it was from the oral calisthenics I'd done or the sting of humiliation I felt at having gone down on someone who clearly didn't want me for more than that. Had I really not realized the guy was only using me to get off?

I felt like an idiot. Like I should have known it was all too good to be true.

"Why not?" I asked anyway, unable to look at him.

His voice came out high and squeaky. "Are you fucking kidding? My dad would kick my ass. And probably yours too."

"He will not. What makes you even say that? Tons of people in this town are gay."

After I used the "g" word, he sucked in a breath. "Will you lower your goddamned voice, West? I'm not gay, you idiot. Are you trying to piss me off?"

"Fine," I said, lowering to a quieter whisper. "You just got blown by a dude. Wanna explain how you're not gay? You asked me out, remember?"

If looks could kill, he'd be sitting next to my corpse.

"I'm sixteen and horny as fuck," he snapped. "Assumed a pretty mouth like yours could suck cock with the best of them, so I decided to test my theory. You've been making eyes at me for weeks. It doesn't make me gay to take someone up on their obvious desire to blow me."

Humiliation bloomed hot all over my body. He hadn't been interested in me, just a willing orifice? I stared at him. "You gave me a hand job first. Not to mention *you're* the one who offered to blow *me* in Spanish class, not the other way around."

"So I got the words wrong. I never was any good at Spanish."

Seriously? The guy was an ass. Why hadn't I seen that? Was I *that* bad of a judge of character? No, mostly just *that* blind with lust and hormones. I felt so stupid. I'd thought it was the start of having my first boyfriend—someone who'd show me off and flirt with me in halls at school. Someone who'd come to family dinner and cheer for me during our family's crazy board game competitions.

Someone who'd smile when I walked in a room and kiss me just because.

I'd been so wrong. So naive.

"Not a word about this, West," he snarled. "You don't want this getting back to my father. Trust me on that."

"What makes you think he's such a homophobe?"

"Because I heard him tell Father Roman that the only reason he wouldn't marry his girlfriend was because of her queer kid. Well, that and the fact the kid's a troublemaker."

"Who?" I asked, knowing pretty much everyone in town.

Curt snorted. "Nico Salerno. That kid's got problems, just like his sister. No wonder my dad can't bring himself to pop the question." He said that last part with a laugh but not before I heard a sharp intake of breath from the next row.

Suddenly a scrawny guy stood up from where he must have been crouched down in the seat in front of us. He whipped his face around to us, eyes flashing and dark, overgrown hair hanging in his face.

"Fuck you," he spat before bolting out of the row of seats toward the exit.

"Shit, he's going to tell the manager." Curt stood to go after him. "Gonna beat his fucking ass if he tells anyone."

I shoved him back into his seat, deciding I was done with this "date" anyway. "I'll take care of it."

I raced out of the theater and caught up with the kid before he reached the lobby. "Wait up," I called.

His steps faltered, and he glanced over his shoulder at me. There was something familiar about him, and I realized with a sinking stomach that I recognized him. He was the kid Curt had just been talking about, the troublemaker. He was a couple of years younger than I was, but had a sister around my age.

"Nico, right?" I asked.

"No."

That was the first lie Nico ever told me. But it sure as hell wouldn't be the last.

I stepped closer, holding my hands out in an effort to keep him from bolting. "Look," I said. "I'm sorry you heard that." And I meant it.

He studied me from under thick, dark lashes, lips tightened in anger and face flushed in embarrassment. He shoved his hands in his pants, and that's when I noticed the bulge straining against his zipper. He'd heard us getting off. It had turned him on.

"Doesn't matter. It's the truth," he said in a huff. "Everyone in town knows it. Makes no difference to hear him say it."

I could see the hurt and anger coming off him in waves, and I hated I was one of the causes.

"The guy's full of shit."

"This whole town is full of shit," he said defiantly.

I couldn't help but smirk at him. Nico was kind of cute with those stormy eyes and pouty lips. I shook my head to clear it of the stupid lust haze. What the hell was my problem? It was thoughts like that that had landed me in that damned movie theater to begin with. *Never trust the lust thoughts, West,* I thought.

"What're you going to do? Leave?"

I'd meant it as a joke, but his eyes darkened at the suggestion.

"Come to think of it, yes," he said. "That's exactly what I'm going to do."

Six weeks later, Nico Salerno disappeared from Hobie, Texas, and his family never saw him again.

CHAPTER 1

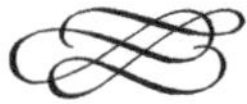

NICO - CURRENT DAY

"Where's the king?" I asked when my best friend Griff and his husband Sam showed up at my tattoo shop empty-handed. I'd been looking forward to their visit to San Francisco all week but was surprised to see them show up without the baby.

"Don't worry, we dropped Benji off at Mom and Dad's so you wouldn't have to deal," Griff said, leaning in for a hug.

"What do you mean, wouldn't have to deal?" I said.

Sam rolled his eyes and started looking at some of the premade designs hanging on the walls. "Everyone knows babies aren't your thing, Nico. Whenever you're around him, you get weird."

My eyes flashed to Griff. "I do not get weird."

"You do. It's okay. I get it," he said with a laugh. "It's too bad though, we could use a competent babysitter. Blue and Tristan have their hands full with their own crew, and Mom and Dad are going to be torn between Benji and Wolfe when we're in town."

What I should have said was that they were wrong, that I was fine babysitting, but we all knew that was a load of crap. As much as I hated to admit it, babies truly weren't my thing. I'd never been interested in them. Maybe it's because they were so damned vulnerable or breakable. Or they were loud and covered in puke all the time. I didn't know, and it really didn't matter. As a single, gay man, it wasn't something that came up often in my life.

Until my best friend had moved to Napa and started a family.

"Well, it's true I don't make a good babysitter, but I can help in other ways," I said, reaching behind the counter to where I'd stashed my notebook. "Here are a few sketches based on Sam's concept for the tattoos."

I opened the book to the page I'd dog-eared. On it was a dragon that looked a lot like the one I'd inked on Griff's shoulder years before. But instead of a large, adult dragon, it was a little roly-poly baby version, and instead of bright green eyes like Griff's, it had warm brown ones like Sam's. Woven into the pattern of the scales on its tail was the name Benji.

Griff gasped from over my shoulder, and I turned to face him. His watery eyes skipped past me and locked onto Sam's.

"Sunshine," he whispered to his husband. "Holy cow."

"C'mere," Sam murmured to Griff, reaching out to pull him into a tight hug.

As they embraced, Griff turned, catching my eye over Sam's shoulder and breathed. "*Nico.* You freaking nailed it."

I nodded and turned away as if to ready my supplies, but really I needed a chance to catch my breath. Their raw intimacy cut through me, exposing parts of myself I never cared to examine very closely. I'd never been one to get close to others. In fact, my friendship with Griff was really the sum total of the close relationships I'd had in the past fifteen years with the exception of one selfish prick I'd been stupid enough to fall for when I was a teenager.

It felt nice to be appreciated for something I was good at. And it was especially good to hear the compliment from my best friend's mouth. It had been a while since we'd had a moment like that. It wasn't that I begrudged my best friend his happiness with the man he loved, it was just that when Griff found Sam, he no longer needed me the same way as before.

I'd spent many years thinking Griff was the man for me. We'd lived together on the streets as teenagers and been tight as teeth ever since.

But when Sam came along, things changed. Griff was no longer mine, and the loss of that imagined future together had left me feeling particularly lonely and set adrift.

I quickly shook off the feeling of self-pity and forced myself to focus on the task at hand. I didn't need what they had. I'd been more than fine for years doing my thing—embracing independence and letting random hookups meet my needs. No one was worth keeping around for longer than a good lay. I'd learned that the hard way years ago. Physical satisfaction from one-nighters, emotional satisfaction from friends and clients. It had worked for me for years. I didn't want the ridiculous, sugar-sweet nonsense with another person, so there was no need to be affected by this.

And screw melancholy in general. No one wanted to spend time with the mopey downner in the group.

"Who's first?" I asked as cheerfully as I could. Griff tilted his head and cocked a brow at me. I gave him a smile of reassurance and gestured for them to follow me back to a private room, leaving my cell phone under the front counter to avoid any interruptions.

By the time the tattoos were done, I felt a strange combination of tired and antsy. The guys asked me to join them for a drink afterward, and we headed to one of our favorite clubs.

"I didn't think you old men would have the energy for dancing anymore," I teased once we found a table with our drinks in hand.

"We don't. We're just trying to pretend so you don't think we're losers," Sam said honestly. Griff barked out a laugh.

"He's right. We only wish we were still cool club types," he agreed. "But now that we're here, I'm definitely going to get Sam's sweet ass out on the dance floor. C'mon. You too, Nico."

Griff took a long pull of his beer while I threw back the two shots I'd gotten. I knew by the itchiness I'd felt earlier at the shop that I needed to find someone to blow a little steam off with once Griff and Sam were gone.

"Okay, let's do this," I said, standing up and turning back to hold my hand out to Sam. "Dance with me. It'll make Griff jealous," I said with a grin.

Sam's face morphed into a mischievous smirk as he took my hand. "Sounds good."

Without looking up from his beer, Griff spoke loudly enough for us both to hear. "You think it'll make me jealous, but all it will make me is horny as hell."

Me too, I thought.

When we found a spot on the crowded dance floor, Sam pressed up against my back and put his arms around my waist and his chin on my shoulder. His deep voice slid into my ears, making me shiver. "As if he's not horny all the time as it is."

I turned slightly so he could hear my response. "Oh please, you guys have been together long enough. Surely things are getting old and boring by now."

He chuckled. "Hardly. What about you? Any prospects? Are we looking to get you laid tonight?"

"Yes please," I said quickly.

"A cute twink, right? Twinkier than you anyway?" Sam teased in my ear as Griff joined us.

I rolled my eyes. Griff and Sam had only ever seen me with little guys, but that night I was in the mood for something different. Something I rarely let myself have.

"No. I'm thinking tonight I wanna be manhandled. Couple of bears oughta do it."

Griff danced in front of me with his hands on my hips, making a Nico sandwich with his husband. At my words, his eyebrows rose up high enough to disappear beneath his curly mop of hair.

"The hell?" he asked.

I shrugged, taking the opportunity to preen back against Sam like I was marking him with my scent or something. Griff growled and pulled me closer to him and away from Sam. I heard Sam chuckle and saw his hand come up in front of me to cup Griff's cheek.

"Simmer down, Foxy," he warned. "You know Nico's not my type."

Regardless, Sam moved around to dance against Griff's back, shooting me an apologetic smile. I winked at him to let him know there were no hard feelings. They both knew I respected the hell out of their marriage and would never do anything to get between them. We'd gone out dancing a million times before, and the two of them learned that they loved using me as their plaything on the dance floor, not only to turn each other on but to convince other men to pay attention to me. It was a game the three of us had gotten used to playing, and we'd discovered it benefited all three of us equally.

Griff's hands came up my chest until they rested on either side of my neck. "Bears? As in multiple big guys?"

I shrugged. "Maybe I like to mix it up sometimes."

"You know you'd have to bottom, right?" Griff asked with narrowed eyes. "You don't bottom. Ever."

Sam grumbled something about not wanting to know how Griff knew what I did and didn't do in bed.

"Not true," I corrected. "And stop asking questions. Just find me two big guys. I don't care if they're bears or not. I want muscles."

"What's going on with you, Nico?" Griff asked. "You have a death wish? Why won't you let us fix you up on an actual date? You know, like with someone you can actually forge a relationship with rather than a one-and-done?"

"Never mind. Jesus, forget about it, find me a little guy."

Sam brought a hand up to cover Griff's mouth. "Don't listen to him, Nico," Sam said. "If you're in the mood for a bear tonight, we'll make it happen. What about that one over there?" He nodded in the direction of a rough-looking man who looked to be about ten years older and fifty pounds heavier—all of it muscles.

"Yes please," I said, trying not to whimper.

"What the hell?" Griff mumbled. "That guy will chew you up and spit you out."

One can hope, I thought.

Sam maneuvered us over to where the man was dancing by himself. I turned my back to Griff, allowing him to dance against my ass as I crooked my finger at the older guy. He joined the three of us, dancing face-to-face with me long enough to encourage Griff and Sam to break away and dance on their own.

"Well aren't you adorable? Love the ink," the man grumbled in my ear. Normally, being treated like a twink drove me up the damned wall. I tried hard to be the dominant one in all my hookups because I never wanted people to think I was small or weak. I'd had enough of being treated as small and weak to last a lifetime. But when it came right down to it, in the dark of night and only to myself, I had to admit that I really did want to be manhandled by someone bigger than me sometimes. I also wanted to be taken care of and have someone to treat me like a spoiled princess, but that was a secret I barely admitted to myself, much less anyone else.

"Thank you," I said to the man, leaning into his chest farther and wrapping my arms around his waist. "What're you looking for tonight?"

"Whatever it is, you're it."

"You have any friends?" I asked, hoping like hell the answer was yes. I couldn't do one-on-one. It was too much, too intense. I didn't want to be anyone's sole focus this evening.

"Sure do. See that guy at the bar with the leather vest?"

I looked over and saw the man he gestured to. A smile appeared on my face like the Cheshire cat. The man looked like he could pound the hell out of my ass and shove my face in the mattress while doing it. The perfect combo for my current mood. "He with you?" I asked.

"My husband," he said proudly.

"No kidding? You think he'd be okay with a third tonight?"

"I know he would, sweetheart. Come with me."

~

SEVERAL HOURS later when I found my way home significantly more relaxed and retrieved my forgotten cell phone from behind the reception counter of the shop, I noticed a missed call and voice mail. It was an attorney from a long-forgotten lake town in Texas named Hobie, calling with a message that Adriana Salerno had died, leaving me sole custody of her baby daughter.

My stomach turned over violently, almost causing me to vomit all over the newly swept floor of the tattoo parlor. I hadn't seen Adriana in what seemed like a million years but was really just fifteen. Since I'd left Hobie for good and sworn I'd never look back.

Oh god.

I replayed the message to see if I'd heard the name correctly. Sure enough, the message said Adriana Salerno.

My sister.

CHAPTER 2

WEST

If there was one thing I wasn't expecting to see in the small Catholic church in my quaint little hometown, it was some crazy-ass, purple-and-blue-haired dude covered in tattoos and piercings. I wondered how the hell he'd transported from the London punk era to modern-day, small-town Texas. Adriana Salerno, for whom we'd all gathered, hadn't ever left the Lone Star state. At least that's what she'd told me during one of those long hours she'd been in labor with Pippa. So how the hell would she have ever met a strange character like that?

Maybe he was in the wrong place. Perhaps he was just passing through town on his way to an emo seminar and decided to stop in and light a candle for the loss of his ability to blend in.

I forced myself to look away. He was too far toward the back of the church for me to pick out any details besides the ink and hair color, so I tried to focus back on the casket at the front.

Adriana.

Hands down the closest friend I'd had in years besides my siblings. I still couldn't even begin to wrap my head around her sudden death.

I looked across the group of townspeople gathered in the church and thought about how many of us had loved her. From her regulars at the bakery to the ladies at my practice who looked forward to her visits and the kids who took her volunteer art classes at the community center. Everyone recognized what a warmhearted young woman she'd become—how cheerful she was and the fact that she'd give you the shirt off her back if you needed it.

And now she was in that fucking box.

She hadn't always been that kind soul. Years before, she'd gone through some bad shit and chosen a rough road. But as soon as she'd gotten out of high school and had to rely on herself, things had started to change. This final year, the one in which she'd gotten pregnant, had solidified the changes in her for the whole town to see. She'd done it for Pippa.

The tiny bundle in my arms squirmed and squeaked. I looked down at the perfect little face beginning to come out of the comfort of slumber, and I quickly reached into the backpack at my feet to find the bottle I'd prepared before heading to the service. I tried desperately to get the formula into the baby's mouth in time, but I wasn't quick enough.

A lusty wail flooded the tiny church building like the very personification of my own heartbreak. Frantic, hungry cries bounced off the walls and shocked the congregation into silence. My hands shook as I tried my hardest to shove the bottle into her little mouth before I dared lose my control and join her in her sobs. A crashing sound came from somewhere in the back of the church, but I could only focus on what was in front of me in order to keep from losing my shit.

Even though I was a family physician who'd worked miracles in the past, I wasn't able to fix this child. To make it better for her. To take her pain away. To go back in time and save her mother. All I could do was feed her and hold her close.

I couldn't tell the little bundle in my arms that her mama was coming back for her, because her mama was gone. Adriana, my strong, beautiful friend, had left forever.

And Pippa was all alone.

Once she had grabbed a few strong pulls from the nipple, she settled into a softer rhythm of suckling interspersed with little breathing sounds. When the short service was over, I passed the baby over to the woman next to me. Goldie was one of the senior nurses at my practice and had been able to get temporary custody of Pippa through her work as a foster parent. I'd given her paid leave as long as she needed it to take care of the four-month-old.

Goldie had spent the entire service bawling her eyes out and moaning Pippa's name under her breath every few minutes. If I hadn't already been dealing with a broken heart, the sounds of her grief would have broken my heart clear in half. I knew that during whatever moments of clarity Goldie'd had during the service, she'd most likely prayed to the Virgin Mary to deliver Pippa into the loving arms of the couple who was so desperate to adopt her.

Jennifer and Daniel Warner were sitting across the aisle from us in the opposite pew. I'd noticed Jenn glance over at the baby every few minutes during the service. She kept her hands either clutched together in her lap or folded inside Daniel's larger ones between them. I had very mixed feelings about the Warners adopting Pippa. On the one hand, I knew they'd been trying for a long time to have a second child, and they were already wonderful parents to their six-year-old son Nathan. On the other hand, I felt a proprietary ownership of Pippa. I'd been there for Adriana's pregnancy, Pippa's delivery, and the first four months of her life.

I'd envisioned helping Adriana raise her—not as a parent, obviously, but a good friend. Adriana had been alone and had never revealed who the baby's father was. She finally confessed the truth about her pregnancy to me the night she died, and she'd made me swear to make sure Pippa knew how much she was wanted.

Adriana and I hadn't been close friends until she came to me for care during her pregnancy. I'd known her, of course. Everyone in Hobie had known her. And she'd been in some of my high school classes growing up. But it wasn't until her prenatal care and subsequent delivery of Pippa that we'd become close. The long hours of her labor had been a bonding experience unlike any I'd ever known. She'd told me all kinds of things she'd never told another soul.

Once the baby was here, I'd become her support system. She was alone, and I knew there was no way a single parent should have to handle everything on her own.

Adriana had just been settling into a routine and needing less help with the baby when she'd gotten the pulmonary embolism that had suddenly ended her life. With Goldie's help, I'd immediately taken over Pippa's care until social services had forced us to turn her over to them. Luckily, it had only taken several hours to process her back into Goldie's care, and I lived in fear of what it would be like when I no longer had access to her whenever I wanted.

I followed Goldie out of the church, noticing the punk dude was no longer sitting in the back pew. Once I stepped into the bright sun of the churchyard, I spotted him standing off to the side, speaking to Honovi Baptiste, an attorney in town. As my eyes adjusted to the sunlight, I noticed the man with the blue-and-purple hair was actually strikingly beautiful in a way that looked familiar to me. Well, he would have been beautiful if he weren't sporting a scowl on his face and wearing clothes that looked like he'd borrowed them from someone's great uncle Melvin.

Despite the ridiculous button-down shirt and khaki trousers, the man was the furthest thing from a traditional Catholic churchgoer. His hair was short and dark on the back and sides but long on top and colored a rich purple with alternating stripes of deep turquoise. He ran his hand through it in apparent frustration, which made the colored locks ripple like an animation of a My Little Pony shaking out his mane. His ear was lined with tiny spikes and hoops, and as I walked closer, I noticed a small silver barbell through one dark eyebrow, a small loop in one of his nostrils, and twin piercings on his full bottom lip. He had tattoos peeking out from his cuffs and collar as well as on his hands and fingers. I couldn't help but wonder what ink and piercings might be hidden by his clothes, and the thought made my dick twitch. I ground my teeth at the inappropriateness of my response to this absurd character at my friend's goddamned funeral.

Fair or not, I blamed the asshole for my response to him. He should have stayed away from Adriana's service and met up with his lawyer some other time. He probably needed someone to defend him from a petty crime. Maybe the outfit was meant to make him look like an upstanding citizen in court. As if that were possible.

Before I had a chance to lead Goldie to where I'd parked my truck, I heard Honovi call out to me.

"West, come over here, will you?" he said. "You too, Mrs. Banks."

Goldie and I turned to join Hon and his client.

The punk saw Goldie holding Pippa, and it was like he'd laid eyes on a horrible ghost of some kind. Or an alien erupting from someone's face. He looked pale and terrified. I wondered who on earth could be so afraid of a tiny baby and more importantly *why* someone could. Or if he was a client of Hon's, maybe he was simply scared about his trial.

Hon reached out to shake my hand before stepping toward Goldie to fawn over Pippa.

"Weston Wilde, Goldie Banks, this is Nico Salerno," Hon said absently as he continued to coo at the baby. My stomach flipped, and my ears began to buzz as his words started to click together like puzzle pieces in my head. Hon continued, "Adriana's brother. He's here to take custody of Pippa."

My jaw dropped, and I stared at the man in front of me. He didn't even look twenty-five years old, and he was so stiff with attitude a strong breeze could knock him over. He was the unlikeliest man in the world to make a decent father for Pippa. *This* was Adriana's long-lost brother? The good-for-nothing punk who'd gotten his precious feelings hurt and taken off when he was a kid?

"Like hell," I growled, reaching over to scoop Pippa and her blankets from Goldie's arms and hold her to my chest.

Hon's eyes widened in surprise, and the purple-haired guy—Nico—did the same. Both men and Goldie looked stunned speechless at my reaction. I was usually the perfect citizen. Mister Manners and the town's friendly doctor. But not this time. Not on the day I buried my friend and was hit with the awful fact of Pippa growing up without her.

There was no way in hell I was letting this stranger take Adriana's baby girl. If he wanted her, he would have to go through me.

And that little emo dude had no idea what I was capable of when my heart was broken.

I turned to mumble an apology to Goldie before I jerked open the door to my truck, strapped Pippa in the baby car seat as quickly as I could, and peeled out of the lot.

CHAPTER 3

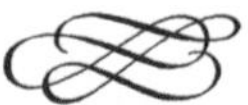

NICO

I stood there staring at the back of the dark truck as it sped out of the lot.

What the hell had just happened?

I felt like I was in a daze. Like everything that had happened since listening to that voice mail two nights before had been a hallucination. I'd flown in on the red-eye that morning and rented a car to make it to the service just in time. I'd snuck into the back row of the church and just tried to keep my head down. I was still in deep denial about everything.

When the baby's cries had rung out through the church, I'd jumped, knocking some kind of brass platter to the stone floor in a horrible racket. It felt like the entire group of mourners turned to stare at me. As if I hadn't already attracted enough attention in the entire town just by showing up.

It had taken every ounce of my courage to return to Hobie after the attorney had given me the details of Adriana's death the morning before.

Adriana Cristina Salerno. My older sister by three years. The sister I'd tried looking up to before I'd left all those years before but who'd repeatedly let me down.

I'd slunk out of the pew and out the back door of the church. I hadn't been able to take it anymore. Too many memories of Sunday services, sitting up straight and trying to stay awake during the incessant incantations of the priest's rituals. I'd sworn to myself I'd never set foot in another church as long as I lived, and up until then, I'd been able to keep that promise.

By the time I'd made it to my rental car in the parking lot, my hands were shaking so hard I would have done anything for a shot of tequila. Instead, I crossed my arms on the frame across the top of the driver's side door and leaned my forehead against them before letting out a deep sigh.

Only a few minutes later, the attorney had found me and introduced himself, pulling me back toward the churchyard to meet the baby. Adriana's baby. My sister's baby.

My baby now.

Well, at least until I could find a way to sign away my rights to her and find her a good set of adoptive parents. Mr. Baptiste had assured me over the phone that there was a wonderful young family ready to adopt her. I just needed to come to town long enough to sign the appropriate paperwork and facilitate the dispensation of the rest of Adriana's assets, including her house and the bakery she owned in town.

When the attorney had called out to a tall man and older woman, he explained that the older woman was the baby's current foster parent and the man was the town's family doctor.

"He was also Adriana's friend," Mr. Baptiste said quietly before the man himself stepped close enough to be introduced.

Weston Wilde. But not exactly the same West I'd had a secret crush on as a young teen.

This West was tall, at least five inches taller than I was, and tight with muscle that didn't quite fit the clean-cut suit he wore. His thick blond hair curled deliciously with waves that begged for fingers in them. Light green eyes bore into me, and I felt my balls tighten inappropriately. I studied the man for another split second before looking up at the deep blue sky and mentally shooting God the bird.

Really, motherfucker? You're really going to dangle a guy like that in front of me in the middle of all this bullshit? Couldn't he have lost his hair by now or some shit?

What a fucking joke.

He was, of course, perfect—he'd aged beautifully with laugh lines next to his eyes that took the tiniest edge off his otherwise aggressively masculine face. He was a fashion magazine's take on a cowboy.

The man's face was etched out of goddamned *man* stone. Like Charlton Heston and Robert Redford got together to chisel a man's man out of desert man granite and came up with this manly version of—

"Like hell," I heard him snap. I blinked and tried desperately to replay what could have happened while I was busy fantasizing about man stuff.

Before I could figure out what the hell was going on, he'd loaded up an arm full of pink blankets and sped off.

"Um," I began.

"Oh heavens," the older lady muttered.

"Dammit." The attorney sighed.

"He'll be at—" the woman began.

"Yep," Mr. Baptiste said gently. "Hop in, Goldie. Nico, why don't you follow me in your car?"

After only a short drive through the little town, I saw the attorney's vehicle pull into a long, familiar driveway surrounded by tall fir trees. My foot slammed on the brakes before I had a chance to make the turn in after him.

My mother's place.

The shit shack I'd grown up in until I left home at age fifteen. I took a deep breath and resigned myself to the memories that were sure to flood me when I came around the corner to see the ramshackle trailer.

As I inched down the driveway, I realized how much more wooded the lot had become in my absence. Trees grew together across the narrow drive to form a shaded canopy, and I took a moment to brace myself for the sight of the shabby, brown box I'd spent my childhood in.

Only, when I came around the final curve, what I saw wasn't what I remembered. Instead of the shit shack, I saw a tidy, light pink cottage with a wide front porch complete with a couple of rocking chairs and hanging ferns. The ferns were like a punch to the gut because I knew Adriana had to have bought them herself before she died.

The house looked nothing like I would have pictured my sister living in. At least the Adriana I remembered from years before. That woman had been hard, dark, and brooding. It didn't make any sense.

I parked my car in the wide gravel parking area to the side of the house and took a moment to look around and orient myself. The small cottage took up much more room than the trailer that had been there before, but in the distance I could still see glimpses of the shining blue water of Lake Hobie through the trees.

Sure enough, the dark pickup truck we'd been hoping to spot was parked closest to the house, and Mr. Baptiste and Mrs. Banks were stepping out of the attorney's vehicle. I joined them as they approached the front door and rang the bell.

"He's probably out back on the swing," the older woman said softly.

The swing. They couldn't mean the tire swing that had been there when I was a child. That thing had been on its last legs years ago. I hopped back off the porch and made my way around back, seeing immediately the swing she'd referred to. It hung from the same enormous oak branch the old tire swing had been attached to, but now it was made of a smooth, wide board hanging from strong, thick ropes.

Just as the woman had suspected, West sat on the swing with the baby in his arms. At some point, he'd lost the suit jacket and rolled up the sleeves of his white button-down shirt and was leaning over, whispering and pressing kisses to the baby's head. Despite the fact he'd basically stolen my niece from right under my nose, something about the scene made my heart hurt. Clearly he loved the little girl.

Was it possible he was the baby's father? If so, why hadn't he taken custody of her?

West's head snapped up as he sensed me approaching, and his eyes narrowed when he realized who I was. I was at a loss as to what to say to him. I didn't want to appear weak—to allow him or anyone else in that shit town to think I wasn't capable of handling my family situation.

"Who's the father?" I asked, nodding in the direction of the bundle in his arms. Might as well get the important part out of the way. If he was the father, maybe this had been a wasted trip and I could get back to San Francisco and my regular life there.

He looked at me but didn't speak, so I continued. "Why isn't there a dad in the picture?"

West seemed to choose his words carefully before replying. "The baby doesn't have a father."

Ah. So that's how it was. Some kind of random-hookup deal. Now *that* fit more in line with the Adriana I'd known.

"I see."

"What does that mean?" he snapped.

I felt my eyes widen in surprise at his defensiveness. "Just that I understand now why I'm the one who got custody of her."

"You're not keeping her," he said. It was a statement, not a question, and it got my hackles up immediately.

"I'll do whatever the fuck I want to, asshole," I barked. "Hand her over."

The time for niceties was gone, as if it had ever been there in the first place. I'd be damned if I was going to let some holier-than-thou Dr. Perfect tell me what I was and wasn't going to do with my sister's baby.

His eyes narrowed to angry slits, and he held the bundle closer to his chest. "I'll hand her over to you when hell freezes, jackass." His voice was a low, thunderous growl, and it brought goose bumps up all over my skin.

Suddenly I had the ridiculous mental image of two rams going at it —butting heads over and over again and ending up with nothing but sore heads. I couldn't help but laugh, which, of course, just pissed the man off even more.

"What the hell is wrong with you?" he asked. "Your sister is dead, your niece is an orphan, and you're *laughing?*"

"Yes, I'm laughing. Because you don't have a fucking leg to stand on in this, and you know it. And I sure as shit don't need to explain myself to you. You have no idea how I feel about losing my sister. Matter of fact, you don't know me at all."

West's nostrils flared, and he hissed his response. "I know that when she was seventeen years old and fell off a boat, she screamed your name. I know that when she was eighteen and her stepfather refused to pay for a girl to go to college, she wished you were there to help change his mind. I know that after she gave birth to Pippa, the first thing she said was that the baby had your crazy-ass ears." He looked at me in defiance, never taking his sparkling green eyes off me. "I know these things because I was here. And you weren't."

My heart felt like it was going to break into a thousand pieces all over again. Adriana needing me didn't make sense. The sister I'd left hadn't needed me for anything. And West mentioning a stepfather I'd never really had knocked the breath out of my chest. But I wasn't about to let that asshole have the satisfaction of seeing me cry. So I clenched my teeth and balled my fists to hold it all in.

"You don't know shit. If she called out my name after falling off a boat, it's because she *pushed me off one* when I was fourteen and must have fucking learned how shitty that was. And if she wanted to go to fucking college, she could have fought tooth and nail to pay for it herself like I had to. So fuck you for thinking you know a goddamned thing about me and my sister."

West's face seemed to soften in surprise, but he still held the baby close to his chest.

"I'd like to meet my niece. Please," I said as evenly as possible. Something inside was clawing at me, pressing me forward to get my hands on the one remaining link between me and my family.

I saw West's jaw tighten, but he stood up and loosened his hold on the bundle so he could reveal her to me—not to hand her to me but to let me get a glimpse of her.

I stepped forward to peek at her face. There, staring up at me, was the smallest human being that had surely ever lived. Her skin was absolute perfection, smooth, creamy white with hints of blushing pink. Her tiny plump lips were deep red, and her eyes were the same mix of green and blue I saw every time I looked in the mirror. As she turned in West's arms to stretch, one tiny ear revealed itself from behind a fold in the blanket, and sure enough, it was a ridiculous Dumbo ear. It was too much.

I swallowed down a sob before mumbling something to the effect of, "Never mind," and turning around to make my way quickly across the dying grass of the back lawn around to the driveway.

I could hear his voice calling from behind me as I walked away.

"Go ahead and leave, Nico. It's what you're good at."

I didn't let the tears come until I was safely back in the car on my way down the familiar driveway and out of that godforsaken town.

CHAPTER 4

WEST

I stared after him in shock. That was *it*? That was the sum total of his reaction to meeting Adriana's beautiful daughter? The only person left in his fucking family—the tiny life he was now in charge of protecting? To walk away again?

Adriana had spent hours trying to convince me that Nico was a decent person worth loving, worth forgiving, but I'd never actually believed her. And there, in the back yard of Adriana's home, I knew I'd been right. He was a heartless asshole who'd selfishly walked out on her when they needed each other most. He'd never looked back. Clearly he hadn't grown up, and all he still cared about was himself.

I began making my way back to the house, knowing I was going to have to hand Pippa over to that selfish prick. Just the thought of leaving her in his care made acid burn in my stomach. There was no way he was capable of taking care of a newborn. No fucking way. I'd bet my entire medical practice on the fact he'd never changed a diaper or given a baby a bottle. Hell, I'd be shocked if he'd even held a baby before. What exactly was he planning on doing while the adoption process played out?

Just as I reached out to open the back door, I heard an engine turn over in the front of the house. A vehicle crunched along the drive until the sound indicated it had driven out of earshot. Who had left? Surely not the man who was supposed to take charge of Pippa. I'd fucking kill him.

As I entered the house, I could see Hon and Goldie peering out the front windows by the breakfast table.

"Did that guy seriously just leave?" I called out. They both spun to look at me, Goldie bustling over to take Pippa out of my arms and Hon nodding his head. "What the hell?"

"I think this has all been a big shock to him, West," Hon said gently. "Nico hasn't been back to Hobie in like fifteen years. Cut him some slack."

"Please tell me he's agreed to let the Warners adopt her," I asked the attorney. "He has to."

"He hasn't confirmed it, but he sounded relieved when I told him about them."

"Thank god," I muttered, sitting down on the overstuffed sofa and running my hands through my hair. As long as the guy was willing to give Pippa the best chance at a good life, I could forgive him for being a Grade A asshole.

Goldie walked over and rubbed my shoulder, giving me the same sweet smile she'd given me at work after a tough case.

"Sweetie, why don't you head on home and get some rest? It's been a long day. I'll stay here with Pippa until Nico comes back."

"Goldie, he can't take care of her himself. You're not going to let him—"

She squeezed my shoulder to stop me from saying it. "I'm going to stay the night regardless. You know better than to ask if I'm going to leave this baby with someone before I'm sure he can care for her. You're tired. Now go home, Dr. Wilde."

I met her eyes and saw in them the stern nurse she'd been since I'd been a child playing in my grandfather's office at the practice. Hell, she'd probably changed my own damned diapers once upon a time.

"Yes, ma'am," I mumbled. "See you tomorrow."

I made my way back out to my truck, taking care to remove the car seat and leave it on Adriana's front porch. I tried not to think about Nico Salerno attempting to figure out how to put it in the back of his rental car and getting it all wrong.

As I drove back the few blocks to the center of town, I noticed what looked like his rental car parked in the empty lot of the small city park off to my left. I didn't see whether or not he was behind the wheel, and I forced myself not to look too hard for him. I couldn't decide if I was disappointed or relieved he hadn't left town.

Two blocks later, I pulled into my own driveway and followed it around back and into the freestanding garage behind the house. I lived above my medical practice in a great old Victorian house near the center of town. One of my grandfathers started the practice in the midseventies and passed it down to me when he retired a few years ago. Grandpa and Doc had tried to gift me the home as part of the practice, but I'd refused. Instead, I was buying it from them with monthly payments that galled them every time they noticed the deposits on their bank statements.

I knew that when the entire thing was paid off, I'd feel an immense sense of pride at owning the gorgeous home, but until then, I felt lucky enough to live and work there every day.

When I'd pulled past the small parking area for patients, I'd noticed a familiar dark SUV parked there. I got out and joined my brother Hudson who was sitting on the back stoop, checking his phone.

"Hey," I said as I stepped past him to unlock the back door to the kitchen. "What are you doing here? I thought you'd be heading back to Dallas."

He was still dressed in the suit he'd worn to Adriana's service, and I realized I hadn't even stuck around long enough to thank my family for coming.

"Stopped by to see if you wanted some company," he said, still looking at his phone as he stood to follow me in. Despite the casual tone of his voice, I could tell there was nothing casual about his offer.

"What's going on?" I asked. "Did Grandpa and Doc send you over here?"

"Yep."

"Why didn't they come themselves?" I asked, walking up the back staircase to my second-floor living space. I tossed my keys onto the kitchen counter and made my way to the fridge for a couple of beers.

"They did, West. We all came," he said, looking up and finally meeting my eyes. I saw kindness and love in my brother's face, and I wasn't quite ready for that level of emotion from anyone just yet. My feelings about Adriana were too raw, and after everything that had happened with Pippa, I felt like the smallest thing could push me over and send me reeling.

"Where is everyone now?" I asked, continuing to focus on opening the beers as if that brief moment of connection hadn't happened.

As I expected, Hudson let it go. He shrugged. "Took off after you didn't show. Figured you'd gone to Adriana's or Goldie's. Grandpa said to tell you he's fixing Chicken Marbella and you'd better be there by six."

I handed Hudson one of the bottles before slugging down half my own at the same time I pulled off my tie. I made my way back to my bedroom and began shucking off the rest of the formal clothing so I could change into something more comfortable for family dinner.

Hudson padded down the hall after me. "Where's the baby? With Goldie still?"

"Yeah."

"Who was the guy?"

I turned around to look at him with my eyebrow raised in confusion. As if I didn't know who "the guy" was.

"You know, the guy with the weird hair and all the ink. I saw you talking to him after the service. Never seen him before."

Just the mention of Nico Salerno had my back teeth grinding together again. "Adriana's good-for-nothing brother," I admitted. "Apparently she left custody of Pippa to him."

"What the fuck? The guy who took off when we were kids?"

"Yeah. Don't get me started, Hudson. Okay?"

I turned back around and slipped my shirt and undershirt off to replace them with an old, soft flannel button-down. I hung up my suit trousers and slid on a worn pair of blue jeans, thankful Grandpa had been a rancher and didn't give a damn about how we dressed for family dinners.

After throwing on some boots, I followed Hudson back out to the kitchen to finish our beer.

"You sure you don't want to talk about it?" Hudson asked. I thought for a minute about how many times he'd been there for me before—just a quiet companion when I'd needed a friend. We'd been brothers my whole life, but we'd also been as thick as thieves. As the two oldest siblings in a family overrun with them, we'd taken the unofficial roles of protectors to our younger brothers and sisters. Instead of burdening anyone else with our problems, we kept them quiet.

And only burdened each other.

I wound up telling him about the punk who'd come in from the West Coast to butt his nose into Pippa's business—the guy who'd abandoned Adriana when she'd been a wayward teen and left her alone with the Billingham boys when Mrs. Salerno married Sheriff Billingham but died only two years later in a car accident. Just the thought of it set my teeth on edge and made me want to beat Nico up even more.

Hudson tilted his head at me and furrowed his brow. "This is really bugging you, West. What's the problem? You said you think he's going to go through with the adoption, right?"

"Yeah. That's what Hon thinks anyway. I guess I'm pissed off that he couldn't bother to show up and be there for Adriana until it was too late," I explained. "She deserved better than that. She deserved someone in her corner. Especially after her mom died."

"She had your friendship this past year, West. And everyone at the bakery. And Pippa. She was happy."

I felt my jaw tighten again and knew I was running out of energy to keep up a brave face.

"I think I'm going to skip family dinner after all," I told Hudson.

A heavy arm landed on my shoulders as he pulled me in close. "Nope. C'mon. I promised I'd bring you. Grandpa and Doc will skin me alive if I show up empty-handed. Let's go. You can cry your eyes out on the way there if you want. I promise I'll pretend not to notice."

"Fuck," I muttered, following him out to his vehicle.

And damned if Hudson didn't keep his promise, as always.

CHAPTER 5

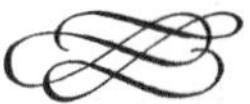

NICO

I didn't get very far through town before I remembered I was a fucking adult and not a petulant young teen who could just run away from his problems. Plus I'd be damned if I was going to confirm that asshole doctor's assumption that I was good-for-nothing.

After pulling into the parking lot of the town park only a few blocks down the road, I turned off the engine and lay my head down on the steering wheel. How did I see this playing out? What were my options?

Adriana's baby girl, Pippa, was alone. Why? Where was my mother? I hadn't had a chance to ask many questions of the attorney before I'd been thrown into the deep end of meeting the people who'd been caring for my niece. And, honestly, I was almost afraid to ask. If my mother was dead too, I wasn't sure how I was going to handle the news.

A sharp rap sounded on the driver's side window, causing me to jump in my seat. I turned to see a uniformed officer glaring at me through the window, so I lowered it and looked up at him.

"See some ID, sir," the officer said in a clipped tone. He kept his reflective shades over his eyes so I couldn't see much of what he looked like other than having buzzed hair and being muscled to within an inch of his life. Gym rat, no doubt.

"Is there a problem?" I asked.

"Seems you're loitering. ID please."

"But I only parked here like three minutes ago," I muttered, reaching for my wallet in my back pocket. Had I not been so mentally exhausted from the events of the day, I would have gotten mouthy with this small-town, piece-of-shit cop.

I handed the officer my license and the rental car paperwork before noticing the name tag on his uniform.

Billingham.

"Are you by any chance related to Sheriff Billingham?" I asked, trying to see behind his shades without success.

"I'm his son. Curtis."

Curtis. As in bully-from-hell Curt Billingham.

"Curt?" I asked. "It's Nico."

"I know who you are."

Uh-oh. That did not sound friendly. Which shouldn't have surprised me, really. The kid had always been a jerk to me, especially after our parents started dating. He'd always thought he was better than I was.

"Then you know I'm in town for Adriana's funeral," I said, refusing to let the asshat intimidate me in his big, important, police officer's getup. "I just pulled over to get my bearings before heading back to her house." Okay, so that was a lie, but still. It was none of his business.

"You need to move along," he said stiffly, extending my license back to me between two beefy fingers. "No one wants you loitering, *Salerno.*" The way he said my last name was like there was a poisonous, furry caterpillar on his tongue.

"Whatever," I mumbled, reaching out for my ID. He pulled it back as soon as the words were out of my mouth.

"What did you just say to me?"

"I said, 'Yes, sir. Thank you, sir.'" I glared at him as I spat the words in his direction. This entire scenario reminded me of one of the reasons I'd sworn never to come back to this shit town to begin with. I hadn't even been in town for two hours, and it was already suffocating me. The whole thing was like a scene out of a cheesy movie.

Curt flicked my ID with his thumbnail, and it sailed past my face to land on the floor of the passenger footwell. I took a deep breath and looked straight ahead, chanting to myself to leave it alone. I knew better than to pick a fight with someone wearing a badge no matter how much of a snotty-assed punk he was.

I turned the engine over and reversed slowly out of the parking spot before making my way out of the lot.

The sooner I got my sister's affairs in order, the sooner I could leave Hobie for good.

Again.

By the time I pulled back down the familiar driveway, I'd stopped at the grocery store to pick up a few things to tide me over until the following day. I hadn't known what to buy for the baby, so I hoped the woman who'd been caring for her had whatever she needed.

When I entered the little house, I saw the woman and the attorney sitting at the breakfast table, drinking from thick mugs. There was no sign of the gorgeous asshole doctor. Which was probably a good thing because I really didn't have the energy to face him again so soon.

"Um, hi. Mrs. Banks? Mr. Baptiste?" I began, feeling unsure of myself and hating it. "I'm sorry I ran out of here like that. I promise it won't happen again."

The woman's face softened, and she stood up to approach me. "It's Goldie, hon. Not Mrs. Banks. And I completely understand why you got overwhelmed. Come here, sweetie."

Before I could react, the older woman had engulfed me in a bear hug, all squishy boobs and warm floral perfume. The gesture was kind —so very different than the welcome I'd gotten from most everyone else I'd encountered that I could feel tears pricking the back of my eyes again. I squeezed her back before quickly untangling myself from the maternal embrace so I didn't lose what little control I had over my emotions.

"Thank you," I mumbled. "I have to admit, ah, I'm not exactly… good with babies. I was hoping you might know of someone who could help—"

"Nonsense," she said sweetly. "Just because you're not experienced, doesn't mean you're not good with them. I'll show you everything you need to know and stick around until you've gotten the hang of it. How does that sound?"

I stared at her. "That sounds amazing, but why would you do that?"

"Nico, honey, there's no way for you to remember this, but I've known you and Adriana since you two were knee-high to a grasshopper. That girl thought the world of her little brother, and until I find out otherwise, I do too. And I sure as heck think the world of Pippa. So I'll do whatever it takes to make sure you all end up okay. Why don't you bring your things in from the car, and I'll show you around before Pippa wakes up from her nap?"

I couldn't speak past the lump in my throat, so I quickly nodded and made my way back out to the rental car to gather my things. By the time I returned inside, I noticed the attorney had spread out some paperwork on the kitchen table and was busy talking on his cell phone.

Goldie showed me around the small home, most of which was one big open room that included a cozy living area with a stacked stone fireplace, the large wooden breakfast table, and a modern kitchen with specialty appliances of some kind. In the back there were two bedrooms. The master was off to the right, and the smaller bedroom, the nursery I assumed, was off to the left. Between the two stood large glass sliding doors to the backyard. My mother's property had never looked better. The backyard had been landscaped with simple, clean lines and basic shrubbery. Even though it was the end of September, the grass looked freshly mowed, which made me wonder who would look after the property now that she was gone.

Oh right, *me.*

I set my things down on Adriana's queen-sized bed and tried not to look at anything in the room. I just wasn't ready to see my sister's personal space yet. When I followed Goldie out of the room, I pulled the door closed behind me, as if I could shut out the reminder of not having known the woman my sister had become. I knew there was no way I was going back in that bedroom anytime soon except to grab my bag out of there once everyone left. One look at her personal items and I knew I'd feel the weight of every year I'd missed getting to know her as an adult.

By the time Goldie finished showing me around, the baby still hadn't woken up, so we joined the attorney at the table. Once he finished his phone call, Honovi began explaining some of the details of the custody situation.

"Wait," I said, holding my hand up. "What about my mom? Why isn't she here to take care of the baby?"

Goldie's soft hand came down on mine, but she let Honovi break the news.

"Nico, your mom passed away several years ago," he explained in a gentle voice. "She and the sheriff were killed in an automobile accident."

I looked at him while the news sank in. "Really? When? How long ago?" I wanted him to be wrong. I wanted him to say, *No, not really. She's just on vacation.* But I knew he spoke the truth. She would never have left her only grandchild.

Honovi glanced over at Goldie before continuing. "Maybe twelve or thirteen years ago?"

"Wh-what? That long? She's been gone that long? What about Adriana? What did she do without my mom all that time? Oh my god." I was babbling, but I didn't know what else to do. My head was spinning, and a small voice inside me kept chanting, *You could have come home, you could have come* home *and been with her.* "Can I see my mom's grave?"

Honovi gave me a smile of reassurance. "Sure you can. Her grave is in the churchyard. Adriana will be buried next to her. She still had Curt and Reeve, Nico. They were her family."

Bile rose up my throat at the thought of the Billingham brothers being my sister's only remaining family, and I shoved it away. While the image of my mother's body in a grave only a few miles away from me settled over my heart, I realized something else. For some reason I hadn't thought of it until now.

"How did you find me?" I asked the attorney. "How did you know how to get ahold of me?"

"Adriana listed your contact information when she made the will before the baby came," he said. His eyes were so kind and I was grateful she'd chosen such an empathetic man to do this legal process.

"But how did she know? I never contacted her after I left."

He shrugged. "Could be she did an Internet search. Or maybe hired a private investigator. If you're living and doing business under your legal name, it's not that hard."

I thought about Adriana knowing how to contact me and not reaching out. I wondered how long she'd known where I was—what she might have thought about me after all these years. While I settled into a complete funk, I heard the beginnings of a baby crying.

Goldie's face lit up as she stood.

"C'mon Nico, let's go meet your precious girl."

CHAPTER 6

WEST

For the next four days it seemed like everywhere I went in town people were talking about "that weirdo from California" who'd come to take Adriana's precious angel from us. It took all my self-control not to show up at Adriana's house all hours of the day to check on them. But both Goldie and Hon had assured me Nico was managing okay with Goldie's help.

It was on the fifth day when Goldie showed up at the office that I freaked out.

"What are you doing here?" I snapped when I saw her come in and put her lunch in the fridge as if it were any old normal day at work.

Her head snapped up, warm honey curls bouncing fresh out of the curlers she still used daily. "Excuse me, Dr. Wilde, but I work here." Her voice was the voice of my childhood, and it immediately put me into kid mode. I tried hard not to whine my response.

"But what about Pippa?"

"What about Pippa?" she shot back at me.

"She needs you. Where's Nico? Who's with him? What if something happens?"

"Dr. Wilde, have I ever done anything to put a child in danger?"

Oh shit.

"No, ma'am," I muttered.

"Then mind your own business, and let's get to work. Leigh Coney is here with JJ, and it sounds like he might have the flu."

I followed her out of the break room to one of the small exam rooms. Sure enough, the five-year-old had the flu. It was our first confirmed case of the season. That meant work was about to get very busy. Once we got him squared away with everything he and his mom needed, we moved on to the next child waiting for her annual checkup. The day remained steady until it was time to close up shop.

I followed Goldie out to the small parking area and opened the sedan door for her.

"So, ah, are you headed to Adriana's house?" I asked as nonchalantly as I dared.

She looked up at me with a knowing smirk. "I think you mean Nico's house, Dr. Wilde."

I felt my jaw tick at the thought of it being his house instead of hers now. "Whatever. Are you going to check on them?"

"Nope. I'm headed home to spend some much-needed time with Gene. If I don't cook something healthy for him soon, he's liable to subsist on frozen dinners until he turns into one."

"But...," I began.

"If you're so worried about them, West, why don't you stop by? I'm surprised you haven't visited Pippa since the day of the funeral. That's not like you."

It was true. Since Pippa had been born, I hadn't gone more than one or two days without seeing her. My arms were itching to hold her, and I was desperate to put my nose to her little head and smell the baby wash scent of her.

"I didn't want to interfere," I explained.

"That's a load of malarkey, and we both know it. Something's gotten into you, and you're throwing a hissy fit. Whatever it is, get over it. She needs us right now whether you're scared or not."

She was right about Pippa needing us. The baby had already spent the past several hours without a familiar face, and I didn't want her to go to bed tonight without being rocked by someone who loved her. I sure as hell knew Nico wasn't that person.

"I'm not scared, Goldie. I'm just worried I'm going to punch that guy in the face is all."

Her eyes studied me as she sat down in the driver's seat. "You sure that's all? You sure it's not about having to say goodbye to Pippa when the Warners adopt her?"

My gut twisted at the mention of her adoption. "I have to get used to not seeing her every day," I said quietly. "It was easier to do it when I knew she was with you."

Goldie reached out and cupped my cheek with her warm palm. "West, you need to stop working so hard and find someone for yourself. Start your own family. You were born to be a dad. That little girl is lucky to have you, but she's going to have plenty of other people who love her once the adoption goes through. I think you should focus on finding someone for yourself. I hate that you're still on your own."

I placed my hand over hers on my cheek and squeezed before moving it back inside the car. "Goldie, hasn't it occurred to you yet that most of the good gay men in town are either my brothers or cousins? I'd have to travel to Dallas or Austin to find someone, and nobody wants a long-distance relationship. Plus I don't have time. I'm married to my job."

She chuckled. "Pfft. Not true about the supply of good men. I happen to know of a certain military base nearby that is full of nice men. And statistically speaking, at least a good chunk of them are gay. You need to get a matchmaking app like the one your sister was talking about so you can find one."

I rolled my eyes and laughed. "Oh my god, you sound as bad as my mother. Don't worry. Hallie made all of us sign up for the one her boss is developing. And we both know she'll force me to make use of it once the program is live. In the meantime, go feed Gene. I'll stop by and check on Pippa."

She smiled and turned the key in the ignition before looking back at me. "West?"

"Ma'am?"

"Go easy on Nico, will you? He's having a hard time with everything."

The concern in her eyes forced me to nod in agreement, but I knew deep down I didn't give a shit about whether or not Nico Salerno was having a hard time. Any hard time he was having was one he deserved.

I made my way to my truck and threw my messenger bag across the cab to the passenger side before climbing into the driver's seat. I wondered what Nico's reaction to my unannounced visit would be. Maybe if I brought the guy dinner, he'd be less able to turn me away. A peace offering of sorts.

After swinging by Lou's cafe, I pulled down the long driveway to Adriana's house. Dark was settling in, and the evening breeze was blowing dried leaves off the trees. I wondered if the cooler weather would come soon.

As I pulled up to the parking area, I thought about how best to approach the prickly man in order to get some time with Pippa. The pasta dishes I'd picked up had filled the cab of the truck with a warm savory aroma, and my stomach began to complain about the unsatisfying salad I'd had for lunch.

I grabbed the bags of food and made my way to the front porch, stopping myself before opening the door. I hadn't had to knock when visiting Adriana, but the cold reminder of her passing washed over me just as my hand grasped the knob.

Before I pressed the doorbell, I saw movement through the narrow glass to the right of the door. Nico was standing in the middle of the main room, cradling Pippa in one arm while lifting up the hem of his T-shirt with his other hand.

The shirt had a giant wet spot on the chest and shoulder as if Pippa had spit up all over him. His face was screwed into a grimace as he struggled to remove the soiled shirt while still holding the baby. As the hem of the shirt came up, it revealed miles and miles of ink over a flat stomach.

And that's when it hit me again like a stroke to the groin. The man was attractive as all hell. For some reason I'd forgotten that little tidbit from the day of the funeral. I hadn't been able to see much past the haze of my grief and anger. But now, seeing him as a regular guy not hidden in the stupid formal clothes he'd been wearing that day, I saw that he was stunning.

I'd always known my friend Adriana was beautiful. She'd garnered plenty of attention for being a lovely woman. But this man—her brother—was something even more exquisite. Looking at him was like looking at a rare gem collection. There were colors, details, and nuances it would take years to adequately appreciate. The hair, the ink, the piercings. The symmetrical features of his lovely face.

And the hooded eyes that held everything from fear and insecurity to loneliness.

Stop projecting, asshole.

I stood there, frozen, as the beautiful man bared his upper body. My eyes didn't even know where to land—there was so much ink, and it was covering a tight, fit male body that was sparking the interest of my very lonely, pathetic dick. My heart rate ramped up as I tried to take it all in.

Tattoos covered almost every inch of his skin with the exception of a small blank area over his heart. The bare skin stood out in its uniqueness, and I wondered why in hell a man with so much art on his body had left a bare spot in the center of his chest.

Just as I'd suspected, there were piercings standing out on his nipples. Little matte black barbells from the look of it, and my mouth watered at the sight of them. I'd never been with someone with piercings like that. I wondered what it felt like for him to have them played with. I wondered what it would feel like to take them into my mouth and tug.

Jesus, fuck. My cock was plumping so quickly I had to shift the food bags to one hand so I could press and rearrange it. How in the world was this strange man making me so goddamned horny? Was I that hard up?

Yes.

Without a doubt, *yes.*

As I stared at him, I realized he'd dropped the shirt on the floor and gone back to cradling Pippa. It was amazing how different he was from the scrawny kid he'd been when I'd confronted him at the movie theater. He hadn't developed into a big guy by any means, but his small biceps and shoulders were defined and flexed slightly as he shifted the baby in his arms. As he lifted Pippa to his shoulder, I saw the bumpy plane of his abdomen and could just barely make out a thin trail of hair leading from his belly button down into the low-riding waistband of a pair of black athletic pants.

The shiny purple-and-turquoise hair on his head was messy and all over the place as if he'd been running his fingers through it. There was so much to appreciate on the man I couldn't look away.

I was still pressing a hand into the tight crotch of my pants when I realized he'd begun singing. Nico was singing a lullaby to my sweet Pippa, and I was practically jacking myself off at the sight of it. What kind of sicko was I?

Jesus, Weston. Head out of the gutter.

But the gutter is fucking glorious.

I remembered my long-standing vow never to trust my initial lust reaction to a hot guy.

Shaking my head in frustration, I reached out to press the doorbell, willing my dick to stand down before Nico could see the extent of my desperation. The man looked up at the sound and spied me through the door. I tried to look bored, but I wasn't sure I pulled it off.

He opened the door and looked at me, not saying a word.

"Um, hi," I said, knowing full well I was about to go into stupid babbling mode. "I have dinner for you. Us, I mean. I brought dinner for you. And me. To eat together. Well, we don't have to eat together. But I brought enough for two. Although I guess I could just leave both portions with you and then you'd have leftovers. And, well, if I did that, I could make a sandwich at home. Matter of fact, why don't you keep this. I'll get out of your purple hair."

Oh my god.

One corner of his mouth tilted up, and I felt my face flush. I quickly set the bags down inside the threshold and turned to go.

Before I could step away, a hand shot out and grabbed my elbow. I froze at the touch but didn't turn around to face him.

"Wait." The voice was soft and sultry, causing even my cock to roll its eyes. Of course the man had a sexy voice now. Goldie was right. I really needed to find someone. This shit was getting out of control.

The voice of my dreams continued. "I think maybe she's sick."

And that's all it took for a change to come over me. Gone was the lust-sick puppy who could almost taste the little black barbells on my tongue, and in his place was the pissed-off physician who loved Pippa and feared for her health at the hands of the inexperienced punk on the porch.

CHAPTER 7

NICO

I wouldn't have ever had the guts to ask that man for help if I hadn't seen the goofy, stuttering side of him he'd presented when I opened the door. It was like I was seeing a completely different man than the controlling bastard I'd met several days before or the cocky teen he'd been when I was a kid.

The asshole doctor had transformed for that one special moment into an adorable human being—someone just as insecure as the rest of us and unable to control his mouth. I'd liked that guy. He'd seemed warm and sweet—approachable. Not the same snooty J.Crew model I'd met after the funeral or the horndog I'd overheard in the movie theater all those years ago.

But the minute I'd mentioned Pippa being sick, he'd turned back into Dr. Prick again.

"Give her to me," he demanded, pushing past me into the house and reaching for the baby. "You should have brought her to me the minute you thought she was coming down with something."

"Hold on there, jackass," I said, feeling my hackles shoot up. "Take a breath. She's not dying. And I only just realized something was off. I was going to call you."

He got a few steps into the house before mumbling to himself and turning on his heel to walk right out again to his truck. I stood there staring after him through the late-September twilight, wondering if maybe he was the one who needed medical attention instead of Pippa.

"West?" I called after him. "You heading out so soon? Thanks for stopping by." I couldn't help but add a teasing tone to my voice even though it made him turn and shoot daggers at me with his eyes.

"Getting my medical bag," he shot back before mumbling, "Smart-ass," under his breath.

When he returned to the house, he closed the door behind us and gestured me over to the sofa. Once I sat down, I looked at him warily, reluctant for some reason to release Pippa into his care.

West removed a stethoscope from a carryall that looked more like a canvas tool bag than a traditional doctor's bag. It was filled to the brim with first aid supplies and served as a strong reminder that this man truly was a physician. While he may have also been a jerk, he'd gone through years of medical training specifically to learn how to help small children like Pippa.

I lowered the baby from my shoulder to the deep cushion on the sofa between us. West immediately peeled back the blankets to check her out.

"Why isn't she dressed?" he asked without looking up. He rapidly rubbed the diaphragm of the stethoscope against his own shirt to warm it up before placing it on the baby's chest.

"I just bathed her. She was—"

"Shh," he snapped, holding up his free hand to stop me from continuing.

I pursed my lips and narrowed my eyes at him. Fucking ass. Such a gigantic prick. Why ask me a question if he didn't want to hear the answer?

As he listened to her heart and lungs, his slender fingers moved the stethoscope around her tiny bare chest. His hands looked gentle and capable despite being attached to someone with a giant ego. I could tell he cared about her or maybe just cared about all kids. I had to assume anyone who went through that much trouble and expense to become a family doctor had to care about children.

Adriana had been lucky to have a friend who liked kids—someone she could count on to help her figure all that baby stuff out. Or, hell, maybe it had come easier to her somehow. Easier than it had me anyway.

Goldie had spent several days of her time and God's own stockpile of patience to help me learn how to do even the most basic things for Pippa. I could now feed her, change her, and bathe her. But giving her the first solo bath without Goldie's help had just about killed me. I'd been convinced I was going to drown her or break her. Babies were slippery fuckers when wet.

I kept thinking about how much Griff and Sam would have cracked up seeing me transforming into babysitter extraordinaire this week. I hadn't told Griff where I'd gone and had brushed off his texts and calls so far. I knew I needed to contact him soon to tell him where I was, but I also knew he'd come running. And I didn't want to take him away from his own newborn to help me with Adriana's.

"What're her symptoms?" West asked in a soft voice. He was peering into her ears now with one of those pointy ear-looker things.

"She keeps throwing up," I explained. "Every time I feed her she spits it all back up again."

West's tongue seemed to twist in his mouth to keep from smirking.

"What?" I asked. "I'm worried about her. She's going to starve if she can't keep her formula down, right?"

He wrapped the blankets back around Pippa and scooped her up onto his shoulder before beginning to pat her firmly on the back.

And that's when I remembered.

Burping the baby. Burping the baby was a thing I was supposed to do after each bottle. *Shit.*

"Uh...," I began. "I think..."

A holier-than-thou twinkle appeared in Dr. Beautiful's smug face. "Mm-hmm. What do you *think,* Nico?"

I felt my teeth grind together at his tone, but there was no avoiding the way my name on his tongue made my groin tighten up.

"I think I may have just not burped her well enough, come to think of it."

"Is that right? What made you realize that?" And as if on cue, a hearty burp came out of Princess Shits-Her-Pants.

I let out a breath and ran my hand through my hair. There was no getting around how bad at this I was.

"So you brought food?" I asked, standing up and hoping like hell the change in subject would wipe the smugness off his goddamned chiseled, J.Crew modeling face.

"I did. Picked up some pasta dishes from Lou's. Hope you're okay with pesto or Alfredo. I didn't know what you liked." West stood up from the sofa and followed me to the breakfast table with Pippa still on his shoulder.

"I like both. Thanks. I really appreciate it. I haven't been out of the house since I got here, so anything from a restaurant is a nice change."

I pulled down some plates and asked if he wanted a beer or soda. "I have some wine too, if you want," I offered hesitantly. It wasn't that I wanted to make nice with the doctor as much as I didn't want to seem like a country bumpkin who only drank beer with his pasta.

"Nah, a beer is good, thanks," he said. "You know… I'm happy to watch Pippa if you need to get out of here for a bit."

I looked up at him, wondering exactly what he was getting at. Was he trying to get me to admit I needed a break? Well, fuck that. I wasn't about to do anything to make him think I couldn't handle the baby when I already knew he thought I was useless.

"Nope, I'm good," I said a little too loudly.

West shook his head. "It's okay to need a break, Nico. Taking care of a newborn isn't easy. I wasn't implying you go out clubbing. I just thought maybe you had errands you needed to run, and you yourself said you hadn't left the house in days."

He was beginning to sound an awful lot like a nice guy, and that didn't exactly fit into my image of him. In fact, there was a part of me that didn't want him to be nice. I didn't want to like anyone in this shit town because then I'd have second thoughts about leaving when it was time to go. And I was sure as hell leaving the minute the adoption process was final.

"What's wrong with clubbing?" I asked. "Surely there's a good club here in Hobie, Texas?"

West barked out a laugh and shot me a twinkling look that nearly brought me to my knees. When his face lit up with a real smile like that, he was truly breathtaking.

"There's a quasi motorcycle club. Does that count?" He snickered. "They meet up at Bud's on the main highway but only on dollar-draft night."

I couldn't help but chuckle right along with him. Now *that* was the Hobie I remembered. Small town full of small-town people.

"I don't think that's the kind of club that would want me as a member," I suggested.

"No, maybe not."

I served us each some pasta from the takeout containers and thanked him again for bringing it. It wasn't until I went to put a napkin in my lap that I realized I was shirtless.

"Oh shit," I muttered, running my hand along my chest to my stomach as I stood. "Be right back. Sorry." As I turned to place my napkin on the table, I caught West staring at my hand moving down my front. I was used to people staring at my tattoos with curious glances, but this seemed different. Appreciative of the body, not the ink.

I knew it couldn't be attraction of any kind because the man screamed straight—from his clean-cut button-down shirt to his boring-ass khaki pants. I had to assume he was a good ole Texas straight boy through and through.

Then I remembered the incident in the movie theater. He sure as hell hadn't been straight then. But he *had* been friendly with Curt Billingham, and that was enough evidence to convict him of being an idiot at the very least.

Instead of taking the time to think about it further, I made my way back to the baby's room where my bag was stashed and fished out a clean T-shirt before returning to the table to eat.

"Why is your stuff in the nursery?" he asked.

I looked up at West before glancing back toward the bedrooms. It would have been obvious to him that I'd turned left instead of right.

"Not that it's any of your business, but I let Goldie have Adriana's room when she was here. I slept on the couch."

"Why didn't you sleep on the twin bed in the nursery?"

I rolled my eyes. Controlling much? Jesus. He didn't need to know that I couldn't sleep near Pippa because I spent the whole night having to mentally breathe for her. Every sound she made was surely her last one, and I'd been convinced she'd died of SIDS two hundred times over already. It was awful.

"Why are you so concerned with where I'm sleeping, Dr. Wilde?"

"I'm not. Forget about it."

We ate in silence. West held Pippa on his shoulder with one hand while struggling to eat with the other. I finally felt sorry for him and offered to help.

"Let me hold her," I said, reaching out to lift her off his shoulder.

His arms squeezed her tighter against his body, and I froze. Our eyes met over the bundle of blankets, and I could see remorse in them even though he still seemed reluctant to give her up. I remembered the day of the funeral, how possessive he'd been. It couldn't be easy to go from being a part of this little girl's world to not seeing her for several days.

"It's okay," I said softly. "I'm just going to hold her so you can eat. I'll stay right here."

"Sorry," he murmured, releasing her to me while he kept his eyes locked on mine. I cradled her on my chest and watched him finally return to eating.

Once he was done, he carefully pulled a sleeping Pippa out of my arms and cradled her against his front as he stood up.

"I'm going to rock her for a bit before putting her in the crib." He looked at me and seemed to replay his own words in his head. "If that's okay with you, I mean."

I wasn't sure what saying those words had cost him, but it seemed a price he was willing to pay to spend time with Adriana's daughter. I nodded and watched him make his way back to the nursery.

As I cleaned up our dishes and put away the leftovers, I could just make out his lullaby wafting across the open space between the kitchen and bedroom areas. The sound was low and sonorous, and it brought goose bumps up on my skin. I recognized the words and realized he was singing "Hush Little Baby." The sound of it in that man's voice was heartbreakingly beautiful.

I found myself inching closer and closer to the back of the house where the doorway to the nursery stood ajar. My body was close enough to the side wall to keep me hidden, and I stood there letting the sexy rumble wash over me like a warm balm.

As much of an ass as I'd still assumed he was, he sure as hell was sweet to my niece.

God, that baby girl was lucky. For just a moment I fantasized about Weston Wilde blowing soft words into my ear as he lay behind me in bed, pressed against my body with those long, warm limbs tangled in mine. I did not whimper out loud at the thought.

But fuck if I didn't want to.

CHAPTER 8

WEST

As I finished doing my rounds at the small county hospital, I couldn't stop thinking about Nico Salerno. It had been three days since I'd brought him dinner, and I'd stopped by every night since then on my way home from work to check on Pippa.

Not that Adriana's house was on my way home. But hopefully he didn't know I lived above my practice.

Those evening visits had been nice. We'd seemed to have found a neutral zone where we could stop hating each other as long as we didn't discuss Hobie, Adriana, Pippa, the adoption, our families, or anything else remotely related to how he was doing with the baby. Discussion subjects allowed were work—his tattoo shop in San Francisco and my medical practice here in town, music—his love of retro rock and my love of acoustic guitar, food—both of our preference for anything we didn't have to cook ourselves, and the weather, of course.

I'd brought him dinner every night, nothing fancy, just something to keep him from having one more thing on his plate. I hadn't wanted things to get weird between us, and I'd continued offering to look after Pippa so he could catch a break. I could tell the man was losing sleep the way a new parent does, and I tried my best to encourage him to nap when Pippa napped. Unfortunately, he seemed to have a need to prove himself in some way and insisted he was fine.

Of course, I hadn't believed it for a moment. He was noticeably paler and may have even been losing weight. Dark circles marred his lovely face under his eyes, and he seemed to have trouble concentrating. They were all signs of the sleep deprivation new parents went through in the newborn months. It wasn't until the night before that I'd actually gotten proof of his exhaustion.

We'd been sitting down for Pippa's bedtime bottle, Nico on the sofa and me in a side chair feeding the baby, when I realized he'd stopped talking in the middle of a story about a tattoo client of his. I looked up from the bottle Pippa was downing and noticed he'd fallen asleep sitting up. Just the realization he'd literally fallen asleep midconversation almost caused me to snort out loud.

The poor guy was wiped out. He'd mentioned one of his employees was handling the tattoo shop for him while he was gone, but he was still having to juggle some of the administrative duties long distance. In addition to the shop, I knew he was starting to worry about Adriana's bakery and the maintenance of her house. I wasn't sure what his plan for her assets was, but I'd overheard Honovi reminding him that there were bills that needed paying and employee payroll that needed to be run.

I'd offered to put Nico in touch with my sister who could do payroll stuff in her sleep, but the stubborn asshole hadn't even let me finish speaking before announcing he was fine. He could do it himself. Apparently, the guy fancied himself a goddamned superhero.

When Pippa finished her bottle, I put her up to my shoulder with a burp cloth. I rubbed her back while watching Nico slowly slump farther and farther down in the soft sofa cushions. Instead of rocking Pippa for a few minutes before putting her down, I just kissed her little, fuzzy head good night and placed her in the crib.

When I'd returned to the living area, Nico had been lightly snoring in a heap on the sofa, and I wasn't quite sure what to do with him. Cover him with a blanket and leave? Try to move him to the master bedroom and tuck him into bed like a child? Leave him untouched and just stare at him like a creeper? Apparently, that was what my subconscious wanted to do since I was standing there gazing at the man like an idiot.

"Right then," I muttered, stepping into action. The physician in me knew that the guy needed a restful night's sleep in a real bed, so I reached around his back and began to lift him off the sofa in a kind of hug maneuver.

Nico smelled like heaven—an intoxicating blend of coffee, raspberries, and some kind of masculine body wash, along with the sweet familiar scent of clean baby. I wanted to inhale that scent into my nose and imprint it on my brain permanently.

As I pulled him up from the sofa and into my arms, he mumbled. His lips brushed lightly against the skin of my neck as he spoke, and I felt the sensation deep in my belly.

"Hm?" I murmured near his ear. I hoped he was still sleeping enough not to remember this, not to register who it was moving him. I didn't want him to realize I was touching him and suddenly freak out.

"The baby," he repeated in a gravelly voice.

"Shh, she's asleep. It's okay. Time for you to sleep too."

He was slight enough for me to lift him in my arms and carry him the short distance to Adriana's bedroom. As I lay him down on the bed, I noticed his long-sleeved T-shirt had ridden up over his belly button, revealing the illustrations permanently marked into the skin of his lower abdomen. For once, I was close enough to see what they were, and I noticed the most odd collection of images, everything from religious icons to Japanese lettering to tribal tattoos. There didn't seem to be any rhyme or reason to what he'd chosen—almost as if he'd just closed his eyes and pointed to the boards each time he'd visited a tattoo parlor.

I rolled him across the bed enough to open up the covers and roll him back in place. It wasn't until I pulled the covers over him that I realized how perfectly made the bed had been before I pulled the blankets back. Almost as if he hadn't slept in it at all. Maybe he was just as fastidious as Goldie was about tidying up after himself when he was a guest in someone's home.

The room was dark, but there was enough light coming in from the rest of the house to see the lock of colored hair that had fallen across one eye. I reached out to brush it back and felt a pang in my chest. He looked so peaceful and vulnerable—no longer the feisty man I'd encountered the day of Adriana's funeral or the one I'd confronted years ago in the movie theater but a sleep-deprived new parent, brought down a peg or two by fifteen pounds of chubby-cheeked baby.

It had taken every ounce of strength I had to turn around and walk out of that house instead of crawling into the bed beside him and curling around his tired body. Despite knowing he was a selfish prick who'd ditched his family as a teen just to prove a point, there was something about the sight of him there, asleep in Adriana's bed that made me want to look after him—hold and protect him. Comfort him.

"Dr. Wilde?"

"Wha—?" I blurted, snapping my head up to see that I wasn't, in fact, in Adriana's house any longer. I was standing at the nurses' station at the hospital with someone asking me a question. I cleared my throat and pulled myself together. "I'm sorry, what did you need?"

The young nurse smiled at me, and I realized it was a woman named Darci who'd been trying to catch my brother Hudson's attention for months now.

"I just wanted to make sure you knew about the bonfire party Saturday night out at Walnut Farm," she said in her usual friendly manner. "There's going to be a ton of people there, and we're doing hamburgers and hot dogs. It's just a BYOB thing, you know? I was hoping you might come by and maybe..."

Here it comes, I thought.

"Bring your brothers and sisters," she finished. I noticed a pink blush rise up on her fair skin and wondered why the hell Hudson hadn't asked her out yet. The woman was sweet as hell and great with the patients.

"Yeah, sure. Sounds like fun. You need us to bring anything in particular?" I asked, shooting her a wink and causing her blush to deepen further.

"Whatever you think would make for a good time will be fine, I'm sure," she said.

"Gotcha. I'll tell the Wilde crew and see you Saturday night. Thanks for letting me know."

I completed the notes in my charts before heading out to the parking lot. I'd intended to drive back home and finish up some paperwork at the office before heading to my grandparents' house for dinner, but of course I found myself heading to Adriana's house to stop in and see Pippa.

When I pulled through town, I spotted Nico's rental car parked out front of the bakery. I wondered if the baby was with him. It felt a little strange to see him somewhere out and about in town. As if he had a life that wasn't limited to looking after Pippa while stuck inside Adriana's little house.

It wasn't really any of my business though, so I kept driving, past the sandwich shop and the bookstore until finally pulling down my own street toward home. Despite knowing what Nico Salerno did was truly none of my concern, I couldn't stop thinking about him. Why the hell was I so obsessed?

On my way to Grandpa and Doc's house a little while later, I realized what it must be. I simply wanted to understand why he'd left town when he did. Why had he left Adriana and their mother at the mercy of the Billinghams? Sheriff Billingham had always been an overbearing son of a bitch, and his two sons were mirror images of the man himself. Had he truly left because of them?

It had only taken Curtis Billingham forty-eight hours after our interlude at the movies to join in with some friends of his, calling my cousin Max a queer after they caught him checking out some guy's package in class. After that, it had taken all my self-control not to out Curt to his supposed friends. Instead, I'd simply rebuked his further efforts to get me to suck him off, and I'd told my family the guy was an asshole, and we'd all done our best to ice him out.

The fucker still hadn't gotten over my rejection nor had he stopped trying to get into my pants every time he had a little too much to drink.

Adriana had always wondered why Nico had left, and I'd always felt guilty for having a suspicion and never telling her. I wanted to know for sure. Had it been because of what he'd overheard us talk about that night in the movie theater?

I felt an ache in my jaw and realized I'd been grinding my teeth in frustration—something I'd been doing more and more of lately. I didn't like not understanding something. Or someone.

When I parked in front of Grandpa and Doc's farmhouse on their sprawling ranch a little ways outside of town, three dogs came leaping off the porch and running toward me. The largest was a sweet old coonhound named Grump and the two little ones I always referred to as Sweet and Salty because of their personalities.

I reached down to greet them with ear scratches when I heard the front door open and the sound of Grandpa's voice calling out to me.

"Get your ass in here before I kill your other grandfather."

I looked up to see Grandpa's narrowed eyes and stiff jaw. I chuckled. "What're you guys bickering about this time? Did Doc forget to turn the car off before going into a restaurant again?"

And just like that, Grandpa's ornery mood dissolved into a smirk. "Oh god, that was the funniest thing ever. Come on in and let's give him hell about it again."

He held the door open while I led the three dogs into the spacious home. I could hear some kind of jazz music playing in the back of the house and followed the sounds until I found Doc in the kitchen.

"Westie, don't listen to a thing that old man tells you," Doc warned. "He's in a mood."

I leaned in and gave him a quick hug before lifting the lid of the fat Santa cookie jar that lived on the counter year round and always had sweets in it that Doc had made. Jackpot. Homemade brownies.

"Mmm, just what the doctor ordered," I mumbled, grabbing a thick brownie before putting Santa's head back on his body. "Why is Grandpa mad at you? He told me you guys had dinner at El Senõr's last night and you accidentally left the engine on the entire time you were in the—"

Doc shot Grandpa a look. "One time, goddammit. I did that one time, and I still blame you for distracting me with those pants. Shut the hell up, you old geezer. Your memory is for shit."

I snorted on chocolate crumbs and glanced back and forth between Grandpa and Doc. They were usually so sticky sweet in love, even after all these years, that it was kind of fun to see them annoyed with each other.

Grandpa pointed at me and laughed. "Get mad at him, not me. I didn't bring it up."

Doc looked at me with a smirk. "He's pissed because I made the brownies with avocado instead of butter to make them healthier."

I choked as the fake brownie got lodged in my throat. "Ew, groth," I sputtered, making my way to the sink to spit out the offending item and take a sip of water from the tap. "That's disgusting."

Doc laughed and elbowed his husband. "Did you see him eat half of it? Now he can't pretend he didn't like the healthy version."

Grandpa couldn't help but join in, laughing at me right alongside Doc until his face was buried in Doc's neck and Doc's arm was stretched around Grandpa's shoulders.

"Har, har," I said, shooting Doc the evil eye. "Joke's on you. I picked up chocolate éclair cake from the bakery this morning before work, and now I'm not sharing it. Wouldn't want to foist something unhealthy on you two bozos."

That just made them laugh even harder until Doc whispered something in Grandpa's ear and Grandpa smacked Doc's ass with an "Atta boy" before heading back outside.

"Where's he going?" I asked, opening the fridge to get a soda.

"Out to the truck to secure your dessert. Hand me a can of that, will ya?"

I got diet sodas for both of us, and we took them to the long farmhouse table between the large kitchen and family room. There was a glass dish of cut up carrots and other veggies already on the table, and I quirked a brow at Doc.

"What's with the healthy stuff? Is something going on I'm unaware of?" I asked quietly, looking out the window to make sure Grandpa wasn't within earshot. Grandpa was over ten years Doc's senior, and I knew Doc worried about him.

"His cholesterol was up at his last checkup, that's all. I'm just making sure he doesn't kick off before me. I'm not sure I could handle that, you know?"

I saw the concern in his eyes and the love shining forth as Grandpa made his way in the back door with an armful of Adriana's chocolate, fat, and sugar specialty I'd been stupid enough to pick up.

"Oh shit, Doc. Sorry about that," I began. "I shouldn't have picked up the éclair if—"

He put his hand on mine where it rested on the table and squeezed. "Nonsense. Nothing says we can't have a treat every now and then. I just want us to get back in the habit of balancing it with good stuff. You know the drill, Dr. Wilde." He winked at me before leaning back and taking a sip of his soda and continuing. "What's new? I haven't seen you in a few days. Have you been by to see the baby?"

I ran my hands through my hair in frustration. "Yes. Every night after work."

"And?" Doc gestured for Grandpa to join us and reached out to hold his hand after Grandpa took a seat in the chair next to him. "How's the new gentleman doing with her? Doing okay?"

I shrugged. "He says he is, but I don't know. I get the feeling he's barely hanging on, you know?"

"Well, it's hard when you're not used to it. Ask any new parent and they'll tell you," Grandpa said with a kind smile.

"He won't let me help. Like, with anything. There's no way he can keep this up," I said. "The guy looks like the walking dead."

"Is Goldie still helping?" Doc asked.

"No. Nico told her he was fine on his own, and she believed him."

I caught Grandpa making significant eyeballs at Doc before Doc spoke. "West, Goldie knows what she's doing. If she trusts the guy to take care of Pippa without help, you and I both know she's right. What's this really about?"

"I don't know," I said. And it was true. I really didn't know. If I had to guess, I would have said I was more concerned about Nico himself than the baby. Nico wasn't getting enough sleep or enough to eat or any kind of stress relief. I had to assume he was a giant combination of stress, malnutrition, lack of exercise and minimal fresh air. "He... he won't let me help him. And no one should have to do all that on their own."

Doc reached across the table to grab my hands and squeeze them while he locked eyes with me. His eyes were the kindest, softest light blue eyes I'd ever seen. They'd looked at me with unconditional love for all my years on earth, and I knew without a doubt that if I was worried about Nico, that's all Doc needed to know to be worried about Nico too.

"I'll handle it, West," he said softly. "Leave it to me, okay?"

I felt something relax inside me then, knowing as always that I was lucky to have family who loved me and supported me like I did. Grandpa was looking over at Doc like he hung the fucking moon, and I thought for the millionth time in my life that if I could just find someone to look at me like that for one freaking second in my life, I could die even happier.

CHAPTER 9

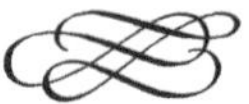

NICO

As difficult as it was to be stuck in the house with Pippa, it turned out that leaving the house to go into town was ten times worse. The minute people saw me, they had noticeable, negative reactions to me. Those reactions varied from simply turning their backs and walking away to outright rudeness and snotty comments about the weirdo from the West Coast.

I heard that phrase so often now I was beginning to think it was a thing. Insult by alliteration. *West Coast Weirdo…* hmm… Wants Weston Wilde.

What? No. *No I didn't.*

But of course I did. He was hot as fuck, muscled in the very best way, and disliked me. It was like a horndog's delight. The trifecta of sex godliness. Oh Jesus, I needed to get laid.

As I found a space to park on Main Street, I spotted a police car lingering just behind me on the road. After I parked and stepped out of my car, I noticed Curtis Billingham pull away. I'd seen the fucker everywhere since I'd gotten to Hobie. He was like a bad penny, always turning up wherever I went.

I pushed the door into the bakery and greeted everyone, not remembering names for shit. I was pretty sure the woman who ran the place with Adriana was called Rox, but that was about all I remembered. As I walked in to say hello, I felt an odd sense I was forgetting something. I realized it was the lack of having the baby with me. This was the first time I'd left Pippa at home with someone else, and I had a different Dr. Wilde to thank for it.

I'd been just cleaning up after breakfast that morning when I had a visit from Dr. and Mr. Wilde who were apparently West's grandparents. They'd just wanted to pop in and visit Pippa, but when Doc had headed back to the nursery to peek in on her, Mr. Wilde had pulled me aside to beg me to let Doc help out with the baby a few mornings a week.

"Goldie suggested it," Mr. Wilde had said. "She and I have both been desperate to find Doc something to do in his retirement. He hates golf, our boat is in for repairs, he doesn't have any interest in joining me in the garden, and the man needs baby time, you know? None of our damned grandkids seem to give a shit that we're ready for another batch of babies in our family. Is there any way you might agree to give Doc a little baby time? Maybe it could be a win-win situation for the both of you?"

Just as I opened my mouth to give my usual "no" answer to any offer of help, Doc came around the corner with Pippa in his arms. The look on the man's face as he beamed down at her was ridiculously sweet, and as a retired family doctor, he clearly knew what the hell he was doing with her.

"Um...," I said, glancing longingly outside through the front windows of the house. "I did kind of need to take care of a few things..."

Doc perked right up then and blurted, "Can we take care of the baby while you're gone? You'll get everything done much quicker without having to worry about Pippa."

"That's true, but—"

"If you need references, we have a few people you could call," Mr. Wilde said with a teasing voice.

I rolled my eyes and grinned at the two older men. "Okay fine. I'm going to take a shower first. If she's still alive when I come out, I guess

I'll give you a trial run. I just have to go deposit some money at the bank, stop off and do payroll at the bakery, and grab groceries before coming back. Hope that's enough baby time for you two softies."

The two men were still baby talking at Pippa ten minutes later when I waved at them over my shoulder on the way out.

Sugar Britches was located in a quaint little storefront in the center of Hobie's town square. When I'd first walked into the bakery, I'd been floored. The Adriana I'd known had been angry, spiteful, and terrible in school. It was hard to pair the adorable shop in front of me with the moody teen I'd grown up with.

Goldie had taken me by there for a few minutes one of the first days I was in town, but we hadn't stayed long. I knew Rox from that brief meeting, and I was sure she'd be wondering where I'd disappeared to in the days since then. She hadn't seemed all that thrilled to even meet me in the first place. I could hardly blame her. She was most likely worried about what I was planning on doing with the place.

And I had no idea what to tell her.

"Well, hello there, gorgeous," a young man's voice said from somewhere off to my left as I entered the storefront. I glanced around but didn't see anyone. "Down here," came the voice again.

Through the glass front of the pastry display I spied a guy on his knees, stocking sweets on the shelves.

"Hi, I'm Nico, Adriana's brother…," I began.

The man stood up, and I realized he wasn't quite as young as I'd originally thought, but was still definitely younger than I was. Maybe he was in his early twenties. The kid had gorgeous porcelain skin, red lips, and dark hair almost shaved off in a close buzz cut. I wondered if he had some Asian ancestors to give him the beautiful combination of dark hair and creamy-smooth skin.

"Nico Salerno," the guy drawled. His voice rolled my name off his tongue like he was fellating it. I fought to keep inappropriate thoughts out of my mind.

"Yes, that's me," I said unnecessarily.

"Well, well. Aren't you a hot piece of—"

Suddenly Rox stepped up and clamped a hand over the guy's mouth to shut him up before he could continue.

She looked at me with an apologetic face. "*Boss*. He means a hot piece of boss. Don't you, Stevie? Please excuse him."

I snorted and held out my hand to the guy. "Nice to meet you, Stevie. Do you work here too?"

"Certainly do, hot stuff," he said once the woman's hand came away from his mouth. His grin was adorable, and I knew right away I could be friends with the flirty man. Finally someone in this shit town who might speak my language.

He was dressed in dark leggings, Doc Marten boots, and some kind of oversized tank top in leopard print. It wasn't anything I'd be caught dead in, but it seemed to suit his funky personality just fine.

"Sorry it's taken me so long to swing back by and touch base with you guys. I kind of have my hands full with the baby," I began.

Rox winced. "How's Pippa without her mama?"

I felt my teeth clack together to stave off the emotion of thinking about Adriana. "She's doing fine. Doc and Mr. Wilde are looking after her for a bit today."

Stevie smiled. "I love Doc and Grandpa. They always throw the best parties. Wait till you see the haunted house they set up in their barn at Halloween. Fuckin' fabulous."

I glanced at Rox and back at Stevie. "Oh, I'll be gone by then. I'm just here temporarily. Are they your grandparents too?"

"Me? No. I wish," he said. "But I'm friends with one of their granddaughters."

"I remember the town being overrun with Wildes when I was growing up. How many are there? Seems like a lot."

At that point, everyone in the shop started snickering. One of the customers, who'd been giving me the side-eye from a small table in the corner piped up. "Oh, honey. Like a million, I think. You've got Weston, Hudson, MJ, Hallie, Winnie, Saint... Who am I missing?"

Another woman chimed in. "Cal, Otto, King..."

My jaw dropped, and I looked at Rox, who just shrugged. "Nine siblings?"

Stevie mouthed the word *Catholic* before closing the cabinet he'd been filling earlier and putting his finger to his chin like he really had to think about it. "No, there are ten I think. Who are we forgetting?"

"Har, har," a young woman said from a mouthful of cupcake at the coffee counter next to the pastry case. She didn't bother to look up from the magazine she was reading but lifted her arm up in the air and shot the guy the bird.

"Oh, right. That last one. Sassy, I believe they call her. Appropriate name," Stevie said, shooting me a wink. "And that's just the one set. Don't even get us started on their cousins."

The woman behind the magazine had a hard time not choking on her cupcake before pulling down the mag to greet me.

"Hi, Nico. It's nice to meet you. I'm Sassy Wilde. West is my big brother. Ignore Stevie. He's not very subtle when he flirts."

Stevie huffed and lifted his nose in the air, twirling around and pretending to busy himself at the coffee pots.

I waved to her across the open space between us. "Nice to meet you, Sassy. Are you sweeter than your brother? He's a bit rough around the edges." *What the hell?* Why did I say something so rude to a stranger?

Sassy's eyebrow rose as she looked at me, but she still kept a smile on her face. "Oh really? What has dear old Weston been up to?"

"Nothing, never mind. I shouldn't have said anything. That was inappropriate."

"No, no. Go on. Tell me what he's said. I'll tattle on him to Grandpa, and he'll get the whooping he so clearly deserves," she teased.

The thought of anyone but me whooping Weston Wilde's muscular ass was unacceptable, and the idea of *me* spanking him was… well…

"Nico?" Sassy asked, breaking me out of my reverie. I wondered if she could tell what I'd been imagining in my head.

"What? Oh, no. He's just… I think he just wants the best for Pippa, you know? And he knows I'm not good with babies," I explained in a rush before trying to change the subject. I turned back to Rox. "Hey, so apparently there's a rumor going around that you guys would like to get paid. I brought the checkbook, and Honovi said you all should have the time sheets here for me."

What I didn't mention was that, apparently, Adriana hadn't been the best at managing her shop's finances and there wasn't even enough money in the accounts to make payroll. I'd had to deposit some of my own money on the way to the shop just to make ends meet. I'd spent several of Pippa's nap times trying to make heads or tails of her convoluted system and finally realized it seemed like a sheer lack of basic bookkeeping knowledge was at fault. It didn't come as a surprise, considering she hadn't gone to college or anything. It was impressive she'd managed to accomplish as much as she had without a degree. I knew how hard it had been for me under the same circumstances.

Stevie handed me a mug of coffee and gestured to the pastry case with a quirked brow. "Like somethin' sweet?" he drawled.

I smiled gratefully and pointed to a thick chocolate-chip cookie. They looked like the ones my mom used to make, and the first bite proved they were, indeed, my mom's special recipe. I shouldn't have allowed the groan of ecstasy to escape my lips, but it was out before I could stop myself. I thought I heard Stevie whimper.

Rox shoved the guy aside and told him to make himself useful washing some dishes. She poured herself a cup of coffee and gestured me to a small table against one of the big picture windows by the front door.

"So, Nico, we've gotten an order for one of Adriana's hand-painted cakes," she began.

"Okay?"

"And, well, I can't do it. It requires artistic skills that I can't fake even if you paid me in tattoos," she said with a smile.

I smiled at her. "You know... I could pay you in tattoos. That's not a bad idea," I teased.

"Unfortunately, my bank doesn't accept those at mortgage payment time. But if you had your shit here, I'd hire you to do one in a skinny minute. The closest ink to Hobie is practically all the way to Dallas."

"Hm, food for thought. Tell me more about this cake."

She pulled out her phone and began scrolling through photos while she spoke. "Adriana had killer drawing skills. Must run in the family. Anyway, she made these cakes that had hand-drawn images on them. She called them painted cakes."

She showed me several photos of cakes with beautiful decorations. Most of them were floral designs, but some were of animals or cartoon characters for children.

"Wow, those are killer," I agreed, scrolling through for more.

She let out a breath and smiled sympathetically. "Right. So do I tell the client Sugar Britches doesn't do painted cakes anymore? People come from all over for them. And she was able to charge an arm and a leg for them too. It was great money."

I thought about the state of the shop's finances while I scrolled through the photos again.

"I'm assuming you can bake and prep the cake? All I would have to do is the painting part?" I asked. "I mean, don't get excited. I probably can't do as well as she did… But I can sure take a stab at it. When do they need to know by?"

Her face broke into a big grin. "The event is in about a week, and they're buying the cake from us regardless. If we can't do the specialty cake, they said they'll just buy a plain one and decorate it with fresh flowers. But they'd really prefer the painted cake. Apparently, it's for some guy who's retiring from Clyde's Garage. His wife is throwing a huge retirement party for him. She fell in love with a painted cake Adriana did for her bridge group luncheon."

"What does she want painted on it?" I asked.

Rox's eyes lit up. "Motorcycle shit."

I felt my heart kick up a notch. "No way."

"I swear. She said he's retiring so he can finally take all the trips he's been wanting to take on his bike. He's in the club that meets up. There's a bunch of guys who ride together, so they'll all be at the party."

"Cool. I'll give it a try. Can you get a cake ready tonight and leave it for me in the fridge? I'll come in early and try to work on it while Pippa takes her morning nap in the car seat. I can stash her in the office, right?"

Rox stood up and took our mugs around the counter to wash them. "Sure. Or you can come after lunch when it's slower and I can watch her while you work. Morning is busy around here since we're as close as it comes to a coffee shop."

"Good point. Okay. Sounds like a plan. Let me get those time sheets and make out some checks before I have to bolt."

Rox smiled at me and led me to a small room in the back off the commercial kitchen where it was obvious Adriana kept a desk and all her paperwork. She showed me where everything was, and I quickly got to work.

Just as I was finishing up and tidying Adriana's files back the way I'd found them, Stevie wandered in.

"So, Nico," he began with a grin. I could tell he was waving his flirt flag pretty high, and part of me perked up in response. I knew I was in dire need of some stress relief, and a blow job would have been just the thing.

"Yes, Stevie. What's up?" I offered him a dish of hard candies sitting on the desk while I waited for him to speak. He took one and fiddled with it between slim fingers before slipping it between those candy-red lips.

"So listen. There's this big bonfire party tomorrow night out at a place called Walnut Farm. It's not really a farm anymore but more of a giant vacant plot of land where people congregate this time of year and put on a big bonfire. Tons of people our age will be there with burgers and beer and shit. I was hoping you might come join us. Have a little fun and get out of the house, you know?"

"Well, I have the baby... but maybe I could ask Doc if he could watch her again." I smiled up at him, noticing a blush sweep across his cheeks.

"Yeah, that'd be cool. Can I pick you up?"

"No, I'm sure I'll have to duck out early regardless, so let me give you my number and you can text me directions. I'll just meet you there, if that's okay."

"Sure, sounds good," he said, stepping forward and waiting for me to scribble my number on a scratch piece of paper. "Got it. Looking forward to it."

"Thanks for including me, Stevie. I really appreciate it," I told him. And I meant it. I'd had so many sideways looks and whisperings going on behind my back around town since I'd arrived, it felt nice to be included for once.

"Well, Sassy's probably ready for a coffee refill, so I'd better go back out there. Thanks for this," he said, deliberately rolling the candy around on his tongue where I could see it. Suggestive little shit. He shot me a wink before turning and waving over his shoulder. "See you tomorrow night."

Thank fuck. After seeing that mouth and tongue, I decided tomorrow night couldn't come soon enough.

By the time I passed out the paychecks and made my way to the grocery store down the street, part of me was itching to get back to Pippa. Maybe I was nervous about leaving her for so long with strangers. What if Grandpa Wilde and Doc weren't who they said they were? What if they were older than I thought and had fallen asleep on the job?

I felt the need to get back to her like an itch under my skin.

After racing up and down the aisles of the little store, I grabbed the basics and checked out as quickly as I could. As I was loading up the car, I felt a presence behind me.

I turned to see who it was and noticed Curtis Billingham standing in my blind spot. He wasn't in uniform this time but stood erect and arrogant, as if he were a cop assessing the riffraff. I wasn't even sure there was such a thing as riffraff in Hobie, but if there was, I was it.

"Help you?" I asked as I set the final bag in the trunk of the rental car.

"Why are you still here in town?"

I looked around me at the small grocery parking lot. Several people were slowing down to stare at us even while they pretended not to. I assumed most people in town recognized Curt and they sure as hell had heard who the new purple-haired tattooed guy in town was.

"None of your business," I responded with a laugh, wheeling the cart back to the row of carts in front of the store. Curt's eyes tracked me as I made my way back to my car and got in the driver's seat. I turned over the engine and waited for him to move out of my way so I didn't back over him.

He didn't move.

This guy was really starting to piss me off. Clearly he was angry for some reason, but what that had to do with me, I wasn't sure. I hadn't been to town in fifteen fucking years—having left before our parents had even gotten engaged.

I rolled down the window and lost control of my patience.

"Get the hell out of my way, *Officer* Billingham," I barked.

Several patrons of the store gasped and stared openly now, squinting at me through the bright sunlight of the cold fall day.

"What did you just say to me?" Curt bit out between clenched teeth.

"You heard me. Unless you have reason to detain me, get the fuck away from my car. This is harassment, and we both know it."

His voice was low in response so that I was the only one who could hear it. "If you think I'm going to do one single thing to make your life easier in my town, Salerno, you've got another think coming. I'll stand here all day if I want to."

I threw the car back in park and turned the engine off, getting out of the car and slamming the door behind me. Every feeling of having been bullied by this fucker and others like him in my life came crashing down on me, and I had to remind myself that I was an adult now. I didn't have to take his bullshit anymore.

"Man up, you chickenshit," I shouted at him. "If you have something you want to say, then say it. But don't hide behind your damned badge or stalk me like a jealous lover. You've followed me all over this goddamned town trying to intimidate me, and it isn't working, you son of a bitch. Grow the fuck up."

At the mention of being my lover, his face turned purple and a vein stood out in his neck. Oh ho, seemed I had found a tender spot in our local homophobe's ego. Had he seriously not owned up to his sexuality in all this time?

He stepped forward and got in my face, his reflective lenses only inches from my forehead. I cursed my lame-ass genetics for making me so small compared to him, but whatever I lacked in body size, I was determined to make up for in attitude.

I gritted my teeth and fisted my hands beside my hips, trying so hard to remind myself that spending a night in the Hobie jail was a really bad idea, especially if it was run by this guy's friends.

"Is there a problem here?" The voice was familiar and soothing, and it came out of the blue from somewhere behind me. Suddenly stupid-ass tears threatened to fill my eyes, and I blinked them back in annoyance.

Weston Wilde.

I closed my eyes for the briefest moment of gratitude before reminding myself I didn't need help. I was fine on my own.

"No, no problem Dr. Wilde," I said. "Just asking my *dear brother* here to kindly step away from my vehicle so I can pull my car out."

When I referred to Curt as my brother, all hell broke loose. The officer lost his shit and pulled his arm back to strike. Before I could do the same or even defend myself, strong arms grabbed me around the waist and twisted me away, out of the trajectory of the meaty fist coming for me.

I scrambled against West and growled at him to let me go, but he murmured words of calm into my ear so low I couldn't catch anything but the tone of them. My breath was heaving, and with each drag of inhale, I felt West's arms tight around me. By the time I caught sight of Curt, two other men had a hold of him and were trying to keep him from coming after me again.

His sunglasses were gone, and his face was so deep red it was purple. He was shouting at me, and all I could make out were the words "trash," "coward," "sister," "girlfriend," and, finally, "faggot."

The men pulled Curt away and convinced him to leave before we gathered even more attention than we already had. My heart was beating so fast I thought it might pound out of my chest and fly away. I was full of a mix of anger, fear, and grief all mixed into one, and Curt Billingham had become the very epitome of all the things I'd felt about my hometown all those years. Hatred, unwelcome, bigotry, homophobia, and violence. It was ugly and awful and reminded me how much I needed out of that place for good.

I twisted out of West's arms and practically elbowed him away from me. I sure as hell didn't need pity from any of these idiots—especially from the aw-shucks, goodie-two-shoes doctor with the kind eyes trying to calm me down.

Fuck that. No thanks.

I made my way back to my car and jerked the door open.

"Nico, wait. Let me help you get home," West offered. The crowd around us had begun to disperse, and I realized my hands were shaking so hard I wouldn't have been able to unlock the car if it hadn't already been unlocked from before.

"I don't need anyone's help. I'm fine on my own."

I said it with such fierce determination, I almost believed it myself.

CHAPTER 10

WEST

I stood in the parking lot staring after him. What the hell had just happened? How had a simple stop at the grocery store turned into a heated confrontation between Curt and Nico? Was Curt seriously holding grudges after all this time? Surely not. Nico hadn't even been around when they'd lost the sheriff and Mrs. Billingham.

Curt still stood several cars away, trying to catch his breath. The men who'd held him back wandered off after several glances back toward me to make sure I wasn't going to cause any trouble. I waved at them to let them know it wasn't my fight, but I walked over to Curt to ask him about it.

"What the hell's wrong with you, Curt?"

"That son of a bitch comes back here after all this time and just, what? Takes over where he left off?" Curt spat.

"What do you mean?"

"Everything Adriana left behind should have been left to us, not him. And that punk-ass piece of shit just waltzes back into town like nothing happened and takes over? Fuck that, West."

"This is about the house? The bakery?" I asked in surprise. "What, did you want the baby too?"

I'd said it just to prove the point that the assets weren't all financial. There were responsibilities laid on Nico's shoulders that Curt wouldn't have wanted if his life depended on it.

"Who's he to you?" Curt asked, squinting at me without his reflective lenses on. He must have lost them in the scuffle.

"A… friend," I said, testing the word on my tongue. It didn't seem quite right. "Why?"

"I saw the way you touched him, the way you looked at him. You want to fuck him, don't you?"

I was taken aback by his harsh language, the f-word sounding completely wrong in that scenario.

"None of your business," I said with a laugh. "And considering you're dating Chloe Metz, it's particularly none of your business. What, is that jealousy you've got going on, Curt? Really?"

He looked around the parking lot, trying to be subtle about it, but I knew exactly what he was doing. The same old scaredy-cat dance.

I rolled my eyes. "Grow up," I muttered, turning to walk into the store.

"I'd stay away from that freak if I were you, West," he called out from behind me. "That family is nothing but trouble. Ask me how I know. Better yet, ask my brother."

I shook my head as I walked away. After a quick run through the store to pick up my own groceries, I made my way back out to my truck and loaded up. Grandpa and Doc drove up in Grandpa's old beat-up truck and pulled into the parking space beside me and rolled down Doc's window.

"This is a surprise. Just getting groceries?" I asked.

"We spent the afternoon with Pippa," Doc said with a grin. My heart did a familiar proprietary flip-flop whenever I thought about someone besides me having time with the baby, but I squelched it. This was my grandfather for god's sake.

"You're kidding? Nico let you watch her? Seriously?"

Grandpa got a twinkle in his eye as he glanced at Doc. "This guy's a miracle worker. The plan worked like a charm. Nico said we can come as often as we want for a few hours a day to get our baby fix."

"What?" I asked, frustrated. "That fucker won't leave me alone with her for one damn minute."

Doc chimed in. "Westie, has it ever occurred to you that maybe he doesn't leave when you're there because he enjoys your company?"

Warmth swirled in my gut at the thought, but I pushed it away.

"Ah, no. No freaking way. The guy hates me, and quite frankly, the feeling is kind of mutual."

Grandpa and Doc exchanged a look before Doc smirked at me. "Sure, West. Whatever you say, boy."

I gritted my teeth. He knew I hated when he called me boy. He did it to piss me off and make me feel like a kid, but I held my tongue out of respect for him regardless.

"So what's he doing now? Did he look upset?"

"Who?" Doc said, all innocent and shit.

I huffed. "Never mind." I turned to get into the truck and slammed the door behind me. Grandpa and Doc were laughing their fool heads off at me, but I ignored them. Bunch of assholes.

Even though I knew I wouldn't be well received, I decided to stop by Nico's place anyway. I wanted to make sure he was okay after the run-in with Curt, and on the way there, I thought about what my grandfathers had said.

Was it possible the guy was attracted to me? Could I get over my annoyance with the guy long enough to consider hooking up with him? And what about my vow never to trust someone I was only physically attracted to?

But I couldn't stop thinking about how good it would feel to touch him, if only for a night.

It wasn't that I was the kind of guy who hopped into bed with any old random person, but I also hadn't had much time for relationships between college, med school, residency, and running my own practice. And I hadn't been kidding when I'd said there were slim pickings in Hobie. Everyone I knew in town who was gay was related to me by blood with the exception of guys I knew too well like Stevie Devore. And Stevie was jailbait. Not to mention way too flirty and sex-crazed for my taste. The guy had known me for all of two seconds before he had my belt open in the back room of someone's Super Bowl party and was lowering himself to his knees despite my protestations. No thanks.

I pulled down the long drive to Nico's place and mentally slapped myself for thinking of it as his place. Adriana hadn't even been dead for two full weeks, and I already thought of her house as someone else's? Maybe this was a mistake.

I parked the car and leaned my forehead against the steering wheel. I was an idiot. Was I really hoping to go in there and get lucky with Adriana's brother? The guy who'd ditched her and left her to face the harassment and belittling of the Billingham family? No, Nico Salerno needed to account for his actions.

Instead of going in there and kissing the guy, I needed to go in there and confront him about what had caused him to bolt so long ago. That was what I needed to do. Make him explain himself.

I felt my jaw tighten in newfound ire as I hopped up the steps to the front porch and knocked.

There was no answer. I knocked again a minute later. Still no answer. By this time, I'd whipped myself up into a frenzy. The fear of him being hurt at the grocery store, Doc's implication Nico might want me, the reminder he'd abandoned my friend into the hands of bullies, and the annoyance of Nico not answering the door all had twisted me up inside until I was ready to boil over.

"Open up this goddamned door!" I shouted, banging my fist against the wood even harder. "I know you're here, your car is here."

The glass rattled in the windows alongside the doorframe, and I had a moment's realization that this kind of behavior wasn't like me. What exactly was my problem?

"Nico, dammit!" I yelled again. "It's West. Let me in."

Still nothing. I turned around and looked back toward our vehicles and the clearing around the cars. No sign of him out front. I began to get a bad feeling in my gut and wondered if something had happened to him. Maybe he was inside and hurt. What if he was asleep and the baby needed him? Maybe he was out for the evening in someone else's vehicle.

Could he have gone out with someone? If so, who? I ran my hands through my hair for the millionth time that day and turned back to peer in the window again. Nico was standing right there on the other side of the glass. I jumped a foot in the air, clutching my chest and trying not to screech like an idiot.

The look on his face was downright menacing, and I noticed he was dripping wet and covered with nothing but a short navy-blue towel wrapped around his waist. Oh shit, he'd been in the shower.

Nico yanked the door open and hissed at me. "West? What the fuck is wrong with you? Do you have any idea how long it took me to get Pippa down so I could take a fucking shower? Jesus Christ, you selfish prick. What do you *want*?"

His slim, inked fingers clutched the two corners of the towel together, and all I could see were miles and miles of Nico's body. The muscles, the inked skin, the drips of water making their way slowly along all the angles and curves of his chest and arms, his thighs and calves. Surely the blood in my cock was pounding louder than my fists on the door moments earlier. I felt my mouth water and my tongue flex as if in anticipation for licking the droplets from his skin.

"West?"

"Huh?" I asked. "What?" I felt dizzy and unsure of what was happening. What was I doing there?

"I asked you what you wanted," Nico grumbled at me. Even his angry voice was like a stroke to my desperate dick.

Your dick in my mouth or your hand on my cock—either way.

It was so clear to me in that moment, but I wasn't about to say it. I couldn't want him. I *wouldn't.* I had to remember it was *his* actions fifteen years ago that had led to Adriana feeling incredibly lonely as an adult.

"I… I…" I swallowed thickly. "I just came to see if you were okay."

Really, West? That's what you're going with? Ask him about why he left Hobie. Ask him about Curt. Ask him if he knows about Adriana and Reeve. Ask him if, god forbid, he left because you're the one who put the fucking idea in his head.

"I'm fine," Nico said. "But I can tell that's not the real reason you came, so spill it."

"Oh, ah. Well… there's this bonfire thing tomorrow night, and… um…"

Oh my god.

Nico's glare turned into a smirk. The sexy edge of his mouth turned up in a teasing way that did nothing to help calm my dick down. "I know about the bonfire. A guy named Stevie offered to take me."

In that moment, I swear to god, I wanted to kill everyone and everything. The day had escalated to a point beyond which I just could no longer maintain my sanity.

"No fucking way," I snapped. "You're not going anywhere with that kid. Forget it."

Nico's eyes widened, and I noticed his jaw tense at the same time.

"Since when did I need your permission, Dr. Wilde?" he sneered back. "You're not my mother."

"No, I'm not your mother," I growled. "In case you forgot, you decided long ago you didn't need a mother."

The minute, the *very second,* those words were out of my mouth, I knew I could never take them back, even though I would have given anything to do so in that moment. I didn't even know what possessed me to say it.

The hard smack against the side of my face came fast and furious, spinning me around with its intensity. I deserved it. I knew I did, but at that point, I had no more control over my mouth than I did my feelings.

"Get out!" Nico shouted at me. "Get the fuck out of my house!" His voice was a cross between angry and horrified, and my heart felt like it was going to shatter right there on the floor.

"I'm sorry for what I said, Nico, but I'm not leaving," I said, pushing my way in and holding up my arms to block his subsequent blows. I was so much bigger than he was I could have easily gotten him in some kind of hold so he couldn't hit me, but I didn't want to use my size against Nico.

"Yes you are, goddammit!"

"Nico, wait," I tried, grabbing for his flailing arms at least. At this point, his towel slipped off and he was completely naked, fighting me. I was both angry and turned on, which in turn made me disgusted with myself.

"Leave! Leave now. You don't know a fucking thing about me." His shouting turned to sobbing like the flick of a switch, shocking both of us. "Get off me. Get away from me, West… *please*."

The last word was a whimper just as he gave up the fight and collapsed against my chest in a heap. His balled fists went from pounding to clutching at my chest. I wrapped my arms tightly around him and slid us both down to the wooden floor, my back against the front door. The clean, masculine scent of his body wash or shampoo swirled around us in the air.

"Shhh," I said into his ear. "I'm so sorry. I'm so sorry, Nico. I didn't mean it. I'm so sorry." My words came out over and over like the rhythmic cadence of his hitching breaths.

He was curled into a ball in my lap, all slender arms and legs. His hair was a damp twist of color, and he pressed his face into my neck as he let out shuddering tears.

"She's gone, West." It was softly spoken, and I almost didn't catch it. "They're both gone and I never got to say goodbye." I realized then that he'd never had a chance to mourn his mother even though she'd been gone for years. As far as Nico felt, she might as well have died just the week before. My heart broke for him.

"I know, baby. I know," I murmured back, trying to calm his breathing and not really realizing what I was saying. "I miss Adriana too. So goddamned much."

"I… I… used to follow her around everywhere. I just wanted her to like me… And my mom… She's the only person who—" His breathing was still catching, and he was having trouble regulating his breath.

"Shhh, it's okay. Just breathe, Nico." I held my arm tightly around his body and used my free hand to brush the wet strands off his face.

We sat in a heap together like that, each of us taking comfort from the other's touch without either of us speaking. I listened to the catches of his breath, felt the warm fingers of his hands grasping my shirt, and pressed my lips to his temple.

My heart felt like it was going to beat out of my chest. After a few moments, I realized his breathing had calmed and he was toying with the buttons of my shirt with his fingers. He looked up at me, and our eyes met. The intensity of the connection between us was like a lightning bolt to the solar plexus, and it was too much. Too much for both of us, probably, but sure as hell too much for me considering my mixed-up feelings about the man.

When I'd seen him through the door, I'd wanted to kiss him, touch him. But now? Now what I wanted seemed like so much more than that.

Things went from natural to awkward in the span of time it took for me to take my next shaky breath. I quickly reached for the towel from where it lay in a damp heap next to us and handed it to him, trying not to look at his groin. There was no way in hell I'd be able to keep my cock in my pants if I caught sight of his, and regardless of what was happening between us, I wasn't about to make a move on the guy while he was clearly grieving.

"I'm… I'm so sorry. I shouldn't have come here. I should, ah… go," I stammered, shifting a bit so he wasn't held so tightly to me in case he wanted to stand up.

After covering himself with the towel, he lifted his head and locked eyes with me again. His were bright, and I noticed the varied shades of green and blue flecked together to make the most exquisite irises. Wet tears were caught up in his dark lashes, and I saw a tiny jagged scar along the edge of his chin next to a freckle. Even in his grief, he was more beautiful than any human being I'd ever seen close up.

I leaned forward and pressed a soft kiss to his forehead, sliding a hand into the hair on the side of his head to hold him still long enough to move my lips from his forehead to his cheek. He smelled clean and felt soft and warm against my skin. Not a single fiber of my being was okay with leaving him there alone.

Nico let out a tiny sound with his breath, and I felt it in the deepest part of my belly.

"Stay," he breathed.

God, how I wanted to.

"I can't. I shouldn't," I whispered. "Not like this. I have to go."

We stayed motionless for a few more moments before I spoke again. *"I have to go."* As if saying it the second time would force me to actually follow through with it.

"Then go," he said quietly, glancing down to where my arm had tightened back around him like a steel band.

I quickly pulled away from him. After tucking his head down and standing up, Nico quickly wrapped the towel back around his waist and secured the ends together.

I stood and turned to face the door, but before I could pull it open, Nico's arms came around my front and he pressed his body against my back. I felt his nose brush against the nape of my neck, and I closed my eyes with a sigh. I grabbed his hand from my chest and brought it up to my mouth.

I kissed his open palm before resting my cheek against it for the briefest of moments. And then I peeled his arms off me and strode out into the night.

CHAPTER 11

NICO

West stayed on my mind long after he drove away. The feel of his arms around me, the scent of him as my nose lay buried in his neck, the way he'd cared for me in that moment and admitted to understanding how I felt about losing Adriana without ever really having a chance to get to know her.

For just that second, I'd felt understood and loved. For just that moment, I'd had a tiny break from the loneliness I'd felt for the past fifteen years. But the moment came and went, and for some reason I felt even more alone now after having had it and lost it.

I'd asked him to stay, and he'd gone. Story of my fucking life.

I turned back toward Adriana's room in search of some clothes to put on. With my luck, Pippa wouldn't stay asleep much longer. Surely the only reason she'd stayed asleep through West's and my fight to begin with was the fact that she'd so recently fallen asleep. I'd learned quickly that those first minutes of her sleep after a bottle were like a coma. Nothing could bring her out of a milk-drug-induced stupor.

As I crossed the threshold into Adriana's room, I looked around and realized being in her personal space no longer upset me. Ever since I'd woken up in there several nights before, I'd felt at peace with being in her room. Of course, I'd never admit to West that he'd helped me cross that hurdle, but nonetheless, I was grateful to sleep in a real bed and not on the couch any longer.

I knew there would come a time I'd have to go through all her belongings and get rid of them—either by packing some away for Pippa or donating them to charity. Just the thought of it made me shudder.

~

THE FOLLOWING DAY, I was scheduled to meet Pippa's prospective adoptive parents at Honovi's office, and I was feeling anxious about it. I started a load of laundry so I'd have some decent clean clothes to wear and then popped leftovers into the microwave for dinner. Once I'd settled in to finish my evening with a movie on television, my cell phone rang.

It was Griff, but before I even had a chance to say hello, he was giving me hell through the phone.

"Are you fucking kidding me right now?" he railed. "I show up at the shop to find out where the hell you've disappeared to, and Mike tells me you have a sister who died?"

"Griff—" I tried.

"No! You listen to me, you selfish asshole. You've been my best friend for almost fifteen years, and you never once told me you had a sister. How could you? How could you go through losing your fucking sister and not tell me?"

I could hear him on the verge of losing his shit completely when I tried again.

"Griff, I'm sorry. Is Sam there? Can I talk to him please?"

A sob came through the line, just like I knew it would. I could kick myself for hurting him like that, and it was sure as hell going to take a while to earn back his trust.

"How could you, Nico? Where are you? I'm coming. Where the hell are you right now?"

I heard him break down fully and finally hand the phone over to his husband. When Sam came on, I could hear Griff's muffled cries and assumed he had his face tucked into Sam's neck or chest.

"Hey, Nico," Sam said in a kind, calm voice. "He's okay. Just give him a minute. For some reason he thinks your losing your sister is all about him."

I could hear Griff grumble something in the background followed by Sam shushing him.

"I understand Griff's reaction, Sam. I knew he'd be hurt," I admitted.

"Then why didn't you tell us? We would have come with you—you know that."

I blew out a breath. "That's just it. I knew you guys would drop everything to come with me, but you have Benji now. I didn't want you to have to leave him or, god forbid, bring a newborn on an airplane. I hadn't seen my family in fifteen years. It's not like we were close. The last time I saw Adriana, she was seventeen and mean as a snake. She fucking hated me." I tried to explain it wasn't quite the same as Griff or Sam losing their sister. They both had sisters they were extremely close to.

Sam's voice stayed steady and calm, and I thought about how damned lucky my best friend was to have found someone so perfect for him.

"Nico, it doesn't matter. Griff's coming there whether you like it or not. I'll stay here with Benji, okay? You know he's not going to take no for an answer. If you fight us on this, all three of us are coming."

"Yeah, okay. Fine. I'm in Texas. I'll text you guys the address, and you can fly into Dallas and rent a car for the drive out to Hobie. But give me some time, will you? I have my hands full with some shit right now and can handle a visit better in a few days."

"Good, here's Griff."

When I heard Griff's familiar voice let out a great big sigh into the phone, I rolled my eyes and grinned to myself. Fucking drama queen. But god, I adored the guy. It was true—he'd always been there for me.

"I'm sorry, Griffin," I said softly. "I didn't mean to hurt you. When I got the call, it really threw me, you know?"

"Yeah, I'll bet it did. I can't even imagine what went through your head. Will you tell me about her? Please?"

So I did. We stayed on the phone for another hour while I told him I'd had a surly teenaged sister named Adriana and a single mother who'd worked her ass off cleaning houses and painting nails on the side at a local hair salon. I told him about my mom falling in love with the sheriff and me overhearing people say the sheriff would never marry her as long as that queer son was in the picture.

Griff cried some more, but that time I did too. We'd both left our biological families and wound up living on the streets of San Francisco. But thinking back on all that was a strange kind of bittersweet —because had it not happened that way, we never would have met each other. And I sure as hell could never wish for that.

"She had a baby, Griff," I said with a wrecked voice. "Her name is Pippa."

"Oh my god, Nico. That poor thing."

"Yeah, so, I have her now, but don't worry. There's a nice couple who wants to adopt her."

There was silence on the line for a long time. I wanted to ask him what he was thinking, but I wasn't sure I really wanted to know.

"Adoption? Wow, Nico," he said. "How are you handling all that? A baby. Wow."

I snorted. "I know, right? Me with this four-month-old baby girl. But we're managing okay. I can't say I'm sleeping much at all."

Griff laughed and turned away from the mouthpiece to relay that news to Sam. I could hear them both snicker on the other end and smiled to myself. I finally knew how they felt.

"Listen, Nico. I'm gonna call Mom and see if she wants to come with me. That way if you need help and I have to get back, she can stay."

"No, Griff. There's no need for that. I promise, I'm doing fine."

"I'm not asking your permission. It's happening. You know she'll insist on coming anyway the minute I tell her."

And I did know that. In addition to being a kind and generous woman, Rebecca Marian had six biological children and three adopted children. She was maternal, loving, and supportive of everyone she'd ever met. If there were any family I'd always wished I'd been a member of, it was the Marian family. And short of legally adopting me too, Thomas and Rebecca Marian had done everything in their power to be there for me over the years, including helping finance my tattoo shop.

I wasn't used to needing others, and I sure as hell wasn't used to admitting it. But maybe it was okay to do it just this once.

"Yeah, okay. I'd like that, Griff. Tell her thanks for me, okay?" I said.

THE FOLLOWING day I showed up at Honovi's office dressed in a clean button-down shirt and the nicest jeans I owned. I tried to look as put together as I could so the prospective parents didn't think there was a lunatic in charge of the baby while they were waiting for the process to begin.

Luckily, Goldie had shown up at the house that morning to offer to stay with Pippa so I didn't have to take her to the meeting. I was uneasy about letting the adoptive parents spend time with her before I had a chance to see what I thought of them. Even though everyone in town sang the praises of the vaunted Warners, I wasn't about to let my niece go into the arms of a couple I hadn't vetted myself.

When Hon brought the Warners into the conference room, their outward appearance indicated they probably were the golden couple everyone said they were. Jennifer and Daniel Warner were like catalog parents. Open up the catalog of perfect adoptive parents, and there you saw Jennifer and Daniel Warner.

Daniel was in software sales, and Jennifer was a middle school science teacher. They were so fucking perfect I wanted to slap them. I wondered what their secrets were. Did he hide a BDSM kink? Or was she secretly sleeping with a student? Were they secretly into prepping and hoarding weapons? Were they related to Hannibal Lecter? Fuck, why was this making me so twitchy? Didn't I want Pippa to go to a loving family?

"It's nice to meet you Nicolas," Jennifer Warner said to me with a friendly smile as I was introduced. I could tell she was nervous, and she'd obviously put as much if not more care into her appearance than I had. She was wearing a slim skirt to her knees and a cardigan set with a simple gold chain necklace. Her shoulder-length blond hair was tucked neatly behind her ears, and her makeup was simple and understated.

Daniel stood next to her with an arm around her waist and one hand outstretched for a handshake. "Daniel Warner. It's very nice to meet you."

"Please call me Nico," I said before shaking their hands and taking my seat at the table.

The meeting was just a preliminary opportunity to meet, but it felt more monumental than that. It made the adoption seem real in a way it hadn't before. I began to imagine Pippa in their arms and tucked away in a tidy, color-coordinated nursery somewhere in their home at night. The Warners already had a son, so Pippa would have a big brother to grow up with.

What if the brother ended up ditching her down the line? What if he was a punk who let her down? Whose selfish actions left her in the lurch?

Nausea began to swirl in my gut the longer I sat with them. It was almost like every nice thing I learned about them made me even sicker. The only negative I'd heard so far was Daniel's comment about being friends with "the baby's uncle Curt." But everyone knew Curt, and you could hardly blame a guy for trying to reassure me he had some kind of connection to the family already. Everything else had been perfect. They were the ideal family for little Pippa.

And it made me want to scream.

This meeting had started the timer on the adoption process, and my remaining moments with Pippa suddenly became limited. On the one hand, I would soon be free to return to my real life in California. On the other, I'd be saying goodbye to the little girl forever. It was a noxious mix of anticipation, fear, and excitement. But most of all, guilt.

By the time Hon had handed me a packet of paperwork to look over and walked me to the door, I wasn't quite sure whether I was going to make it home without vomiting or breaking down in tears like a child.

"Nico, as of right now, we're just waiting for the birth certificate to be sent from the registrar's office. If Adriana had received a copy of it already, we weren't able to find it in her things. I would expect it to be here in a day or two at the latest. So that means everything will be ready to move forward legally, and then we'll just be waiting on your consent. Take some time to think this through, okay? It's a big decision. The Warners understand this is a lot to take in all at once. I'm sure they can be patient if you need more time."

"It'll be fine," I said in reply. "It's not like I'm going to take a newborn back to California and raise her over a tattoo shop." I'd been trying to lighten the mood, but my attempt fell flat.

The attorney shot me a sympathetic smile and wished me well.

After the short drive home, I walked in the door to the house, fully intending on grabbing Pippa up from wherever she was and just holding her, but before I had a chance to even close the front door, Goldie took one look at my face and pulled me into a strong hug.

"The baby," I said in a rough voice against her shoulder. I wasn't quite sure if it was a statement or a question, but it didn't really matter.

"Pippa's fine, but you aren't, honey. And that's okay," she said. "Just let it out, sweetie."

I didn't cry, but I did let myself indulge in her loving embrace for several long beats.

"Why is this so hard?" I muttered.

Goldie chuckled softly as we pulled apart. Her eyes were kind as she patted one of my cheeks. "Love always is, Nico. Love always is."

That word was enough to get my attention. *Love*. I didn't love her. I barely knew her. There was no love involved in this for me. Sure, I'd loved my mom and my sister Adriana, but I'd left them so long ago.

And the one time I thought a man loved me the way I'd wanted… no, *needed*… to be loved at the time, I'd been dead wrong.

Did I love Pippa? It wasn't possible. She was just a tiny nothing of a thing. Fifteen pounds of milk and poop, who had the ability to make my ears bleed at the drop of a hat. Love? Surely not. And after watching goddamned Weston Wilde walk away from me the night before after the tempting promises of his touch, I knew there wasn't even the hope of love for me in Hobie fucking Texas.

And I couldn't wait to get out of there the first chance I got.

CHAPTER 12

WEST

The next day at work seemed to last ten days. All I could think about between patients was the feeling of having Nico Salerno in my arms. Holding him had made everything in my life fall into place—as if my body had been waiting for his before it could finally relax. It was a shock to me. After all, people weren't supposed to have those feelings for someone like Nico.

Wanting to sleep with him? Yes.

Wanting to hold him and care about him? No thanks.

Nico was a proven flight risk. An angry, surly man who had a history of choosing himself over others. The kind of person who could pawn off his own niece onto a pair of strangers so he could go back to his own self-centered life. He wasn't a kind, sweet man but an instigator with a chip on his shoulder against all things Hobie. And Hobie was my life, my home. I was born and raised in Hobie, Texas, and my entire family went back years in that small town. How could I want to be with someone who hated something so integral to who I was?

I couldn't want him.

Which was all well and good except for one fact.

I wanted him.

When work was finally done for the day, I made my way upstairs to my kitchen and saw my brother Hudson sitting at the table working on his laptop.

"Hey, I didn't know you were here. Why didn't you come find me downstairs?" I asked.

He looked up and smiled. "Didn't want to bother you and I had some work I needed to finish before the weekend." Hudson's eyes narrowed at me briefly. "West, is something wrong? You look tired or something."

"I'm fine. You still up for going to the bonfire tonight?" I asked, pulling down a bottle of whiskey and opening the fridge in hopes I had a can of Sprite in there.

Hudson nodded and then gestured to the whiskey. "Make me one too?"

"Yeah. Who else is coming? Any of the cousins?"

"Not sure about the cousins. Sassy and Hallie for sure. Cal wants to come, but he knows I won't let him drink around me until he's twenty-one."

I finished mixing the drinks and handed one to Hudson before taking the seat across from him at the table.

"What about King?" I asked, referring to our younger brother who usually kept to himself. The rest of us had spent several years trying to lure him out of his self-imposed solitude, but nothing seemed to work.

Hudson just shot me a look.

I blew out a breath, trying not to think about my other siblings who were currently scattered around in different cities. "Okay, so, the usual suspects then. You, me, Hallie, Sassy and Cal if he doesn't drink."

"We both know he'll drink. He'd better just make sure I don't see it."

"You're worse than Mom and Dad," I said with a laugh. "They never gave a shit if we drank at aged twenty. Jesus."

"Yeah, well, as long as they're overseas, I'm in charge," Hudson said with a wink. He took evil pleasure in bossing our siblings around now that Dad was working in Singapore.

"That nurse who has a crush on you is going to be there," I told him, deliberately not mentioning her name to see if I could trap him. "Can't remember her name though."

"Darci?" he said.

Gotcha.

"Yeah, sounds right," I teased.

He rolled his eyes and blew out a breath. "Good. It's been fucking ages since I've been out on a date."

"Bullshit."

"Well, it's been ages since I've been out on one that I was remotely interested in possibly having a second with," he corrected with a chuckle.

"Better. So you're going to ask her out?" I took a sip of my drink and set it down on the table long enough to grab a bag of chips out of a cabinet for us to share. Happy hour, bachelor style.

Hudson shrugged and furrowed his brows. "Guess so."

"What's your hesitation? It's not Charlotte is it?" He'd dated the woman for several years and gone through a nasty breakup the year before. I'd wondered if his inability to find someone he liked more than one date's worth was because he was having a hard time getting over her.

"What? No. God no. That's not it. We'll see. Darci seems nice enough, yeah?"

"I think so. Super sweet to the patients and great with kids. She'd make a good mother to your children, Hud," I teased. The guy had always wanted a family. It was just a matter of finding the right woman.

He swatted me on the shoulder and told me to fuck off. We gave each other hell for a little while longer until it was time to get going.

"Come on, let's go pick everyone up and see if Doc and Grandpa want to come with us," I said, standing up and grabbing my coat and scarf in case it got colder later.

"Doc and Gramp are babysitting for Pippa tonight, aren't they?" Hudson asked. "That's what Sassy told me anyway."

I thought about what Nico had said the night before about going to the bonfire with Stevie Devore, and I wanted to punch something. Instead of saying anything though, I pushed my anger down until a couple of hours later when the bonfire was in full swing.

My siblings and I had arrived together and greeted many of our usual friends. We'd all gone to high school in Hobie and still kept in touch with our classmates who'd stayed in town. It seemed like the same old group of people our age congregated at certain events throughout the year. Saint Patrick's Day green beer fest at the pub, Fourth of July fireworks at the lake, first bonfire night at Walnut Farm, the Halloween party at Doc and Grandpa's place, a holiday happy hour the night after Thanksgiving. It was events like these that made me fall in love with my small town all over again.

When I'd first sat down on a long tree trunk set up to form one of the giant benches around the bonfire, I'd wound up talking to my brother Cal for a while. King had reluctantly come too, and was sitting quietly on my other side. Cal was "taking a break" from college while he tried to figure his shit out. Mom and Dad were none too thrilled, so I tried to gently inquire what his plans were. Currently he was working at the marina as a jack-of-all-trades. He'd gone to fancy sailing camps during the summers growing up and was desperate to get a job on a boat somewhere.

While we were talking, I noticed Nico arrive. Sure enough, he was with Stevie who was clearly in seventh heaven on the arm of the exotic new guy. I could hardly blame the guy—there weren't many good options for someone as different from the mainstream as Stevie. I was sure seeing someone like Nico waltz into town was like taking in a fresh breath after living under smog.

But that made no difference to my unreasonable sense of ownership of the purple-haired man next to him. Because I sure as shit wasn't about to sit there and watch Stevie tee Nico up as his boy toy for the night.

"Excuse me, guys, I see someone I want to say hello to," I said to my brothers.

"Wait, West," Cal said, grabbing my arm.

I settled back on the log and looked over at him. "What is it?"

"If I knew something bad about someone… should I tell… someone?" he asked. I could see how unsure he was, but that wasn't quite enough information to know how to answer the question.

"What do you mean? What kind of bad? Like a crime?" I asked.

He blew out a breath and looked at his fingers, which were twisted together between his knees. I felt King lean forward to listen in.

"I found out a married man in town is having an affair. They were, ah, in one of the boats, you know?" He reached down for the soda bottle he'd set on the ground between his feet and fiddled with the label. "It's just… It would be bad if it got out but, like, if it didn't… that would kind of be bad too. Right? I mean, there are kids involved."

His nerves had brought back the insecure teen in him, and I could tell he was really upset about the situation.

"Does anyone else know? Did anyone else see?" I asked.

He shrugged. "Not sure."

I thought for a minute, unsure of what to suggest. "Normally, I'd say to stay out of someone's marriage. But there are certain exceptions to that rule."

"Such as?"

Movement flashed in the corner of my eye, and I turned to see Stevie running his fingers through Nico's hair as if to style it. But it was clear to anyone looking, he was just trying to get his hands on the guy. "Assault or abuse," I said without really paying attention to our conversation anymore.

"New guy's cute," King said softly from my other side.

"Huh?" I said, whipping my head around. "No he isn't."

What was I even saying? Of course he was cute. He was fucking gorgeous.

Cal barked out a laugh, making me jump slightly. "You're smoking crack, brother. Every gay guy here has been watching that dude. Not to mention, many of the women. He's fucking beautiful. Like a rare bird or something."

My heart sped up as I realized Nico could have his pick of the people around that damned fire, including the brothers sitting on either side of me.

"The only other gay guys here besides me are you two and Stevie."

"Yeah. And?" he asked with a knowing grin and a wink.

Goddammit.

"How do you know who he is?" I asked, distracted by the sight of Nico laughing at something Stevie had said. "Did you hear about him from Doc and Grandpa?"

"Maybe."

"Well, the guy's too old for you, so forget it."

"He's like twenty-nine, West. Hardly too old for me." He laughed again and leaned his shoulder into mine. "Think I should go over there and introduce myself?"

"Fuck you," I muttered, standing up. "He's thirty. By the way, next time you put a rum and Coke in an empty soda, don't use a Sprite bottle."

Cal looked down at the brown liquid in the green-labeled bottle and winced before flicking his eyes over to where Hudson stood talking to Nurse Darci. Hudson hadn't noticed Cal's faux pas yet, so Cal had time to fix his mistake. He scurried over to the coolers to find something else to put his drink in.

As I made my way to where Stevie and Nico were standing, I was stopped by several people offering condolences on the loss of Adriana. Some gave me hugs, some clapped me on the back and told me they were glad to see me at the bonfire. Every single one of them made side-eyes at Nico and tried to talk to me about "the brother" being back in town. Not one of them seemed to have anything nice to say, and they all seemed to think he was a punk.

Which set my teeth on edge, because I knew that I, too, had assumed he was a punk when he first arrived. I, too, hadn't given him any credit for having a heart or respect. But when I'd seen him break down and cry for his family, I realized there was more to him than I could begin to imagine. I was hit with the tardy reminder that you couldn't judge a book by its cover and why in the hell had I allowed myself to fall prey to that immature behavior in the first place? I knew better.

With the anger, frustration, and desire all churning inside me, I was a time bomb just waiting to be set off.

By the time I got to Nico, just the sight of him was a soothing balm. I wanted to walk straight into his arms and lose myself in his warm skin—skin that smelled like coffee and raspberries and clean baby. I wanted him desperately.

And it was time to take what I wanted.

CHAPTER 13

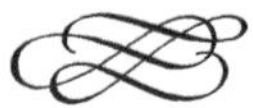

NICO

I was standing in a small group of people, being flirted at aggressively by Stevie. While I appreciated being the center of someone's positive attention, the guy was doing absolutely zero to my dick. On top of that, I was beginning to recognize people I'd gone to school with, and every single one of them studied me like I was a bug pinned to a display board.

And of course Curtis Billingham was there. He kept shooting hate lasers at me from his spot by the bonfire. I was surprised to learn from Stevie that Curt was dating a nice woman named Chloe. She was the petite red-haired woman who'd approached me earlier to ask me for Adriana's chocolate-chip-cookie recipe. I'd politely refused, wondering idly how long it would take before she realized her boyfriend preferred his cookies with nuts.

Just as I was about to beg off and go home, I spotted a pissed-off Weston Wilde storming my way. The look on his face was downright feral, and he came at me like a stalking panther.

"I need to talk to you," he said in a somewhat menacing tone. His eyebrows were furrowed, and his gaze was intense, like he was royally peeved about something. Whatever it was, it was clearly all my fault.

"No thanks." I sighed, not wanting to deal with his surliness on top of everything else.

West froze for a beat before narrowing his eyes even further. I wondered idly if smoke might come trickling out of a nostril or ear canal.

"That wasn't a question." This time his voice was a deep rumble, the kind that had my dick finally waking up and realizing it was time for action. Fucking idiot dick.

Being bossed around by the highbrow doctor in front of the rest of the people our age in town set my teeth on edge. Two could play the asshole game.

"I don't give a fuck. The answer is still no. Now go away. Stevie was just introducing me around. He said there were a few other guys here I needed to meet too. Your brothers, I think?"

Stevie had said no such thing, but I'd heard through the grapevine that West had several gay brothers, and I assumed at least one of the guys he'd come with tonight was one of them. Of course, they were all hella gorgeous. Like the genes had been bestowed upon their parents as gifts from the gods. I could see Doc's genetics in the Wilde kids but not Grandpa Wilde's, and I wondered not for the first time what their story was.

At the mention of his brothers, West's face got even stormier, and I could tell he wanted to grab me up by the shirt and shake me.

Yes please.

"Nico. May I *please* have a word in private?" he said through clenched teeth.

I studied him, wondering how much I should push it. The memory of his arms around me warred with the knowledge that he didn't want me even long enough to stay for a quick fuck the night before. And everyone standing at that bonfire knew full well that I would never be good enough for Dr. Weston Wilde—vaunted member of the famously historic Wilde family who may as well have fought at the Alamo for all I knew.

"Nope," I said breezily, turning my back on him to pretend to pay attention to Stevie again.

Little hairs rose on the back of my neck, informing me West had stepped in close behind me. I tried not to close my eyes and feel for his heat.

The voice was a breath carried in the night air straight into my ear. It was no longer angry, but filled with promise. "Come with me now voluntarily, or I will throw your sexy ass over my shoulder and take you by force. Is that what you want, *Nico*?"

I did close my eyes then and prayed to the god of wood to tell my goddamned dick to stand down. My heart rate was pounding in my cock, and my balls were on their knees begging for more of that sexy voice in my ear.

The most secret part of me imagined what it would be like if I said no again—just refused him and forced him to manhandle me back to his cave where he would make me submit to his every pleasure. That secret part was not helping soften my cock. Not one single bit.

"Stevie," I croaked before clearing my throat and trying again. The guy's eyes went wide in front of me, and I saw them glance at the alpha male spraying his pheromones all over my back. "Stevie, sorry to leave you so soon. Another time?" I tried to play it cool, but surely no one was buying my bullshit.

I felt a strong hand land on my hip, fingers digging in to push me toward where the cars were parked. Maybe I could let him have his way with me just this once. For sex reasons.

For filthy, bossy, play-doctor-with-me, sex reasons.

"Give me your keys," West demanded as we walked in the direction of my rental car. I didn't see his truck anywhere, and before I knew what the hell I was doing, the key to my car was in West's large hands.

Oh, who the fuck was I kidding? Before the night was out, that wasn't the only thing of mine that was going to be in those strong, capable hands.

We didn't say a word until he pulled the car around back of a huge Victorian home I'd seen in town. I vaguely remembered having been there as a child but couldn't remember why.

"Where are we?" I asked.

"My house. Wilde Family Medicine."

He got out of the car and slammed the door closed behind him. As I glared after him out the window on the driver's side, I felt the door on my side open behind me. West leaned across me to unbuckle my seat belt, and I bit back a groan at his nearness. The fabric of his coat brushed against the side of my throat, and I wondered if that was precome I was feeling in my pants.

"*Fuck*," I muttered under my breath.

His eyes met mine, and I could tell he'd heard the word as a request rather than a curse. His eyes were like lust lasers pointed straight into my libido, and my cock hammered even louder in my jeans. When the hell had these things gotten so tight?

The man smelled like bonfire smoke and whiskey, and I wondered why no fragrance company had bottled the combination before. It was the very essence of this man from Texas, and I wanted to drink it down one small sip at a time.

I opened my mouth to say something. I wasn't sure what, but it was surely something ridiculous and embarrassing. By the time I got a sound out, West had yanked me out of the car and thrown me over his shoulder just like he'd threatened to do at Walnut Farm.

Unfortunately, I squeaked like a baby bird and grabbed on to his back in fear during the brief moment it took me to regain my senses and fight him.

"Let me go, goddammit. I'm not a child." I grunted.

"Aren't you though?" he spat back.

Fucking asshole.

"No! I'm not. I'm a grown-ass man. Put me the fuck down."

"No."

"What?" That may have come out as another squeak. I hadn't taken him for someone who'd deny a request to remove his hands from my person. He was Mister Polite after all.

"It's a word you established knowledge of quite clearly a little while ago in front of our neighbors. The word means... your request has been denied."

I bumped along like a sack of potatoes, speechless. Stairs receded behind us as we went up into a higher level of the historic home.

The fuck?

Was this guy seriously taking me straight to his bedroom? When I really thought he wasn't going to let me go, I struggled a little more out of nerves or fear. Fear of what, I wasn't so sure. It wasn't that I was afraid of West himself, because I wasn't. Maybe I was afraid of what would happen if I got a taste of him. If I let *him* get a taste of *me*.

Or maybe I was afraid of getting a taste of something I'd want more of. Afraid of awakening a hunger in me that had always lain dormant just waiting for the right temptation to come along.

Either way, my body was sending me every message that I wanted this man. And my brain was nodding its fool head like an idiot. It was only my heart hiding over in a corner by itself whispering, *Please don't do it—you know I can't take it again.*

In the end, the vote was two to one in favor of allowing Weston Wilde to do whatever the fuck he wanted to me. So when he put me down in what I quickly realized was his kitchen, I was all in.

But just because I was all in, didn't mean for one minute I intended to make it easy for him.

CHAPTER 14

WEST

Now that I had Nico Salerno in my kitchen, what exactly was I expecting to do with him?

I stared at him, feeling a powerful urge to dominate the man. The urge was unlike anything I'd ever felt before. Had you asked me a few hours before what I was like in bed, I would have said I was pretty much plain vanilla. Boring as hell—give, take, whatever. Little bit of both, mostly and always done with manners and polite respect.

But with Nico? I didn't want to give, I wanted to *assault*. I didn't want to take, I wanted to *command*. My muscles thrummed with the need to overtake him. To grab his shoulders and force him to his knees in service of my raging hard-on. My teeth wanted to bite and nip every last inch of him, and my tongue wanted to slide into places on Nico's body I'd never even laid eyes on before.

I didn't want to sleep with the man.

I wanted to own him.

While my head had been swirling with thoughts of taking him, my body had been stalking forward slowly until my chest bumped his body back against the kitchen wall. Nico's eyes were wide and his pupils blown. He wanted me as much as I wanted him. I could feel it as easily as I could feel the warm breath of his exhales against the skin of my neck.

"Take off your coat," I said gruffly.

His eyes narrowed, but he did as I said. I watched the twin hoops in his bottom lip and knew they were my first target as soon as I had the green light to put my mouth on him.

"What are we—" Nico began, but I cut him off.

"Shoes next."

"What?"

I stepped back, crossed my arms in front of my chest, and looked down at him. "Take off your shoes."

Nico's nostrils flared. "Like hell I will."

Very slowly, almost in slow motion, I moved my hands to the wall on either side of him and my lips to his ear. Our cheeks brushed lightly against each other, and my nose felt the cold metal of his multiple ear piercings. I breathed hotly into his ear. "Take. Off. Your. Shoes."

His entire body shuddered against me, and I felt him kick his shoes off to the side with the movement of his body's tremor. Something about his following my orders made my cock even harder, and I knew I was playing with fire.

I kept our cheeks together and nuzzled my nose under his ear before whispering again. "Now take off *my* coat."

He bristled but did as I commanded, muttering the whole time about what a bossy motherfucker I was. It took all my self-control not to snicker.

I could tell he was trying to decide whether or not to fight me. It was like there were two Nicos there—the one who wanted to fight me and the one who wanted to fuck me.

And I was fine with fighting *and* fucking. In fact, if I was being honest, I wanted him to struggle. I wanted him to want it of course, but I was okay with him being angry about wanting it. I was a little angry about wanting it too. I wasn't supposed to want Nico Salerno—punk-ass tattoo artist from California who wasn't all that keen on babies. But we didn't always get to choose who pushed our buttons. And he sure as hell was pushing all mine.

Hard.

I kicked off my own shoes and ran my hands from his shoulders down to his wrists. "What do you want, Nico?" I asked in a low voice. "Tell me."

He looked up at me in surprise, unable to believe I'd ask for his feelings on the matter. I could see his thoughts jamming up in his brain as if he was unable to decide what he wanted, much less how to answer me.

I leaned forward again until our foreheads were pressed together.

"Let me tell you what *I* want then. I want to fuck you. I want to dominate you. God help me, I even want to throw you around a little. You drive me up the fucking wall, but I want you more than I've wanted anyone in a very long time, if ever. Let me have you."

His aquamarine eyes were huge and dark, and his breathing was coming faster and faster.

"Please," I whispered against his lips. "Please, Nico, let me take you."

The moan that came out of him was full of want and need and desperation. But most of all, it was one hundred percent capitulation and acceptance. The minute I heard it, I sprang into action.

My hands were still holding his wrists, and I brought them up above his head on the wall where I took both of them into one hand and held them tightly. My mouth landed on his in a crush, and I swallowed his whimper while stamping down one of my own.

His mouth tasted like strawberries, and I licked into him to find more sweetness. I used my free hand to cage his throat so I could devour that mouth as long as I wanted to without him moving. Nico's hips tried to thrust into mine, but I pulled my lower body away. Lord only knew why I refused him the satisfaction of rutting against me, but I did.

I spent full minutes exploring his mouth and then softening the kisses to toy with the little hoops in his bottom lip. I licked and pulled and fiddled until Nico was panting short breaths against my mouth.

By the time I had to pull away from the kiss to catch my own breath, he made a sound of frustrated disappointment.

"Let me touch you," Nico said, arms still pinned above him.

"No thanks," I teased, mimicking his response at the bonfire.

I saw his nostrils flare again and knew that angry Nico was getting ready to come out to play.

Game on. I fucking loved angry Nico.

"Let me touch you goddammit," he snarled, pulling at my grip to get his hands free.

"Nope," I mocked again. This time I leaned forward and licked along the edge of one of his ears before speaking into it. "You didn't really think I was going to let you control this, did you?"

He made a quick attempt to knee me in the groin, but I anticipated it. I spun him around quickly until he was facing the wall and I was plastered along his back, one hand holding his wrists above our heads again and my lips against the back of his neck. My knees were bent a little on either side of his legs so I could stay pressed against him while I kissed his nape. My cock settled perfectly against the crease of his jeans.

"Say the word 'stop' and all this ends, okay?" I promised him, flexing my hips into him. "I have no interest in fucking around with someone who doesn't want me."

Nico didn't say a word but nodded. Good, we were on the same page.

There was some kind of tribal tattoo along the side of his neck, and I traced it with my tongue. I slowly moved my free arm under the hem of his shirt and around to his abdomen.

All his muscles clenched in anticipation of my next move.

"God, you feel so good, Nico," I murmured. "I want to touch you everywhere. Lick you everywhere. Shove my cock so deep inside you all I can hear is your voice screaming my name."

"Jesus, fuck," he moaned. "Please."

I moved my hand down his stomach to his waistband and flicked the button open before sliding just my fingertips under the very edge of his underwear band.

"You want me to touch you, Nico?" The sound of his name on my tongue tasted like the carrot that had been dangled in front of me since he'd waltzed into town the week before.

"Yes," he breathed.

"Mm-hm?" I nuzzled into his hair, smelling a mix of bonfire smoke and the shampoo smell I'd noticed earlier. My fingers lowered farther, and I felt the wet tip of his cock against them. I groaned against his skin. "So fucking sexy. You're already leaking for me?"

I heard a sharp intake of breath and felt his cock jump out and lightly slap the back of my hand.

"Please, West… I want to touch you," he asked again—only this time I felt like I was hearing the real Nico behind the words. So I let his hands go and moved my hand from his wrists down into his pants to grasp his erection.

CHAPTER 15

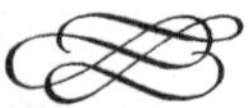

NICO

It was quite possible I was going to come the minute I felt those warm fingers wrap around my stiff cock. I gasped and quickly dropped my own hand down to squeeze the base of it just as he reached for my shaft.

"Stop!" I barked before I could stop myself.

Within a split second, West was gone and I almost fell on the floor from the loss of him. I reached out to grab the wall for support. There were no longer hands in my boxer briefs. No longer a strong body pressing me against the wall. No hot breath on the back of my neck raising goose bumps all along my skin.

"W-West?" I asked, turning around to look for him.

He was standing several feet away with a look of regret on his face. Was that because of me? Had I done something to make him change his mind about this?

"Nico, I—" he began.

"What the hell just happened, West?" I asked. "Where did you go?"

"What?" he asked incredulously. "You said stop! Dude, you said to stop so I stopped, just like I said I would. What did you expect me to do?"

I played back the past few moments in my head and burst out

laughing. "West, I said stop because you were gonna make me come. Jesus. I only said stop for you to let go for a minute and let me stave off my goddamned orgasm."

The corner of his lip quirked up on one side. "Really? You didn't really want me to stop?"

"Hell no, I didn't want you to stop. Are you fucking kidding?" I stalked closer to him and brought my hands to the hem of my shirt. "I thought we were just getting started. I simply wanted it to last longer than five seconds." I yanked the shirt over my head and threw it to the side.

West grinned at me then, and it was the cutest fucking thing I'd ever seen. My heart did a stupid little flip-flop deal, and I resisted the urge to hug the man. Instead, I leaned in and let my mouth trail kisses along his jaw, his neck, and down into the open collar of his shirt.

"Take off your shirt." Now I was the one commanding, and he was the one whimpering in response.

The turnabout only made me hotter because I realized he didn't mind. He hadn't been interested in proving a power dynamic between us, and he was clearly willing for the rules to change so long as it suited both of us.

His fingers scrambled to his buttons and began undoing them as fast as he could. As soon as the last one was undone and the shirt was on the ground, I leaned in to whisper against his ear. "Put your hands on the counter behind you."

"Fuck you," he said with a grin in what I supposed was his "mocking Nico" voice as my hand found the bulge of his cock in the front of his pants and grabbed ahold of it. His hands quickly went behind him to grip the edge of the counter so he could thrust his hips into my hand. "Don't stop."

"Not gonna stop. Gonna drive you fucking crazy. Just watch."

His eyelids were at half-mast, and his breaths were coming in ragged pulls. I placed my right index finger on the hollow at the base of his throat and slowly ran it down the center of his chest to his abdomen, his belly button, his blond happy trail. All the while, his throat made little noises of pleasure and his muscles contracted in waves.

"Nico," he panted.

I smiled to myself as I opened his pants and ran my open palms down into the back of them, cupping the round globes of his ass.

"Nico, oh my god," he groaned again. His voice was beginning to come out rough and the broken sound caressing me like a hand on my cock. My own pants were still open, my hard-on pressing against West's belly. A clear, glistening string of precome ran between my tip and his abdomen.

My lips went to his muscled chest, and I licked, nipped, and kissed my way down until I got to his open fly. As I knelt on the floor, I looked up and met his wide eyes while my hands shucked down his pants and underwear.

"I'm negative," I said softly. "I need to know if—"

"Yes, same." He breathed quickly, making clear eye contact with me.

I nodded, knowing he, as a doctor, understood the dangers but needing to put it out there regardless. It was something I took seriously, and I needed to make sure he did too.

When I finally ripped my eyes away from his intense gaze and looked at his cock, I barely refrained from an audible gulp. It was a nice fucking cock, but it was thick enough to intimidate me just a little.

I looked up at West again and saw a completely different look on his face. It was less intense lust and more… I wasn't sure. Softness? Sweetness? It was enough to make me pause and wonder what had changed. Whatever it was, I wasn't sure I liked it.

He quickly pulled his pants back up, crouched down in front of me, and slid his hands onto either side of my face to cup my jaw.

"Nico, will you let me take you to bed, please?"

His voice was velvety smooth, and something about the situation made me feel like there was suddenly a boulder sitting on my chest.

I'd never in my life had someone sink to the floor to stop me from sucking them off because they wanted… *more*?

My eyes met his, and I saw a gentle kindness in them I'd been trying so hard not to notice before. My body still wanted him, my brain was still bobbing its fool head, but my heart…

My heart was shaking its head from side to side and muttering to itself.

Just as I suspected. Now you've gone and done it. My poor heart, urging me once again not to let this man in.

But I went ahead and did it anyway.

Because I was a stupid motherfucker.

CHAPTER 16

WEST

If I wasn't so intent on getting Nico into my bed, I might have laughed at how mixed up my emotions were. I was two sides of a convoluted coin when it came to Nico. The horny "fuck him, fuck him now" side and the lovesick "wrap him up in your bed and hold him" side. One wanted to bark at him to strip and get on his hands and knees. The other wanted to run a bubble bath and rub his fucking feet.

I'd never in my life felt both those things so strongly for another person.

When I'd seen him kneel for me, it was too much. I wanted my cock in his mouth desperately, but I didn't want him like that—a quick suck on my kitchen floor with half our clothes still on.

So I asked if he'd let me take him to the bedroom, and he'd looked at me like I'd asked a deckhand if he'd wanted to keep the yacht for himself. Like he couldn't believe his luck. Like he was being offered something he didn't deserve.

Which just made me angry. Why didn't he think he deserved to be treated better than a blow job on the floor? What had happened to him in his life to make him think he wasn't worth being treated with kindness and consideration?

He slowly stood and looked at me like a skittish colt, ramping up my heart rate even more with an unfamiliar feeling. And when he reached out for my hand to help me up, I felt it even more. It was like a happy crush. As if I was truly beginning to have feelings for the man.

And all that shit scared me stupid since I hadn't been looking for anything like that with Nico Salerno. I'd brought him to my house to sleep with him, not to fall for him. I needed to get us back on track with the sex-only plan.

Once I stood, I pulled him in and kissed him briefly before leading him toward my bedroom.

In the short time it took us to get there, I'd become even more determined to shed the feelings part of what was happening between us and just focus on the physical stuff. I could worry about the deeper shit later. Or not.

"Or not" would be better.

I led him into my bedroom and quickly pulled him against me again for another kiss. His lip rings brushed my mouth, pulling more sounds of pleasure from both of us while my hands made quick work of the rest of our clothes.

Once we were completely naked, I lay him down in the center of my big bed and crawled over him. His tattoos stood out in sharp contrast from the stark white bedding, and I took a moment to run a hand over some of the images.

"So much ink," I murmured. "Why so many different designs?"

A shadow passed over his face, and he looked away, turning his head to the side to take a breath. I quickly leaned down and nuzzled into his neck, trying to find the space under his ear that had seemed to make him feel good before.

"I'm sorry," I said quietly. "Never mind."

"Less conversation," he said gruffly, exactly the way the Nico I'd met on day one would have responded. But he was right. We weren't there to chitchat. We were there to fuck.

I began to press kisses along the tendons of his neck, following them down to his shoulders and arms and over to the piercings in his nipples. I tentatively flicked at them with my tongue, and when Nico's gasps of pleasure ramped back up, so did my confidence. I played with the piercings until he was sucking in breaths; his knuckles were white where he clutched handfuls of my bedding.

Finally my mouth made its way to his cock, which was still fully hard and dripping onto his skin. My mouth watered at the sight, and I moved farther down his body until my mouth was propped right above his dick.

We locked eyes again as my tongue came out and lapped the precome up. Nico's long fingers threaded into my hair as he tried to keep from bucking in response to my mouth on him.

I continued licking and softly sucking along his tip and crown until Nico began to beg.

"West. West, please," he gasped. "Swallow it goddammit. *Please.*"

Hearing him beg made me feel bubbles of happiness in my gut, but I wouldn't allow them out for fear of pissing him off and ruining the moment. In any nonsexual situation, I knew he'd be *damned* if he'd beg anyone to do anything. But that's what made me feel so powerful right then.

I finally had mercy on him and lay the flat of my tongue along the underside of his shaft—drawing it up the entire length until his head was turning from side to side and his fingers were fisting in my hair. His thighs were trembling, but I held them down with my arms and took his entire length into my mouth and throat.

"Fuck! Oh god," he blurted.

I bobbed up and down, sucking his cock as well as I could to bring him the most pleasure possible. After bringing a hand up to cup his balls, I felt the cool bump of something metal against my fingers. My mouth released him so I could investigate. There under his sac were three solid metal loop piercings in a stack on his perineum.

My eyes must have shown my shock because the edges of his lips turned up in amusement.

"Never seen a guiche piercing before, huh?" he asked.

"Definitely not," I mumbled as I studied them some more. I reached my finger out to fiddle with the little silver-balled hoops.

"What feels good?" The question was meant to ask how he liked stimulation to the piercings, if at all, but his answer was teasing.

"Having your face between my legs," he admitted with a shit-eating grin.

I smacked his ass cheek and leaned in to run my tongue up from the piercings to his balls to his shaft and took him into my mouth again. There was not enough patience left in the room for me to learn the ins and outs of genital piercings right then, but I was damned sure planning on doing it at some point.

His hips tried to thrust up into my throat, and I let him, keeping my head still and cupping his ass to encourage him to fuck my mouth.

After softening his grip on my hair, Nico's hands came around to my face and held my cheeks reverently while he thrust into my throat. I looked up at him the entire time until I could see the moment of no return.

"West," he gasped as his eyes widened.

I closed my eyes in a nod of sorts—the only way I could think of to let him know it was okay, that I wanted him to come in my mouth. My fingers tightened into the flesh of his bare ass.

"Mpfh. Fuck, fuck. I can't..." Hot fluid filled my throat as he released into me with a cry. I held on to him and swallowed his release until all that was left were the sounds of our harsh breathing in the quiet room.

I wiped the back of my hand across my face and moved up on the bed to lie beside him, running a hand through his hair to brush it off his face and appreciate the flush across his skin.

Those blue-green eyes looked up at me in sated wonder, and I leaned in to press a kiss on his cheek.

"You're beautiful, Nico," I said softly.

He looked down and away, anywhere but at me. I wondered how it was possible for someone like him to experience insecurity. Was that what it was? Or could it have been regret? God, I hoped not.

He finally met my eyes and must have seen something in them because he turned into me and buried his face in my neck, wrapping his arms around me and pulling me against him.

Good god. Whatever foolish part of me had thought I could dial this encounter back to "just sex" had been batshit fucking crazy.

I wanted to ask him if he was okay, but that wasn't what this night was. We were practically strangers, slaking a lust. We weren't going to talk about our damned feelings. We were going to fuck. He'd even demanded less conversation. So why couldn't my thoughts get on board with the plan?

I reached down to shift my cock into a more comfortable position, but before my hand got there, Nico's hand gripped my wrist.

"Nuh-uh," he grumbled. "Mine."

I felt my lips turn up in a grin and leaned back to look at him. His face was flushed pink, but I wasn't sure if it was left over from his orgasm or new blushing from his possessive statement.

"Yours, huh? Well, what are you going to do about it?" I teased.

"I'm waiting for Mr. Controlling Bastard to follow through with all that cocky talk about taking me." His voice was the same sultry one that had spoken straight to my dick since almost the first moment we'd met.

I didn't take the time for a snarky or even flirty response to his challenge. I simply grabbed him and flipped him over onto his front, shoved his knees under him and opened up the most perfect rounded ass cheeks I'd ever had the good fortune to lay my hands on.

And then I put my mouth on him again, turning his smart-ass mouth into a babbling fountain of garbled nonsense.

CHAPTER 17

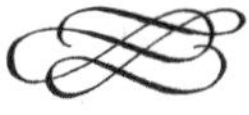

NICO

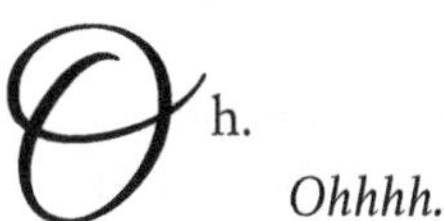h.

Ohhhh.

That was exactly what I'd been waiting for. Someone to take fucking charge of me and shove my face into the mattress. My ass was in the air, in West's mouth even, before I realized I was no longer nestled in the curve of his neck.

"Yes," I hissed into the soft bedding under my face. This was more like it. Fucking. I could do the fucking. *Yes, let's get back to just the fucking.*

His tongue seemed like it was everywhere on my ass, wet and strong and biting. A finger lightly brushed the guiche piercings, and I almost shot off right then. Just the idea of him playing with me there made my head spin. I felt him lean away for a moment and heard the table rattling beside the bed before he was back. This time his fingers were slick and cool and toyed with my hole until, once again, I was begging like a fool.

"Hurry," I gasped. "Want to feel you."

He leaned over my back as his fingers seduced my entrance. I felt the roughness of his whiskered cheek against my jaw as he snuck in a kiss to my chin. "You want my cock, Nico?"

Only desperation kept me from rolling my eyes. Of course I wanted his fucking cock, was he crazy?

"Fuck, fuck," is what came out of me instead as his skilled finger grazed just the right spot and sent a shudder through me. "Do that again," I said on a long groan.

His fingers stretched me with gentle strength, and I got lost for a moment in the thought of those doctor hands. Long, capable fingers and intimate knowledge of the human body. Clearly the man knew what was where.

I felt him shift on the bed beside me, and I turned back to watch him roll on a condom. His eyebrows were furrowed in concentration, and his thick blond hair was sticking up all over the place. West Wilde was hot as fuck. The kind of hot that meant he could just wink at any human being and have them begging for his cock. And there I was getting ready to take it.

He looked up and met my eyes, quirking his brow in question. I quickly turned my face back around and buried it in the thick comforter. Strong, warm hands smoothed up and down my back before squeezing my ass and pulling me open again. Only this time instead of his mouth or fingers, it was that fat cock pressing in, and I clenched with last-minute nerves. Griff had been right. I didn't usually bottom. It was too intimate, too vulnerable.

His body came back down over my back and his soothing voice was back in my ear. "Shh, it's okay. Let me in, baby. Please."

The feel of his solid warmth around me and his gentle hands rubbing appreciatively along my skin were my undoing. I shoved back into him suddenly, forcing it before either of us had a chance to overthink it or be sweet about it any further. We both grunted and groaned in response and began rocking together naturally after the initial shock.

West's strong arm came around my chest and held me tightly to him as he thrust in and out. My own arm reached up to the headboard to keep me from bumping up into it—the other arm reached back over my shoulder to the back of West's head to keep him close.

We came together over and over as the pulses inside my channel made me babble like a fool. Everything about him from the weight of him, to the smell of him, to the sounds of his pleasure in my ear were driving me to the edge of an impossible climax.

Only his hips moved as he flexed in and out of me in firm, steady strokes that lit me up inside. My cock had hardened again as if I hadn't already come from the blow job before, and I removed my hand from West's hair so I could jack myself off.

As soon as my hand came around my shaft, West's was there too, gripping over my hand and stroking with me.

"Jesus, Nico. Your body. I want… *fuck*."

I felt him tense up and move his hand from my cock to caress my balls as he came. It was just a light brush of his fingers, but it was enough. My cock shot onto the bedding as I felt his pulse inside me. My brain seized up and my breathing spiked. My skin prickled with the intensity of the climax, and I saw similar goose bumps appear all over West's skin.

When it was done, he collapsed onto the bed next to me and roughly pulled me into his side, leaning in and pressing a kiss to my forehead before settling into the mattress. I let myself sink against him just for a minute and swore I'd get up and leave as soon as I caught my breath.

Apparently, I didn't catch my breath for five damned hours.

WHEN I AWOKE, I panicked. All I could think about was having left Pippa at home with Doc and Mr. Wilde. I was tangled in long limbs and bed sheets, and I scrambled to figure out how to get out of the damned bed.

"Nico, wait," West mumbled beside me, tightening his arms around me.

"Gotta go—Pippa," I said, moving again.

"I got her," he said. "She's here."

I turned to look at him in confusion. "What? What do you mean, she's here?"

He sat up, rubbing his face with his hands. His hair was so wild I wanted to run my hands through it just to be a part of the crazy.

"I went and got her so Doc and Grandpa could go home."

My heart jumped up into my throat. "I don't... what? You went and got her from my house?"

West nodded, bringing his hands down on his lap before squinting up at me. Clearly he'd been deep asleep and I'd woken him.

The edge of his mouth turned up in a sweet, shy smile. "I didn't want to wake you."

It was the nicest thing any hookup had done for me, and it absolutely freaked me out. I jumped out of bed and began scrambling for my clothes—shoving them on any old which way just so I could get the hell out of there.

"Nico? What are you doing?" he asked.

"Gotta go."

"Wait, no. Please, don't go. I'm sorry if I overstepped."

I tried to ignore him, tried to find my shoes, but they weren't anywhere in his room. I remembered toeing them off at his command the night before and felt a shiver vibrate through me.

I looked around the room for anything I could be overlooking. I didn't want to have to come back. Fuck if my stomach didn't twist at the thought of never coming back there, but I was determined. Nothing good would come of my getting too used to Dr. Sweetheart's good bedside manner.

Just before I made it to the doorway, I felt his arms come around my middle from behind. My eyes squeezed closed, and I took a breath.

"Nico," he said softly. "Stop. Please talk to me. You know the baby is better off staying asleep right now. It's three in the morning. This isn't about Pippa. What's it about?"

I felt myself begin to tremble, and I really didn't want to lose my composure in front of the kind of guy who probably didn't even know what it was like to lose his composure.

"It was awfully presumptuous of you to go over there and get Pippa, don't you think?" I asked defensively.

"Yes, I see that now. And I'll be honest. It was a purely selfish move on my part because I didn't want to wake you up. I knew you needed sleep, but it was more than that. I wanted you to still be curled up in my bed waiting for me when I got back. I wanted... *want* you to be curled up in my arms when I wake up tomorrow. I'm not ready for you to leave, Nico."

I tried slowing my breathing down to keep from panicking and running. I was getting too old to run away from uncomfortable situations. I needed to face them head on. Like West was doing. He was talking to me like a normal human being. Like an adult.

I turned around in his arms and put my hands on his bare chest before looking up at his face. Dim light was coming in from the hallway through the cracked doorway. "But I *am* leaving. I don't live here. This was just sex, West. I don't do... whatever the hell other thing means you go and get someone's baby from their house."

"It was. It *was* just sex," he agreed.

Despite my brave words, my heart fell and shook its fool head in defeat.

"Then what... then what..." I couldn't even finish the question because I realized he wasn't having the same mixed-up feelings I was having. The kind that said it was supposed to be just sex, but it felt like maybe it wanted to be more than that. I looked down at my fingers threaded through the light hair on his chest.

"I'm not ready for you to go yet, Nico. Just stay the night. We don't have to figure any of that other shit out right now, okay? Just get back in bed with me and suck me off. It'll make you feel better. I'm sure of it."

My gaze snapped back to his face, and I noticed his twinkling eyes.

"Jackass," I muttered, pushing him off me and making my way back to the bed to crawl under the covers.

"Ahh, there's the Nico I know and lo—" He stopped suddenly before the word was out. I didn't turn back to face him but smirked nonetheless. "Lust."

The smile stayed on my face while he snuggled up against my back and pulled me tightly to his chest. Maybe I wasn't the only one having mixed feelings after all. But at least he agreed it was just sex. Regardless of the mixed-up feelings, it was *just sex*.

"Lust, huh?" I asked, threading our fingers together in front of my heart.

"Bet your tight ass," he grumbled against the back of my neck, arching his soft cock against said ass.

"You sure Pippa's okay?" I asked after a few minutes.

"She's in a Pack 'n Play in the other room. I gave her a bottle as soon as I got her over here, and she went right back to sleep."

"What the hell's a Pack 'n Play?" I asked.

I felt the rumble of his laugh through my entire body. "Go to sleep, Nico."

"What did your grandfathers say?" I couldn't help but ask in a teasing voice. "Did you tell them you had a naked man waiting in your bed and you needed to fetch his baby to guarantee you'd get a round two in the morning?"

"Something like that. Now shut the hell up and go to sleep."

CHAPTER 18

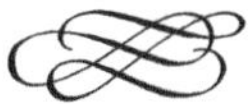

WEST

I awoke to the sound of a baby crying, which meant I was on call in the emergency room. After jumping up and banging my hip into the corner of my bedside table, I realized I wasn't, in fact, in the ER.

"What the hell?" I asked, looking around for where the sound was coming from. I saw Nico's colorful hair sticking out from under the edge of the duvet and remembered what had happened the night before. I felt a huge grin stretch my face as I realized I'd gotten my wish—sleeping with the gorgeous man tucked up against me all night.

"It's your turn," I heard him say from under the bedding. "I was up with her, uh, a little while ago. Or something," he mumbled.

I laughed. "Like hell you were, slacker. Get your ass up."

He pulled back the covers and sat up, hair going everywhere like a very angry Troll doll. His face was fucking adorable, and the little hoops in his pouting lips made my damned mouth water as usual.

"Jesus," I muttered, eliciting a glare.

"Sorry if I'm not Mr. Put-Together first thing in the morning, Your Highness," he snapped, misunderstanding my curse.

"Dude, are you kidding? You're fucking sexy as hell. I was trying to stop myself from going at you again before you've had a chance to fully wake up."

His mouth opened, but no sound came out. Finally I heard him say, "Oh."

Shaking my head, I glanced around for something to put on so I could stop the insane crying still going on. "Got a damned pissed-off Rainbow Brite in my bed," I muttered, giving up on the clothes on the floor and opening my dresser.

I felt a pinch on my bare ass and yelped. "Ouch! What the hell?"

Warm breath landed on the skin of my back as Nico's lips brushed my shoulder blade. "Just making sure you were real. Thought maybe last night's sexcapade was a dream."

"Thinking you're dreaming means *you* need to be pinched, not me," I retorted, trying to hide my smile. His voice was so sexy it was making my cock fill again. "Go get your baby so I can concentrate on what I'm doing and fix us some breakfast."

An arm appeared in front of me to grab a pair of plaid flannel pajama bottoms from the open drawer I was rifling through.

"Don't mind if I do. Thanks, Doc," he said.

"Don't call me that."

"Yes sir, *William Weston Wilde*." My full name on his tongue sounded like he was savoring warm liquid chocolate.

More cock-filling.

I wondered how long it would be before Pippa would agree to go down for a morning nap.

~

Once we got some comfortable clothes on and made our way into the kitchen, Nico fixed Pippa's bottle while I started the coffee maker and pulled out some eggs. We moved around the small space intent on our own tasks until we found ourselves sitting across from one another at my kitchen table with a hot breakfast, coffee, and a baby sucking greedily from a bottle.

Suddenly we both realized what a ridiculously domestic picture we'd created. Our eyes locked onto each other as if one of us had stepped on a landmine and neither of us knew how to proceed.

A loud fart noise ripped through the silence. I knew it had come from the baby, but the baby was resting squarely on Nico's lap.

"Feeling okay?" I asked Nico with a straight face.

His cheeks bloomed pink before he shot me a dirty look.

The awkward moment was gone in an instant as both of us cracked up until tears were leaking out of my eyes.

The rest of the breakfast passed in comfortable conversation. He began to open up more about what he was going through with trying to handle Adriana's bakery.

"She was terrible at bookkeeping, West. I mean, I don't get it. You don't have to be good at math, necessarily. Just have basic organization skills," he said, setting the bottle down and moving Pippa onto his shoulder to rub her back.

Nico was bare-chested, and my stomach tightened at the sight of him holding her against his colorful skin. Little muscles moved as he burped her, and I could make out more of the designs in the light of the morning sun coming through my kitchen windows.

"She barely graduated from high school, Nico, so I'm not surprised she struggled at running a business. Why don't I help? We could go to your place and work on it together. I don't have anything planned today," I suggested.

Nico's hesitation was clear, but he must have really been concerned about it. "Yeah, okay. I mean, if you don't mind. You knew her better, so maybe you can figure it out. I hope to god I'm overlooking something because the bakery is seriously in the red."

I reached over and squeezed his arm. "No worries. I'll take a look." After offering to change Pippa's diaper, I disappeared into the guest room where the portable crib and her supplies were. I made quick work of cleaning her up and changing her into a fresh sleeper outfit from her diaper bag before returning to find Nico finishing up with the dishes.

"You didn't have to do that," I said in surprise.

He smiled shyly before looking back at the plate he was scrubbing.

"You didn't have to fix me breakfast either. Thanks."

"You're welcome, but it's not like it was anything fancy. Your standard *thanks for staying over* breakfast," I said on a chuckle, attempting to lighten the mood.

Even though his face was turned away, I could see him tense up. I shifted the baby into my left arm and slid my right around his front so I could lay my chin on his shoulder.

"What is it?" I asked softly.

"I don't stay over... Ever."

There was a beat of silence while I digested what he was telling me.

I tried turning him in my arms but couldn't manage it while holding the baby. Instead, I walked over to the sitting area and strapped Pippa into her car seat on the floor by the sofa and came back to where Nico was still standing at the sink.

After reaching in front of him to turn off the faucet, I grabbed a towel and dried off his hands before turning him around and lifting his chin. Blue-green eyes narrowed at me in defiance, and I saw clearly the punk he tried so hard to portray to the world.

"Then I am one lucky motherfucker," I said. My voice sounded hoarse, but I tried to speak with the conviction I felt.

I didn't give him a chance to argue with me or walk away. Instead, I took his mouth in mine and spoke to him in the only language that mattered.

A kiss.

A COUPLE of hours later we were at Nico's with Adriana's company books and receipts spread out all over the kitchen table and the baby settling down into her morning nap in the nursery. Nico had changed into sweatpants and a hoodie when we'd arrived, and I was wearing my most comfortable jeans and a T-shirt. October was coming in with slightly cooler days, and I noticed two pairs of socks doubled-up on Nico's feet.

He sat on the chair next to mine, and I pointed to his bundled-up feet. "How are you not burning up? It might be October, but this is still Texas."

"I run cold," he admitted, typing on the old battered laptop I'd given Adriana when I last upgraded my own.

"I beg to differ," I replied. "But if you do, you should never have left Texas and gone to the Bay Area where it's chilly all the time. You should have just stayed here." I was sorting through payroll notes when I realized what I'd just said. I looked up. "I mean… ah…"

Nico's jaw ticked. "It's not like it was a choice."

"Wasn't it?"

"What did Adriana tell you?"

"That you probably had a good reason."

"And you didn't agree?"

"It's not that I didn't agree," I began. His face darkened at my lie, and I sighed. "No, that's a lie. I was pissed at you for abandoning her, regardless of the reason."

His jaw flexed some more, and he looked away. "Fair enough," he said before peering back at the laptop.

I could tell there was more to it than that. Of course there was. Why the hell had it taken me so many years to realize just how hard it would have been for a fifteen-year-old boy to leave his home? And where the hell had he lived at age *fifteen* for god's sake?

My heart ramped up as I watched him. It was like seeing him through fresh eyes.

"Please tell me it wasn't because of that night," I said softly.

He grunted an acknowledgment of my words but continued looking at the screen.

"Please, Nico," I said louder. "Jesus fucking Christ. You heard what Curt said at the movie theater. And then I opened my stupid fucking mouth. Is that why you left?"

Without saying a word, Nico stood up, closed the computer gently, and turned to go to the bedroom.

"Don't want to talk about it. I'll figure this shit out later. You don't have to stick around," he said over his shoulder.

CHAPTER 19

NICO

It was a shitty thing to do. I knew that. I'd sounded like a goddamned brat. But it wasn't something I particularly wanted to discuss, and I wasn't sure I could say why without bursting into tears like a baby.

I shuffled back to the bedroom and peeled off all the bulky clothes until I was in a T-shirt and boxer briefs before slipping between the cool sheets under the heavy duvet. With one of Adriana's supersoft pillows bunched up under my head, I closed my eyes and faced away from the bedroom door. My traitorous ears couldn't help but search for signs of West in the house—wondering if he'd left like I'd told him to or if he'd stayed and was going to force the issue.

My eyes squeezed closed in memory but not the memory of the night at the movie theater. It was something else that had happened a few weeks later.

It was a hot summer day, perfect for the lake. The sun was shining, and the sky was a deep blue. Sheriff Billingham had taken us out on his speedboat for the day in an effort to help the four of us kids get to know each other. Or some shit like that.

It was the town's Memorial Day celebration, and vendors were lined up along the marina docks and shoreline to celebrate. Farmers' market stalls were filled with produce and homemade jams, colorful signs and flags and artwork were posted here and there to showcase artist booths set up. Groups of kids chased each other with cotton candy and other treats from the food stalls. And there were piles of whipped cream and empty pie tins stacked on folding tables left over from the pie-eating contest that morning.

The sheriff had suggested taking the opportunity to watch the evening's fireworks from the boat so we'd have the "best seat in the house" despite the fact all our friends were on shore having fun without us, and the four of us kids at least were less than thrilled.

We were speeding through the warm wind, laid out along the side benches in our swimsuits, when Curt's brother, Reeve, had asked his dad if he could drive the boat for a little while.

Both boys were proficient at handling the boat. In fact, I wasn't sure any of the kids from Hobie couldn't *handle themselves on a motorboat. So it surprised me when the boat suddenly lurched toward shore, tipping so far sideways as it crossed its own wake. Water splashed over the edge onto the bench. I scrambled at the side of the boat to grab hold of the gunwale when I heard snickering coming from Curt several feet down the bench from me.*

"Jesus, I thought we were going over," I said with a nervous laugh. Despite being uncomfortable with Reeve at the wheel and still pissed at Curt for what he'd said at the movies, I was trying to be polite and respectful. My mother had warned Adriana and me to be on our absolute best behavior for the outing.

By then, both the boys were regular tormentors of mine in school. They found little opportunities here and there to tease me and poke at me when they could. None of it was serious enough to warrant saying anything—it was more the repetition of the barbs that hurt. Like death of a thousand cuts.

But I'd put on my game face that day for my mom's sake. I knew she'd fallen head over heels for the sheriff not long after the widower and his sons had moved to town earlier in the year, and Mom had been daydreaming of becoming his wife ever since. I imagined how much easier our lives would have been without her needing to work two shitty-ass jobs and struggle to make ends meet. I thought about what it would be like for her to be able to walk through town as the sheriff's wife instead of the trailer-trash widow of a good-for-nothing drunk.

Curt leaned his cocky face toward me and whispered low enough for only me to hear. "He's trying to impress your sister."

The admission startled me. I glanced at Reeve Billingham at the wheel, noticing him looking proud as a peacock. The guy was seventeen, the same age as my sister.

"That's gross," I'd said.

"Tell me about it," he'd scoffed. "He could have any girl he wanted. What the hell's he gotta look at a skinny chick with no tits for?"

I felt bile rise up in my throat at the thought of anyone looking at my sister in any kind of sexual way. The use of the word "tits" in relation to her made me want to blow chunks off the side of the boat.

The boat lurched again toward shore, and that's when I saw who Reeve was really trying to impress. The entire track team and all its fans from the high school were standing on the shore preparing for the massive water balloon fight. Reeve was their star pole vaulter, who'd apparently had to skip out on the team's fun to hang out with us. He was pulling stunts at the helm of the boat to get his buddies' attention on shore.

Adriana looked pissed, so I carefully made my way over to where she was sitting on the other side of the boat.

"You okay?" I asked quietly.

She nodded but didn't open her mouth. Long strands of dark hair blew around her face from where they'd escaped her ponytail holder.

"The guy's a jerk," I muttered.

She shrugged. "Meh, he's okay. I just wish we could go tubing or something fun. This sucks."

I looked over at my mom who was sitting in the circle of the sheriff's arms and gazing at his face with rapt attention while he pointed out parts of the boat. My mother had grown up around boats all her life. Her father had been a commercial fisherman out of Galveston, and yet she stared up at the sheriff as if she didn't know a propeller from a cleat.

"The point is for us to become best friends with these rodents," I said under my breath. "As if that's going to happen in this lifetime."

Adriana blew out a breath, squinting for a minute before turning to me. "Nico, don't fuck this up for us."

I couldn't believe my ears. "You want Mom to actually do it? Marry the sheriff so we can all be one big happy Billingham family?"

She looked away, off toward the horizon away from the shore. "If it's what she wants... And shit—maybe then I could afford to get the hell out of here and go to school in the city."

She ran a tanned hand across her face in a useless attempt to clear the strands of hair from her eyelashes and lips before looking back toward shore.

I took another glance at our mom just as she leaned her head back in a laugh. The sun was shining on her, casting a glow that made her seem lit up from the inside. It was a rare moment of seeing her in full relaxation mode. She was snuggled against the much larger sheriff, who was busy telling a joke and making her laugh.

Everyone in town seemed to think the sheriff was a cantankerous old grump but the kind who was also somehow endearing. I'd never seen the endearing part. Just the cantankerous part. But then again, I wasn't the kind of kid he was predisposed to like. I hung out with the different kids. The kids with weird clothes and weird taste. The ones who didn't wear golf shirts and show up for youth classes at the church. The ones who got caught sneaking cigarettes and cheap-ass beer behind the concession stands at the local high school football games.

Just then the big man turned and caught me staring. In a rare instance of singling me out for a good reason instead of a bad one, he told Reeve to stop the boat so I could take a turn at the wheel. For a brief moment my heart swelled. Maybe I was wrong about his opinion of me. Maybe he didn't think I was a good-for-nothing. Just for a second I felt like one of his kids—a son he wanted to teach how to drive the boat.

I shot him a grateful smile and stood up to make my way to the wheel after Reeve pulled back on the throttle.

And that's when two things happened at once.

My sister decided to take my turn at the wheel and pushed me back toward my seat. At the same time, Reeve watched me stand before shoving the throttle forward and whipping the wheel hard to port. The giant boat seemed to rotate on its axis out from under me, and I was in the air before I had a chance to grab ahold on something.

Not only was I thrown overboard by combination of the moves, but I also banged my side hard enough on the edge of the boat to knock the breath out of me and crack a rib. When I hit the water, my surprise incapacitated me for a moment, and I began to sink fast. It was only through the quick-acting people on shore and on the docks that I was recovered.

After it happened, not one of the Billinghams came to visit, apologize, or even just call to check on me while I recovered from the injury. The only thing I ever heard them say about it was when the sheriff asked my mom why I hadn't been smart enough to wait for the boat to stop before standing up.

As I lay in Adriana's bed remembering the humiliating event, I forgot about West for a little while. I allowed myself to slip into a familiar self-pity that disgusted me. After pulling my knees up to my chest, I moved the pillow from under my head to over it. Maybe blocking out the world for a little while would help me calm down.

One side of the bed sagged as I felt West climb in next to me. My teeth ground together as I tried to think of what to say when he asked me again about my reasons for leaving.

But he didn't say a word—just slid in behind me and wrapped one arm around my waist, pulling me in close to his front.

"I won't say anything," he said in a quiet voice. "Just let me hold you."

I removed the pillow from above my head and slid my arm over his, linking our fingers and squeezing to let him know he was welcome company.

We didn't speak after that for a long time, but I no longer felt alone. And that was all I'd really needed.

CHAPTER 20

WEST

When Nico had escaped to the bedroom, I'd had to have a serious conversation with myself about boundaries. It was none of my business what Nico's reasons for leaving Hobie were. It was more that I was curious because of what his actions had set in motion for Adriana.

After Nico had left, the sheriff had married their mom and Adriana had thought her life was just beginning. But before she'd had a chance to go on and do great things with her life, the accident had happened and she'd been left alone. With nothing but two useless stepbrothers.

Nico's mom had been at the wheel on the way home from a party at a friend's house when they'd hit a tree. Both she and the sheriff had been killed in the accident, and alcohol had been found in both of their systems.

Once Adriana's mom was gone, the Billingham boys were all she had left.

And they were shit—incompetent and unwilling to take responsibility for helping support Adriana. Thanks to the fluke of being paired with my sister MJ on a school project senior year, Adriana had begun spending time at our place after school. Long after the project was completed, she'd continued hanging out at our house, and if my parents had noticed, they hadn't cared.

Both the sheriff's boys had enlisted in the military. Adriana had been forced to find her own way without any help. Once the boys were gone, she was left with no one. Even my sister MJ had gone off to college and then law school.

By the time I returned to Hobie for good after becoming a doctor, Adriana had turned a part-time job at a coffee cart in the local grocery store into a side business of baking pastries, cakes, and specialty desserts for people all over town. At one point, a tropical storm had come through town and flooded her mom's old trailer, so she took the insurance money and put it toward the construction of her little cottage. After it was finished, she finally had a decent kitchen with a commercial oven and a huge table to spread out on. I'd thought she had everything she'd wanted. Her life finally her own.

Little did I know, she'd been lonely as all hell. Lonely for family—for Nico.

I remember wondering at one point what had happened to him, where he'd gone at so young an age. It turned out, he'd gone to San Francisco and built a life for himself on his own. How in the world had he managed it? Nico was way more complex and capable than I'd originally given him credit for.

I'd been curled up around the guy for at least a half hour before I could no longer keep from running my hands under his T-shirt and into his boxer briefs. He sucked in a breath and pushed his cock into my hand.

"Lie back," I whispered.

He turned on his back and looked up at me, a purple lock of hair falling across his face. His dark eyelashes were beautiful and set off the varied colors of his eyes.

"And here I thought your sister was the most beautiful person I'd ever met," I murmured before leaning in to brush a kiss across his nose, across the flat of his cheekbone, down the side of his jaw. I took a moment to strip his shirt and underwear off before returning to where I'd left off.

I trailed soft presses of my lips down the length of a coiled snake on his chest, across the brushstrokes of random script, and down again along a tattooed image of rosary beads until I came to the top of his trimmed pubic hair. My eyes came up to gaze at him while my tongue snuck out to search for that velvet skin I was hungry for.

Nico's face was intense as he watched me wet my lips and draw them up and down his shaft. While I worked to increase his pleasure, he watched me silently as if studying something perplexing and unchartered. His pulse jumped on his neck as his climax raced in. His eyes widened and nostrils flared. His breathing was erratic and heavy. The cock against my tongue was heavy and throbbing, and I did my best to wrap my tongue around it to pull the orgasm from him by force if need be. I wanted to see him lose his composure, lose whatever was keeping him tied up in knots.

I wanted to see him let go.

He came with a shout that, thankfully, I saw coming just in time to stretch up and slam a pillow over his face. My intention was to keep his shout from waking the baby, but I realized a second later that I'd basically slapped him in the face just as he was getting ready to experience the heady escape of his release.

When he finished coming all over his chest and stomach, I gave him a few final strokes and licks until he caught his breath and yanked the pillow away.

Twin beams of annoyance glared at me from his flushed face. "Are you fucking kidding me?"

"Um. Sorry about that," I said with a wince. "I didn't want to wake Pippa."

"Yeah, I get that, but a nice gentle hand would have done the trick. Or even a goddamned ball gag would have been kinder. You almost suffocated me."

I climbed up to kiss him on his mouth and spent the next several minutes trying to make him forget about the damned pillow.

After the kissing, we lay there entwined together, his fingers moving in lazy shapes under my shirt along the skin of my back, when he spoke.

"It wasn't just the thing that happened at the movie theater," he said into the quiet room. "It was something that happened a few weeks later, at the lake."

I tried to lift my head up to look at him, but he moved his hand into my hair to stop me. After I settled back on his chest, I asked him something I'd always wondered.

"When Reeve dumped you overboard?"

"When I fell off the boat," he corrected. "Like an asshole."

"You didn't fall. You were knocked into the water by that jackass on purpose."

I felt Nico's hand stop its movement on my back. "How did you know that?"

"Because you wouldn't have fallen otherwise. I hardly think you would have stood up unless you thought he was slowing down or stopping."

"Maybe I was the idiot everyone claimed me to be," he said. His voice was so defiant I laughed.

"You weren't. You grew up in Hobie. No way did you stand up to move around a boat without knowing exactly what you were doing. Plus I knew Reeve Billingham and he was an ass. Still is, if rumors are to be believed."

Nico let out a deep sigh. "Yeah, they were both assholes. I have no idea why Curt still has a problem with me after all these years."

I had an idea, but I chose to keep my thoughts to myself. Nothing good would come of telling Nico any of it.

"He's a jerk. Stay away from him, Nico, okay?"

He shifted out from under me and sat up, moving to sit against the headboard so he could look at me.

"What are you not telling me?"

"I'm just saying—"

"Yeah, West. I hear what you're saying. What I don't hear is what you're *not* saying. Tell me."

I sat up too, sliding back until I was sitting against the headboard next to him. "He has a shit ton of attitude toward your mother for what happened to his dad," I told him. It wasn't the whole truth, but it was true nonetheless.

"Why? What do you mean?"

"How much do you know about the accident?"

Nico rubbed his hands over his face before looking over at me. "I didn't ask for any details when Honovi told me she died in a car accident. I was already overwhelmed with Adriana and Pippa and everything."

I took one of his hands and kissed the back of it before holding it between both of mine.

"She was driving under the influence, Nico."

His entire face fell, and my heart went out to him. I couldn't imagine being in his position hearing all this shit.

"Are they sure she was drunk?"

"They'd both been drinking. People remember them leaving the party after drinking, and everyone assumes maybe she'd had less to drink than he had. That's probably why she drove."

"Oh god. Why was she even drinking? She didn't drink. Not after my father..." He trailed off and seemed to stop to think it through. He took a deep breath. "My father drank himself to death. She hated the stuff. Did she start drinking after I left?"

I tried to catch Nico's gaze, but he seemed to look anywhere but at me.

"Don't do whatever it is you're doing right now, Nico," I ordered.

His jaw tightened, but he still looked away.

I moved swiftly to straddle his lap, grabbing hold of his face in both my hands. "Don't you dare take on the responsibility of her choices. Don't you dare."

Everything that had ever broken him in his entire life was in his eyes, and I wanted to scream from the intensity of it.

"She started drinking when I left?" he asked in a small voice.

"Nico," I breathed. "No. It wasn't your fault. Your mother chose to drink at a party. That's all it was."

"But you think Adriana's abandonment was my fault, so why won't you let me think my mom's death was my fault? Curt clearly does."

"Why did you leave?" I asked softly, stroking his cheeks. "Why did you leave Adriana and your mom?"

The tears in his eyes overflowed, and had I thought my heart felt broken before, I was so very wrong.

CHAPTER 21

NICO

West Wilde was a mirage—a phantom empath hovering nearby during my epic journey home. I'd decided he was too good to be true. But god, how I wanted him to be.

"I don't think you want to know," I told him. "It's so fucking pathetic, West."

His thumbs brushed away the tears that had leaked out, and I couldn't help but lean in and lay my face against the softness of his T-shirt.

"I want to know. Of course I want to know. And even if it is pathetic, I promise to remember it was a teenage kid making that decision," he assured me.

I let out a shaky breath. "The movie theater thing happened first. Curt's comment about the sheriff not marrying my mom as long as I was in the picture. Then on the boat that day, Adriana made a comment about wanting them to get married so she'd have a chance at being able to go to college. It all started coming together to make me feel like I was the one thing preventing my mom and my sister from getting what they'd always wanted."

"But Nico, can't you see—"

I reached up to put fingers over his lips. "I know that now.

Remember when you said you'd try to remember it was a stupid kid making the decision?"

"I don't think those were my exact words," West teased against my fingers with a soft smile.

"Well, two more things happened after that. The first was just a random fluke. Mom sent me to a neighbor's house to pick up some hydrangea clippings the woman had saved for her. When I approached the screen door, I overheard the neighbor talking to another woman at their kitchen table. The conversation was about my mom and the sheriff. One woman told the other that the sheriff sure was sweet on my mom. But then they both agreed that he'd never pop the question and take it to the next level as long as I was in the picture."

West stiffened and looked down at me. "You're kidding? It wasn't just Curt spouting that bullshit?"

I shrugged. "No. I mean, I know I wasn't the best kid. I didn't make good grades, I hung out with all the weirdos who always seemed to attract trouble, and everyone knew I was queer at that point. It wasn't like I hid it."

"Even if those things were true, Nico, that's no reason not to accept you as part of your mom's family. God, how awful."

It warmed something inside me to hear him say those things. To finally, after all these years, have someone besides Adriana know what happened and say it wasn't okay.

"Yeah, well, I made the mistake of telling Adriana, and she went fucking ape shit." I couldn't help but smirk at the memory of unleashing the hellcat.

West laughed, and the deep rumble felt amazing against my chest. "She was a feisty little shit when she wanted to be. Sweet as honeysuckle most of the time, but stung like a hornet when she got riled up. Was she that way when you were little?"

I loved it when his voice lulled into his soft Texas burr. It was a sign of relaxation, and it washed through me like a sweet buzz.

I nodded. My fingers found the hem of his T-shirt and snuck under it to run along his skin. "When she was little, you're right.

Sweet as honeysuckle. As a teen, though, she was a moody bitch. Mean as a snake. But when the anger was in defense of me… well, it felt fucking amazing."

"What was the other thing that happened?" he asked gently.

"The sheriff threatened to arrest me," I said.

West's silence lasted for a beat. "What for?"

"Stealing the sign from Ritches' Hardware Store," I said and couldn't help but start laughing.

West smiled at me. "That was you? What's so funny?"

"Oh my god. I just realized the bakery… oh my god." I was laughing so hard I could barely stop. "Sugar Britches. She named it after me."

"She told me it was an inside joke, but she never explained it. Tell me."

"Do you remember the sign on the hardware store used to look like it started with a B because of the font Mr. Ritches used?"

West nodded. "Everyone knew that's why it was stolen so many times. So some kid could have a dirty word sign on his wall. It took like ten signs before the guy wised up and changed the font."

"Right. Well, Adriana and I got into a huge fight and I called her the b-word. She went batshit fucking crazy. One of my friends came up with the idea to steal the sign and hang it on Adriana's bedroom door so when she woke up one morning, it would just be there. The whole thing started off as a joke."

"You're kidding," West said. "You really stole it? How?"

"I didn't even mean to, but I was walking by the store one day after school and there was a flash rainstorm. Everyone dashed into the closest storefront in town, and I headed for Ritches. Just as I approached the door, it banged closed from whoever had gone in before me. I swear to god, the sign fell right off the door and splashed into a huge puddle."

"Liar," West accused with a laugh.

I shrugged and grinned back at him. "Not kidding. I had to decide in that moment—take it for the gift it obviously was, or turn it in and hope I didn't get accused of ripping it off the door. Obviously I took it."

West tilted his head at me as if he wasn't sure whether or not to believe me. "Then what happened?"

"Curt saw me with it. I didn't find that out until it was too late, but apparently he did. Meanwhile, I took it home and hung it in my sister's room. When she woke up and saw it, she screeched so loud I realized it was worth any punishment I could get. She was griping at me about it at breakfast when Mom heard her say bitches. Mom yelled, so Adriana said, 'Mom, I was calling Nico my little Sugar Britches.' She called me Sugar Britches after that. I can't believe I'd forgotten that."

My voice trailed off as I felt the true gesture hit me. My sister had named her business after me. Even after all those years.

"Didn't the sheriff find out? Did Mr. Ritches press charges?"

"Oh, they never charged me. Sheriff Billingham gave me a long lecture about being a disappointment to my mother and how that one action proved I was well on my way to being a petty criminal if I didn't change my tune. Then he shook his head and muttered a bunch of shit under his breath about how he could never marry a woman with a criminal for a son even though he probably should since I clearly needed a father's firm hand."

"What a jackass." West hissed.

"Yeah, well, he was the jackass my mom was in love with. And I was suffocating in this small town. I knew I was gay, I knew I was different, and I knew I'd leave town the first chance I got anyway. So I realized I might as well do it sooner than later and save everyone the trouble. It was the last straw."

West's eyes narrowed at me. "You're kidding? You let that fucker intimidate you into leaving your family? You gave up your mother and sister for that guy?"

I felt my hackles rise and my anger kick up. "No. You don't fucking understand. I gave up my mother and my sister for them to have a better life, you idiot."

I got up and began searching for my clothes. Whether Pippa was awake yet or not, I was going to go get her and busy myself with giving her a bath or something. As if I needed the stress of a slippery baby on top of the stress of dealing with West. Whatever.

West stood up too and came over to clasp my arm. "Wait. Stop. I'm sorry. You're right. I don't understand. But I'd like to. Will you sit back down and talk to me?"

His voice was kind, and his touch was gentle. After letting him guide me back onto the bed, I turned to him to try to make him understand.

"West. We didn't grow up like you, with enough money and family support to be comfortable. After my dad died, my mom had to get any job she could. She cleaned houses in town and made shit for money. My dad had already been making shit for money as it was, and we lived in a run-down trailer for god's sake. The only way they could even afford what little we did have was because this piece of land and the trailer had been my grandfather's getaway spot when he wanted to take a break from his wife and kids in Galveston. He'd come up here with his buddies and fish and drink beer. It was just a scrubby lake property with a double-wide trailer on it, so it was a step up from camping, you know?"

West held one of my hands in his and toyed with my fingers. It felt good.

"So when Dad died, we had nothing. My mom cleaned houses. Adriana babysat, and I mowed lawns to help out where we could. Sometimes the church helped us out, which was nice but humiliating. It sucked. It was awful watching my mom and sister work their asses off and still live in a shitty, bug-infested trailer with one moody window air-conditioning unit and no money for anything other than thrift-store shit and ramen noodles. If you had a chance to sacrifice yourself so your mom and sister could live in a decent house and have new things, wouldn't you at least consider it?"

"I guess I would, Nico. But why didn't you tell them the truth?"

I knew the minute the words were out of his mouth he knew the answer to his question.

"Sorry," he murmured. "I guess you worried they'd feel responsible."

"Yes. And that my mom would break up with the sheriff before letting me go," I admitted. "I wouldn't have been able to live with myself, knowing she gave up her chance for happiness and comfort for me."

"The sheriff put you in an impossible situation, didn't he?" West's words were so kind I wanted to tell him to stop. "But you told Adriana something?"

I laughed. "No, not really. Curt made sure to let it slip around town that I had stolen the sign. After Adriana found out, she was pissed. Anyway, when I decided to leave, I told her there were just too many crappy things about Hobie for me, everyone thought I was shit, and I wanted a fresh start. She knew the truth though. I had told her about overhearing the neighbor, remember? I'm sure she put two and two together even though I swore to her that wasn't why."

"Why didn't you stay in touch at least?" he asked.

I took a breath and let it out slowly, trying to decide whether or not I could get into that part of it with him. Luckily, Pippa began her precry whimpering in time to spare me the decision. I jumped up to slip on my clothes and make my way into the nursery, hearing West's teasing warning from behind me.

"We're not done here, Nicolas Salerno."

I smiled to myself as I reached for the baby in the crib. The unique way he emphasized the "Nico" in "Nicolas" made my heart flip-flop. It was incongruent with his preppy cowboy shtick, and I wondered what other words he pronounced that way—sultry, dirty, exotic…

Promising.

CHAPTER 22

WEST

I let him go. There was no doubt in my mind he wasn't used to sharing his personal crap, so I dropped the subject as soon as he retrieved Pippa from her room. Part of me felt like I'd pushed him into a kind of intimacy that wasn't my place. Why in the world would he want to open up to someone like me when I was the very epitome of the town and people he resented so much?

After I joined him in the kitchen, I began straightening the paperwork we'd left out from our earlier work on the bakery bookkeeping. Whatever the reason for the discrepancy, it was clear Sugar Britches was in the red just as he'd suspected.

I'd noticed from the receipts that he'd made a deposit that week from his own personal accounts in order to make payroll. There was no way of knowing how much of a sacrifice that had been for him, but since he'd told me about being the main tattoo artist at his shop, I had to assume him being gone this long was going to seriously cut into his income back home. I wondered if he needed help—financial or otherwise.

"Nico, is there anything you need to do at the bakery or in town today? I could watch Pippa for you," I offered.

He walked to the sofa and sat down with the baby in his arms, seeming to think through his response.

"Uh, yeah. Actually, if you don't mind, I'd like to paint a cake today. Rox has a client who wants one of Adriana's painted cakes, so she asked me to try one. I practiced on one the other day, but I'd love to get some more practice in before having to do the real thing."

"No problem," I said, walking over and taking the baby. "Why don't you go now? I have a shift at the emergency room starting at six tonight, so I'll need to leave here a little before then."

He smiled up at me with gratitude, and I realized we'd somehow found a new middle ground. Less antagonistic back and forth and more attempts at understanding each other. It wasn't really friendship, and it wasn't really intimacy, but it was a start.

Once he was gone, I tried to tackle the bookkeeping again. I found some massive expenses the bakery had incurred shortly before Adriana's death. When I looked at the notes, I discovered the payments were for the mortgage on the building. She was attempting to purchase the building the bakery was in.

I was stunned. Why the hell hadn't she told me? And why hadn't she just continued renting it from the man who owned it? John Gravely was a prominent businessman in town who owned several commercial properties on the square. He was known for being fair. Had he tried to list the property for sale?

After digging through bank statements, I saw that the mortgage payments were made out to WWR, LLC. My heart lurched. The only WWR, LLC I knew was Weston Wilde Ranch. Grandpa's ranch holdings. Had she been running her bakery in the red because she owed Grandpa money?

I looked around for Pippa's car seat and found it on the floor by the front door. After snatching the backpack with her diaper supplies out of the nursery, I strapped the baby into the seat and loaded her up in my truck. I shot Nico a quick text, telling him I was running over to Grandpa and Doc's so he wouldn't freak out if he came home and found us missing.

When I pulled into the ranch, the same trio of goofballs came running out to greet me with their cacophony of barking. I unbuckled Pippa and told her she was in for a treat.

As soon as we walked through the door, they were on her. Both Grandpa and Doc were like kids in a candy store.

"There she is! Give her here," Doc said.

"Where's her bag? In the truck? I'll go get it," Grandpa interjected. I handed Pippa to Doc and pulled the backpack off my shoulders to hand to Grandpa. We made our way into the kitchen, and I was relieved to see coffee made. There was also a familiar face at the kitchen island—my brother Hudson.

And he wasn't alone.

"Hi, Darci," I said, waving my hand to the young nurse. She beamed and hooked her elbow through Hudson's, leaning in to him and winking at me. Hudson lifted his hand in a wave and greeted me with a smile.

"We got volunteered to be guinea pigs for Grandpa's chili," Hudson explained.

Doc turned to face me, Pippa tucked into the curve of his arm. "Your grandfather is bound and determined to beat Clyde Ogilvie at the chili cook-off this year. I told him he's fighting a losing battle."

"Shut the hell up," Grandpa grumbled, swatting at Doc's ass with a dish towel. "You don't have to eat it if you don't like it. No one asked your opinion."

Doc leaned over to kiss Grandpa with a quick peck on the lips. "I'm just teasing and you know it. Although, I'm not sure our sex life can take many more of your bean-based experiments."

I groaned, and Hudson reached over to cover poor Darci's ears.

"Oh my god, you two. Gross," Hudson moaned. "There's a lady present, if you don't mind."

At least Doc had the decency to look a little pink around the ears. "Sorry, hon."

I walked over to Grandpa and reached out to put a hand on his shoulder. "Grandpa, can I talk to you in private for a minute?" My brother looked at me funny but didn't say anything, knowing I'd most likely tell him what he wanted to know later.

"Sure. Fix your coffee, and we can sit down in my office. You want Doc to join us?" he asked quietly.

"No, it's fine. You can talk to him about it later if you want to," I said, noticing Doc showing Pippa off to Darci. The nurse's eyes were lit up with baby love, and I wondered if Hudson had finally found a new girlfriend.

Once we were seated in the comfortable sofa and chair in his dark-paneled office, I told Grandpa what I had found. "Was she buying the building from you? And if so, why? And why didn't you tell me?"

Grandpa seemed to choose his words carefully. "Yes, she was. John told her he was going to sell and she had to either come up with the money to buy or find another retail space. It would have cost her a fortune. Her hope was to sell her house and move into the space upstairs from the bakery, but you and I both know she could never qualify for a commercial loan regardless."

"Why didn't she come to me?" I asked.

"She didn't come to anyone. I heard about the situation from John at the Rotary Club meeting. He said he had an offer on the place from a developer from out of town. I talked to Doc about it, and we decided to buy the place to keep control of part of the historic downtown in local hands. Plus we had the money, so why not help her out?"

"But she was killing herself making payments to you. Why? Why didn't you let her make smaller payments?" I knew my anger was coming out, but I was unable to hide it.

"West, take a breath and think for a minute. Do you really think that's what happened?"

I thought about how my grandfathers hadn't wanted a single dollar from me for the medical practice and Victorian home I lived in. I remembered countless people in town over the years Grandpa and Doc had helped financially. Grandpa had made a killing in cattle ranching while Doc had run a successful medical practice for years. They were some of the wealthiest and most generous people in all of Hobie, Texas. There was no way they'd ask her to pay more than she could afford.

"I'm sorry," I said finally. "Please explain."

"I didn't know she was struggling to make the payments, West. Adriana is the one who set the payment amount, not me. I told her to pay what she could afford. Everyone in town goes there for breakfast, so I assumed she was doing well enough to afford what she was sending me. If she wasn't, this is the first I'm hearing about it."

I let out a huff and slumped in my chair. "I don't know. I agree she should have been doing better. It doesn't make any sense."

"Does it matter at this point? What is Nico planning on doing with the business?"

"Good question. I guess you're right. I'm not sure Rox has any interest in owning her own business, and I think she's been afraid to ask Nico what his intentions are. I'll ask him when I get home."

Grandpa raised his eyebrow at me, and I realized what I'd said.

"I mean, I'll ask him when I get *back*. To drop off Pippa. Don't look at me like that."

"What's going on between you and the new guy, Westie?"

Doc slipped into the office without the baby and came over to sit next to Grandpa on the arm of the couch. I assumed he'd left Pippa in Darci's capable hands.

At the mention of Nico, I felt my fair skin heat up and betray me like a jackass.

Grandpa's lip curled up in a grin. "Is that right, West? Care to elaborate, son?"

"No," I said stubbornly.

"Has a certain someone we know and love been taking an intimate course in body piercings?" Doc chuckled as he realized what was going on.

Was it hot in here, or was it just me? I thought about the piercings I'd discovered on Nico and knew, just knew, the babbling was going to start if I didn't get out of there soon.

Grandpa's grin grew wider. "Just tell me one thing, West. Does he have a Prince Albert? I went through a period of time in the eighties when I begged Doc to get one."

I sputtered and stood up, desperate for my escape, but Doc and Grandpa continued like everything was normal.

Doc put a finger to his lip as if in thought. "You know, now that I'm retired, maybe I'll try it. I wonder if we know anyone who could do it for us. Think Nico would take a *stab* at it?"

The idea of Nico having to handle my grandfather's junk made me ill.

"You two are disgusting. That's... ugh. Stop. Please," I begged.

"So does he?" Grandpa asked.

"Does who, what?" I muttered.

"Does Nico have any interesting piercings?"

Doc chimed in. "Or ink in private places? I've always been particularly fond of tattooed asses myself. Just seeing all that—" His hands came up to squeeze invisible butt globes. "Nngh."

"Yes! Okay? Yes. All those... things. But— I mean, no. No Prince Albert. But other things and, well, the ink. Okay? Yes, there is ink. Lots of..." I took a breath that came out as more of a sigh. "Lots of ink. In places."

Grandpa and Doc looked at each other with obvious amusement before Doc asked one more question. "What's on his ass?"

I shot him a look.

"Pretty please? I've been sleeping with the same old saggy butt for almost fifty years. Let a man dream."

Grandpa elbowed him. "It hasn't always been this saggy. Need I remind you, there was a time when you thought it was downright bite—"

"Enough!" I blurted. "Fine. It's ah... like, ah... big colorful peacock feathers on one side and a..." I blew out a breath, trying very hard not to get an erection in front of my grandparents. I looked up to the ceiling in hopes there were angels who could deliver me from the conversation. "A coiled snake on the other."

The hooting and hollering that came out of those two was enough to send me scuttling from the room.

CHAPTER 23

NICO

The cake painting went much better than I'd expected, and I lost myself in the rhythm of creating images from my imagination. By the time I got back to the house, it was time for West to leave for his shift at the hospital.

"I'm sorry I kept you so long. I didn't mean to lose track of time like that," I told him.

West's hands came up to cup my face before he leaned in for a kiss. "It was fine. I slept when Pippa napped. You look happy and relaxed. I'm glad you stayed if that's what came of it."

I let out a breath and smiled. "It did. After I did the practice cake, I painted some cupcakes Rox had set out for me. Nothing special, just flowers and shit. But it was cool. I never knew you could paint on frosting that way."

"You sound like your sister," he said, running his hands through my hair. "She always had a sketchbook with her. You two had that in common."

I felt my heart shutter at the thought. Why hadn't I reached out to her? I could have at least done it when I was finally settled as an adult. But I knew the real answer to that question. I'd been ashamed. I knew she'd ask me about those intervening years, and there was no way I could tell her what I'd had to do to survive on the streets. She wouldn't have been able to bear it.

West's finger tilted my chin up so I was forced to meet his eyes. "Hey, where did you go?" he asked softly. "I lost you."

I shook my head and forced a smile. "No, I'm good. You should get going though. It's late."

"Shit, Nico. I'm sorry. I didn't mean—"

"No, it's fine. Really. I promise. Thanks for watching Pippa for me." I twisted out of his grasp and went to check on the baby in the nursery. I heard West sigh behind me, but he didn't come after me. Why the hell was I disappointed by that? I had been in his arms already. If I'd wanted to be with him, I could have stayed in his arms instead of pulling my usual turtle routine.

What the hell was my fucking problem?

I didn't want to be that passive-aggressive asshole. Before I reached the crib, I turned around and returned to the main living area. West had already walked out, so I hurried to the front door and swung it wide open.

"Wait!" I called out, my heart thundering. He stopped before reaching for the door handle of his truck. I balled my hands into fists and said what needed to be said. "I'm sorry. That was shitty and moody. Forgive me."

I'd never heard such reasonable words come out of my fucking mouth, and it almost made me laugh. West cracked a small smile.

"C'mere," he said, holding out his arms and walking toward me. I swallowed my pride and jumped off the porch, jogging the few feet remaining between us and throwing myself into his arms.

The move was weird and unexpected. We barely knew each other. Neither of us wanted a relationship with the other, but I wondered if that's why we were both willing to cling to whatever this connection was. There was so much less at stake than a normal coming together that maybe we thought we could find in each other whatever comfort and fun we wanted in the short term.

West held me in a tight bear hug—my face naturally pressing into the curve of his neck. He smelled amazing, as usual. "What time do you get off work?" I asked into the warmth of his skin.

He leaned back enough I had to tilt my face up to see him. "Six in the morning."

"Come over after? A little postwork relaxation sex maybe?"

His face relaxed into a beautiful smile, and my heart thudded harder than normal. "Yes. Fuck yes. I'll be here at six-oh-five. Leave the door unlocked so I don't wake you up."

He leaned down and kissed me then—soft lips nibbling on mine until his warm tongue brushed the seam of my mouth. I opened for him and let him devour me to his heart's content. Eventually he pulled away. His face was flushed, and his eyes looked semiglazed in the rosy evening light from the fading sun.

Suddenly I felt awkward. Unsure of what to do or say and unwilling to look like an idiot in front of the guy.

"Okay, well, uh... I hope things run smoothly tonight in the ER. See you tomorrow."

"Pippa's been asleep since half past three, so she's probably going to wake up any minute starving to death," he said with a wink.

I gave him a thumbs-up and backed toward the house, almost tripping on the stairs to the porch like a lovesick fool because I didn't want to take my eyes off him.

What the fuck had I gotten myself into? Whatever it was, it felt strangely amazing.

And I wanted more.

~

EARLY THE NEXT MORNING, I was just falling back to sleep after the millionth middle-of-the-night Pippa wake-up call when I felt West's cool body slide into bed. My body shivered in reaction, eliciting his low chuckle.

"You're fucking freezing," I mumbled against my pillow.

"And you're nice and toasty. Roll this way," he said, pulling my back against his chest. "Warm me up."

I turned around in his embrace until my face was mashed against his chest. "How was work?" The minute the words were out of my mouth, I felt the domesticity of them and almost laughed. If any of my friends back home could see me welcome a man, a Texas doctor slash cowboy for that matter, into my bed so early in the morning just for sleep, they'd die laughing.

"It was fine until about nine last night when a four-year-old came in with a drug overdose. Apparently, he'd gotten into his grandmother's blood pressure medicine. It was awful, but we got him stabilized."

"Jesus. How scary. His poor parents must have been terrified." I thought of what I'd do if something like that happened to Pippa. Just the thought of her in pain made my stomach cramp. "How did it happen?"

"Grandma didn't have childproof caps on the bottle because she has arthritis. You should have seen her, Nico. She was beside herself with guilt. I finally had to give her a sedative and find her a bed."

I ran a hand up to his shoulder and rubbed the tight muscles between there and his neck. "Lie on your stomach," I said softly.

West leaned in and pressed a kiss to my forehead before doing as I'd suggested. I crawled over his ass and straddled him just below so I could rub his back.

"How was your night with the Pipsqueak?" he asked.

"Awful. She's a menace. Takes after my bratty sister."

West snorted and reached a hand back to squeeze my leg. "You sure it's not *you* she takes after?"

I thought about how Pippa had my DNA also. Hell, those ears alone were proof enough. I wondered what other traits of mine she might end up with over the years.

I'd never know.

I'd be back in San Francisco living my life alone. Working, visiting Griff and his own little family. Watching my friends move on with their spouses and children. What would that be like? I already knew what it was like to watch my best friend fall in love and become closer to his partner than to me. Would the same happen with my other friends back home?

I had always been satisfied with my life. Proud of my tattoo shop and happy with the handful of friends I had. I was close to the big Marian family even though I wasn't technically a Marian. But what would it be like if I had my very own family? What would it be like if I could stay with Pippa and be her family?

The idea was ludicrous. No one in their right mind would want me as a father. I'd make a terrible parent. And how would I ever balance work with having enough time for her? A little voice in my head reminded me that's exactly what Adriana had been planning, so why wasn't it okay for me to do it?

West flipped to his back to face me—the movement sliding our cocks against each other and forcing a groan out of both of us. My eyes lifted to his in question.

"What are you thinking about, Nico? You're being awfully quiet," he said, running his hands up and down my thighs.

Out of habit, I began to brush him off, but my gut told me to speak the truth.

"Do you think it's unfair to deliberately raise a child as a single parent?" I asked.

West sat up and reached for me, sliding me off his lap so I was sitting next to him in bed. "What's this about? Adriana? Are you upset about her having a child out of wedlock or something?" His brow was furrowed in confusion.

"No, god no. Never mind. It's stupid. Turn back over and let me finish. I didn't even get to the good parts yet. Namely, that glorious, fucking ass."

"No distracting me with offers of fondling. Something is on your mind, Nico. What is it?"

I loved the way my name sounded when he said it. Surely the man could make me come just by saying my name over and over without even touching me. *Maybe I should ask him to try.*

"Huh?" I asked.

"Why are you asking about single parenting? If it's not about Adriana, is it your mom?"

"No, not at all. Although, now that you mention my mom… she

did an amazing job raising us on her own," I admitted, remembering how I'd never once felt as though I was missing out after my father died and it was just the three of us. Maybe that was my answer.

I continued thinking out loud. "I just assumed Pippa was better off with the Warners than with me, you know? I mean, what kid would rather be raised by a perma-bachelor who lives above a tattoo shop in an urban commercial district? But then I think about family… biology. And it's hard. The idea of the last living person connected to me by blood going to live with strangers… Never seeing her again…"

West reached out and pulled me into his lap again, wrapping his arms around me and running his hands up and down my back. "I know it's hard, Nico. I mean, I can't imagine what this is like for you. Losing your mom, Adriana, and Pippa all at the same time. But you have to think about what's best for her and what all is involved in raising a child."

"I know that."

"It's expensive, exhausting, heartbreaking," he began.

I joined in. "Messy, loud, and stifling. Plus it would crimp my style in the clubbing and hookup scene," I joked pathetically. "Not sure anyone would want to play with a man who has a kid."

I felt West's body stiffen and wondered if he had a problem with the club scene. He was probably a snob about people who didn't meet at the fucking golf club or whatever.

"When you have a kid, Nico, your entire life revolves around them. It's a massive sacrifice. Very different from the life you live now."

"True," I said, deciding he was right. Maybe I wasn't cut out to be a parent. It had been a silly daydream anyway. I knew the reality of parenting was nothing like the fantasy.

"I've learned from watching families at my practice that being a single parent is lonely as hell too," West cautioned.

I glanced at him, wondering why he was trying to talk me out of the idea. Little did he know, those last words weren't an argument against parenting in my mind, because he didn't know the truth.

There was absolutely no way raising Pippa on my own could be lonelier than the life I'd already been living before she came into it.

CHAPTER 24

WEST

Before we had a chance to discuss it further, Pippa began to make her morning noises. Nico rolled his eyes and muttered. "Jesusfuckingchrist, I was just up with her before you got here."

He got up and slid some pajama pants on before pulling a T-shirt over his head. "Get some sleep," he said before turning to leave the room. I reached out to grab his wrist before he walked out of range.

"Just give me a couple of hours, then I'll be good, okay?" I asked. He nodded, looking adorably sleepy with his crazy Troll hair sticking up everywhere. I couldn't help but pull him in for a kiss on the lips before letting him go. "Good morning, cutie."

He smiled shyly back at me, the stress from our previous conversation melting away. "Good night, sexy doctor," he said before turning to leave and closing the door behind him.

I rolled over to settle in and reveled in the smell of him on the bedsheets. Was it possible to hyperventilate from sucking in that smell as much as I did? It was to that comforting scent and the soft, familiar sounds of him cooing to the baby that I was able to drift into a dreamless sleep.

When I came awake a couple of hours later, I was surprised to find myself wrapped around him again, our naked bodies as close as possible under the bedding. My stiff cock was throbbing against the cleft of Nico's ass, and the hunger for him in my belly was overwhelming.

I arched my cock into him, hard, and felt his responding thrust backward. Both of us groaned, and I murmured into his ear, asking for supplies.

"Over there. Your side," he said in a groggy voice.

"How long has Pippa been—"

"Not long; we have plenty of time," he responded, reading my mind. I left my legs tangled up with his while I twisted to reach for the supplies in the bedside table. I tried to ignore the other items in the drawer but couldn't help but laugh.

"Shut up. Don't you dare mention my sister's sex crap if you want to get laid," he grumbled.

"But—"

"No. My sister, West. My *sister*. Gross. Fuck, I lost my hard-on," he complained, slapping at my thigh in frustration. "Goddammit."

I turned back around, stashing the condom and lube under the pillow before taking Nico's chin in my hand. "Dude, if you think I can't find the hard-on you just lost, you have zero faith in my abilities in the bedroom."

My eyes stayed locked on his while I moved my hand down to his throat and clasped it firmly but gently. Nico swallowed and widened his eyes before I continued teasing him.

"Now, you are going to turn over onto your hands and knees like a good little Nico, and I am going to blow your fucking mind—among other things. *Capiche*?"

"Si, signore," he murmured as he scrambled over onto his belly and pulled his knees in. I couldn't help but run my hands appreciatively over the coil of snakes and the plume of peacock feathers.

"God, you're the hottest fucking thing I've ever seen," I said under my breath. Nico arched his back and pressed his ass closer to me, naturally opening himself up until I was looking at exactly what I wanted. "Oh, and will you look at that?"

I leaned over and put my lips against his lower back before reaching through his legs to grasp his cock.

"Seems I may have just found that erection you lost."

The whimpering sounds he made into the pillow revved my heart rate up to the stratosphere. I leaned in to lick a stripe from his balls up the bumpy piercings, across his hole to his lower back and heard him suck in a breath.

"Like that?" I asked before taking a soft bite of the flesh of his ass and running my tongue along the captured skin.

"West... *fuck*, yes. Like that."

I loved the way his voice changed when I gave him pleasure. It was the only time I felt like Nico truly let himself be vulnerable to me. And I was beginning to think that the man wasn't used to making himself vulnerable to anyone. He seemed desperate to keep up a prickly outer shell, and I wondered if that was just here in Hobie or elsewhere in his everyday life back home too.

I wanted to know more—learn more about who the real Nico Salerno was behind the purple hair and the spiked earrings and the tatts. Was he happy in his life? Did he miss anything about his hometown? Did he have someone special back in San Francisco? What had made him start to think about keeping Pippa and raising her on his own?

My mouth was teasing his opening while my brain circled around thoughts of the man himself. I realized I wasn't giving his pleasure my full attention and forced myself to push those thoughts away. Once I did, I speared him with my tongue and reached again for his cock.

By the time I was ready to enter him, I was afraid I'd blow on the first stroke. I popped open the lube before sliding cool fingers into his hot body. His sudden intake of breath accompanied his body's clench, and I felt all the air leave my lungs.

I couldn't wait any longer.

"Turn over," I told him. "Want you on your back."

He did as I said and moved onto his back in the center of the bed. Colorful hair went every which way, his chest was heaving from rapid intake of breaths, his hand had reached down to stroke his cock as he waited for me, and his eyes were shining like flecks of obsidian—all pupil and very little color.

I maneuvered between his legs and leaned down over him, dragging my lips up his chest to his neck to his studded ear. His hand moved from his cock to my hair, fingers threading through it before pulling my head back enough to meet his eyes.

Something was there between us—something unspoken and important. But I couldn't grasp what it was, only that it made my heart hurt when I looked at him all flushed and wide-eyed, panting and desperate. Whatever it was, it settled over us for a moment, causing our eye contact to go on longer than normal, like an acknowledgment that something was off or something was waiting just out of reach that needed to be claimed.

"West," he breathed.

"Mmm?" I responded, lips unable to keep from brushing against his. His cock jumped against my abdomen, and mine pressed hard into the bedding beneath me.

He didn't say anything else, so I met his eyes again. There was still something in there I couldn't name.

"What is it?" I murmured. "You okay?"

His eyes searched mine some more before he blew out a short breath and gave a small nod. "Yeah. Yeah, I'm okay."

I bent my knees up under his legs so I could lean in farther and hook my arms under his shoulders. "Talk to me," I asked softly, leaning in to flick one of his lip piercings with my tongue. "Something's on your mind."

"I never asked if you were seeing anyone," he admitted with furrowed brows.

The comment was so mundane compared to what I'd thought was happening between us I couldn't help but bark out a laugh, causing his eyes to widen further.

"What's so funny? I don't want to be some kind of home wrecker," Nico explained defensively.

"I'm laughing because I wondered the same thing about you a few minutes ago. You've been to my house, Nico. You know I live alone.

Believe me, you would have had many, many tongue-lashings in town by now if there was someone in my life. After the way I claimed you at the bonfire, are you kidding?"

His face relaxed, and I felt his fingers begin to move slowly up my spine. "Okay, well… I mean, it's not like I'm looking for a boyfriend or anything. I just don't want to fuck up someone else's relationship if I can help it."

"That's very kind. And what about you? Is there a Mr. Salerno back home in the Bay Area? Someone covered in ink and matching scrotal hoops, perhaps?"

I was teasing, but the idea of it made my stomach sour nonetheless.

He seemed to hesitate, which only caused my stomach to knot even more and my heart to stutter. No. *No.* It didn't matter. Why did it matter? It was just sex. If he was cheating, that was his problem, not mine.

"I'm married to—"

I was scrambling away from him before I knew what I was doing. I tripped over my ass and fell halfway onto the floor. His mouth froze open for a split second before he finished his sentence.

"To my job, Weston. Jesus. I'm married to my tattoo shop. What the fuck?"

Nico was on his knees peering down at me in shock.

"I…" What the hell was I supposed to say? "I, ah, sorry. I just thought…" I stopped spluttering and started laughing.

His face turned to surprise. "Wait, you seriously thought I was *married?*"

"Well, no. That's not what I meant." I moved back up to the bed and knelt in front of him. "I'm not surprised you'd have someone special, so when you said you were married, my stupid head grabbed on to it and I freaked."

He rolled his eyes. "Bullshit."

"Nico, it's true. Fuck. I'm sorry. Please. I didn't mean to say anything to upset you. It was just my nerves about it that caused that stupid reaction."

His look was skeptical, and I tried to figure out how in the hell to fix the situation in which we found ourselves. I reached out to grab his hands in mine.

"Look, I know you aren't looking for a relationship. And, honestly, neither am I. I'm married to my work too. In addition to my practice, I work those shifts at the hospital. So can we stop all this fucking talk and get back to the fucking fucking?"

I batted my eyelashes at him for good measure, and he let out a breath before cracking a smile.

"Fuck yes."

I pounced on him with a full-body slam into the bed. He let out a grunt and grabbed my shoulders to keep from flailing. We kissed while laughing, and it was a combination of relief and joy that seemed to bubble up through me.

After that, I didn't think about Nico with someone else. I didn't think of him wanting more than I was prepared to give him. I just enjoyed the moment of loving on his body to the best of my ability.

Well, not love exactly. But attention, adoration, gratitude, and a healthy heap of lust. I doused him with as many kisses, licks, bites, and touches as I could possibly give the man.

By the time I was again poised to enter him, he was begging for my cock, breathing my name between shuddered gasps, and pulling at me with greedy fingers. My mouth was locked on his, and my tongue danced between us.

"Want you so badly," I admitted into his mouth. "Need to be inside you."

"Fuck. Fuck, yes. Same here. Please. Inside."

I loved it when he babbled and begged—so different from his usual attitude.

After slipping on the condom and pressing into his body, I looked up to see if he needed me to slow down.

His eyes watched me, and his hands came out to hold my face. We made that crazy connection again through our eye contact—the one that had derailed us just a little while earlier. I knew I wasn't imagining it, but whatever it was, it simply didn't fit the casual scenario we'd agreed upon. I didn't allow the moment to happen again. I couldn't.

So I did the only thing I could think of. I slammed my cock into him and latched my mouth onto his, swallowing his scream and pressing his body deep down into the mattress.

CHAPTER 25

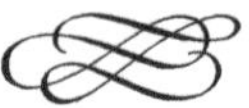

NICO

As much as I wanted to figure out what in the hell was developing between the two of us, all I could feel in that moment was West's glorious fucking cock sliding in and out of my body. My brain short-circuited when the head of his dick stroked over my prostate, and I almost swallowed my tongue.

Okay, I almost swallowed *his* tongue. Same difference.

He pummeled into me so rhythmically I couldn't think or feel or reciprocate. I clutched his legs where they knelt on the bed beside my hips, and I could feel the muscles moving with every thrust into me. God, his legs were amazing. His entire body was amazing.

I could smell the sleepy scent of him and taste the salty tang of his skin. My fingers could feel the rough hair on his legs, and I could hear his deep rumble of pleasure as I tightened my body around him. Once I opened my eyes to watch him, I saw his beautiful face staring down at me again with that look.

The look that told me I was something special. Something wonderful and unique, precious and rare. It was unlike anything I'd ever known before, and it scared the fucking piss out of me.

Had I managed to control my body, I might have lost my erection out of sheer stark terror. But I didn't. Weston Wilde owned my body in that moment, and there wasn't a damned thing I could do to order it to stand down. Every cell was lit up, every muscle was contracting in anticipation, and my cock was jackknifing against my body in preparation for coating the ceiling with my release.

"Oh god, oh god," I blurted as West shifted so he could peg my spot again and again. "Oh god," I choked out one more time.

"Fuck, Nico. Jesus," West groaned before sucking a mark hard into my neck. "You're going to make me come. Fuck."

His voice cracked on that last curse, and that was all it took for me to explode. My hands were still on his skin, but my cock didn't seem to notice or give a shit.

The tingles along my spine seemed to shrink to nothing before suddenly bursting out in a giant explosion that shook through me from head to foot. I cried out his name as I arched into my release and felt his mouth pressing soft kisses all over my face as his hands cupped the back of my head.

West's hips thrust two more times before they wound up pressed so tightly against me his cock felt like it was in my throat as it twitched out his own release.

His voice was in my ear within moments of his climax. He whispered sweet words about how amazing my body was, how beautiful I was, how lucky he was to be with me in that moment. Even though I knew they were stupid postorgasm words, I felt them hit my heart like traitorous Cupid arrows.

I lifted my hands from his legs to his head and ran my fingers through his thick, blond locks. Our chests were glued together with sweat and semen. Our breathing was still rapid and uneven. But my heart was steady and my mind was calm.

West's body was curled on top of mine, his face pressed into my neck and his softening cock still inside me. The way we lay together was heavy, sticky, and uncomfortable, but I would have paid any amount of money for him to stay like that as long as possible.

I swiveled my head to kiss whatever part of him my lips could reach. It turned out to be a lock of hair stuck to his forehead. "Take a shower with me after this?" I asked.

He lifted his head with a small grin. "Yeah, I'd like that."

After an extremely handsy shower, we emerged clean if not completely well rested. Pippa was awake, so I grabbed her and changed her, emerging to the kitchen to discover West standing there holding the bottle ready. I let out a chuckle.

"What's so funny?" he asked.

"I'm just thinking about all the women in the world who would pay big money to be in my shoes right now. Hot, muscled doctor in his underwear fixing a bottle for their baby? Jesus Christ. It's like every woman's wet dream. Look at you."

He turned and flexed his muscles like he was modeling for a calendar. "Does this make it studlier?" he asked.

"No." I laughed. "It makes you dorkier. Gimme that bottle."

West handed me the bottle before turning back to the coffee maker. He began singing in a teasing voice. "He thinks I'm a hot doctor. I'm Nico's wet dream... He wants me..."

I bit my tongue to keep from grinning like a fool. "You're insane. Are you sure you didn't sneak a little something-something from the opiate supply at work this morning before you left?"

He continued to dance around the kitchen in his underwear, shaking his gorgeous fucking ass as he gathered supplies for the coffee. Pippa squawked in my arms, and I realized I'd pressed the bottle's nipple into her cheek instead of her mouth.

"Sorry, baby girl. I was busy staring at a fine man's ass. One day you'll understand," I promised her under my breath. I settled down with her on the sofa and pulled a blanket over my legs. "You want to watch the game?" I called out, grabbing the remote.

West stopped dancing and gawped at me. "*You* watch football?"

I raised my eyebrows at him as he spluttered to cover his misstep. "No. I mean, *yes*. Cool. I'd love to. I just didn't..."

"You didn't think a queer from San Francisco enjoyed watching the Forty-Niners crush the Cowboys? Are you fucking nuts?"

West's face changed from guilt to a shit-eating grin. "Let the record show, those aren't my words, queer boy. They're yours. And if you think for one minute your team is crushing mine, you're in for a rude awakening. You're talking about a low-ass ranked team beating a top-ten team."

I rolled my eyes. "Oh please. The Niners are just waiting for their time in the sun. Get ready for a pummeling. We've been holding back until it was the right time to strike."

The sound of West's rich laughter warmed the open space between us, and I felt myself relax farther into the sofa after clicking on the remote and finding the right channel. Pippa's tiny blue-green eyes stared up at me, and I smiled down at her.

"Hey cutie-patootie. How was your sleep?" I murmured to her. She reached out a hand toward my nose, and her tiny fingers curled in an attempt to grab on. I gave her my index finger to grab instead. After propping my feet on the coffee table, I settled in to watch the game.

West joined me a couple of minutes later with two mugs of coffee and a couple of sandwiches he must have pulled together from stuff he found in the kitchen.

"This okay?" he asked, sitting down next to me and pulling part of the blanket onto his legs.

"Thank you. It's perfect."

We drank and ate in companionable silence, passing the baby between us as needed to keep the hot coffee away from her. West had been right, of course. The Dallas team crushed the San Francisco team. At least he was a good sport about it, only giving me a gentle elbow to the ribs every time his team scored.

Eventually I found myself dozing off against one of his shoulders while Pippa dozed on the other. Once again, I thought about how sticky sweet the scene was and wanted to scream from the irony of my life. If only Griff could have seen me then. Me and the perfect man curled up in our underwear watching Sunday football with a baby. It was ridiculous.

I felt him shift me off him at one point so he could put the baby on a play mat on the floor with hanging toys. When he settled back in beside me, I drifted off again.

"This is amazing, Nico," he murmured after a while. When I cracked open my eyes and saw him flipping through a familiar spiral notebook, I jumped up and grabbed for it, accidentally elbowing him in the shoulder and falling over his lap in the process.

"Ow. What the hell?" He gasped, rubbing his shoulder.

"Give me that," I said, grabbing the notebook out of his hands.

I stretched to put it on the other side of the sofa from where he sat so that he'd have to go through me to get to it again. How stupid of me to have left it on the coffee table. I hadn't been thinking.

"You're writing down memories of Adriana," he said gently. "Is it for Pippa? To help her get to know her mom?"

A thick lump in my throat threatened to choke me, so I just nodded. West reached out and slid an arm around my waist, pulling me over until I was straddling his lap so he could pull me into a strong hug.

"I think that's amazing. Why don't you want me to see?"

I shrugged, tucking my face into his neck and taking comfort in the warm feel of his skin against my nose and cheek.

West continued, "I don't mean to make you self-conscious about it, but the drawings are spectacular. You're really talented. I'd love to see and read more sometime, but I understand if you'd rather me not look at it again. It's your business. But just know it's very thoughtful and loving. Pippa is lucky to have you."

I squeezed my eyes closed and let out a breath. There was that L-word again. "Thanks."

Large hands rubbed up and down my spine until his strong fingers threaded into my hair.

"Fuck this. Let's pack up the Pipsqueak and go somewhere—maybe a walk down by the lake before I have to be on call again at the ER. What do you say?"

I thought about how easy it was to be in his company sometimes. How nice it felt to spend down time with someone like West—smart, kind, happy. I pictured us walking along the lakeside trail with Pippa in the stroller and how incongruous the image was with my real life. No city crowds or noise. Nothing but the clean, fresh air blowing off the water and through the trees and the light sounds of the water lapping along the shoreline. The quiet companionship of Dr. Sweetheart by my side.

"Yes please," I said before reluctantly peeling myself out of his embrace.

The rest of the afternoon passed easily with the hot doctor whose bedside manner was beginning to settle around me like a healing balm. Spending time with West made being back in Hobie feel almost like a good diversion from my regular life. It made me wonder if perhaps I'd fallen into a rut back home of busting my ass at the shop and forgetting that there should be life outside of work. Friends and family. Fresh air and the late afternoon sun sparkling warmly off the lake water.

Spending time with Weston Wilde was supposed to have been temporary—like a stick-on tattoo at a child's birthday party. But with every touch of his fingers in my hair and every brush of his lips over mine, I found myself wanting to cement those feelings into my skin forever with permanent ink.

I had to remember it was a delicate house of cards. And when Tuesday morning rolled around, all it took was one surprised phone call from Honovi Baptiste to send the whole thing tumbling down.

CHAPTER 26

WEST

After spending Sunday with Nico, I probably walked through my shift at the hospital that night with cartoon hearts floating around my head. I felt like a lovesick fool, but I didn't care. I was content to enjoy the feeling as long as I could before he left and my life went back to normal.

Not only had we had hot sex on and off all weekend, but we'd also talked for hours. I felt like I finally had a glimpse into the person Adriana had implied he was. Nico was the guy who tried to protect his family in the only way he knew how—by leaving. And now here he was having to do it all over again. He had to spend this time bonding with Pippa, just to hand her over and walk away from Hobie for the second time.

I had grown up with nine siblings, armloads of aunts and uncles, and more cousins than I could count. Grandpa and Doc were like a second set of parents to me, and half the town was close enough to me to be considered family. And there was Nico—the complete opposite. After leaving Hobie, he'd had no family. None.

While he'd dozed on the sofa, I'd noticed the spiral notebook lying on the coffee table. It had Adriana's name on it, so I reached to flip through it to see what was in it.

I'd been shocked to read page after page of Nico's childhood memories of his sister. Funny things she'd said, crazy hijinks they'd gotten up to together, and even what her bedroom had looked like when she was younger with posters of her favorite bands and handwritten inspirational quotes by Maya Angelou stuck around her cheap vanity mirror.

He'd drawn cartoon versions of some of the things he described, and some of the drawings had even shown the funny crinkle of Adriana's nose when she was frustrated with someone. The love he had for his older sister shone through those stories and drawings like hot beams from the sun. He must have spent all his waking hours on that book since he'd been there taking care of Pippa.

And I had to admit that after seeing it, I'd fallen just a tiny bit in love with Nico Salerno.

When my shift had finished, I'd stumbled back to my place for a few hours of sleep before the first patient appointment later that morning. I showered, slept, and woke up for a quick bite and coffee before making my way downstairs to begin my day.

Mondays after weekend overnights at the hospital were never fun. The practice was slammed with patients who'd gotten sick or injured over the weekend but didn't want to pay hospital rates to visit the emergency room.

I hit the ground running and didn't stop until I poured myself into bed that evening. The next day, the craziness started all over again as soon as I got downstairs to work.

There were more cases of the flu that kept me so busy I didn't even notice when Honovi arrived. Goldie pulled me aside to let me know she'd let him back to my office, so when I got a break between patients, I joined him there.

"Hey, West," he said in his gentle timbre. "I need to talk to you about something pretty important. Do you have a few minutes?"

"Only a few. Things are crazy today. What can I do for you?"

"It's about Pippa." He seemed to speak with hesitation despite the fact we'd been friends for years. "Her birth certificate arrived this morning, and I… I didn't realize you were listed as her father."

Suddenly I got that warm tingly rush that usually hits before fainting, but I stayed steady and just blinked at him instead.

Hon cleared his throat. "Yeah, so anyway. Needless to say, this changes things. Legally, Pippa is yours, not Nico's. So, ah… depending on what your intentions are, the adoption process would need to shift to—"

As he spoke, I must have tuned him out. All I could think about was Adriana listing me as the baby's father. Why hadn't she told me? She'd done it months before her death. Why? Not only did I wonder why she hadn't told me, but I also wondered why she'd done it in the first place. If it was for easy custody transfer in case of emergency, why list Nico as Pippa's guardian in her will?

Suddenly I realized what this meant. Nico was going to hate me. He was going to lose his ever-loving shit. "Hon, have you told Nico yet?"

Hon's eyes widened as he looked up from the stack of paperwork in his lap. "Well, yes. When I couldn't get in touch with you first thing, I went over to the house—"

"Shit. Shit, *shit.* I gotta go," I blurted. "I'm sorry. Can I call you later?"

Before he had a chance to respond, I rushed out the office door to the reception counter out front. Our receptionist was in the process of handing out a sticker to the little girl I'd just given vaccines to.

"Morgan, I have to go out for about an hour. Goldie can cover me until I get back. Tell her to call me only if it's critical, okay?"

She nodded in surprise, and I sent up a prayer of thanks that Goldie was a certified nurse practitioner who could handle most things without me when needed.

I bolted out the door and drove as quickly to Adriana's as I could. When I pulled down the driveway, I noticed an unfamiliar rental car parked next to Nico's, and movement by the front door drew my attention.

There stood Nico, completely engulfed in another man's embrace. He was crying into the man's shoulder, and the stranger's hands were rubbing Nico's back and hair in an effort to comfort him. I could tell by the body language between the two of them, it was a touch born of years of familiarity.

My entire body seemed to fold in on itself. My heart jammed into my throat, and I wasn't quite sure what to do with myself. Who the hell had his hands all over Nico? Who the fuck was comforting Nico?

I wanted to rage—to scream and yell and claim Nico like some kind of caveman. But of course, it wasn't my place. Nico wasn't mine, and he wasn't staying. I had no claim on him, and after the news about the birth certificate, I'd be lucky if he even spoke to me again.

After stepping out of the car, I closed it with a loud enough noise to get their attention. They jumped apart, and Nico turned puffy red eyes on me. My heart lurched at the sight of him—the sadness, disappointment, and anger were palpable.

Before I could even step toward the house, he was racing out to the driveway, screaming at me to leave. The stranger on the porch stood frozen in shock, as if he'd never seen the fiery Troll doll between us.

"You're Pippa's father?" he screamed. I heard a faint gasp from behind me and saw our local mail deliverer, Mrs. Parnell, at the top of the driveway, leaning out of her vehicle to put mail in Nico's box. I opened my mouth to contradict his words, but she zoomed off before I could get the words out.

I turned to Nico, feeling my anger surface. Now the whole town was going to think Pippa was mine.

"Nico," I said, but he cut me off.

"Leave, you jackass!" he snarled. "I can't believe I didn't see this coming a million miles away. You're a liar. And a coward. Probably a seducer and a… a…"

I held out my arms in the global gesture of *Stop, please* and began walking toward him. "Wait, Nico. Let me explain."

He reached me with pummeling fists and flying tears of rage. "I don't need your fucking lies. I'm not going to believe a word you say anyway. No wonder you didn't tell me who the father was. No wonder you were so attached to her." Nico sucked in a breath on a sob, and I couldn't take it anymore. I wrapped my arms around him and held him tight enough that he would stop hitting me.

"Stop, stop. Just let me talk to you. Please. She's not mine."

"Liar," he spat. "You're a fucking coward who doesn't even have the balls to claim her. I never took you for a coward, West."

"Nico, you're wrong."

"Why would she lie? It makes no sense. Did you really think this whole adoption thing was going to go through without people finding out? What, you're too afraid to claim her and screw up your perfect reputation in your perfect fucking little town? Weston Wilde, beloved doctor and member of the perfect Wilde family knocks up a girl from the wrong side of the tracks? No wonder you were there for her delivery. No wonder you were—"

"Stop," I growled in his face. "You're pissed. I get it. But you're spouting a bunch of bullshit you know nothing about. Calm the fuck down, Nico."

He was hiccupping the way he'd done before when he'd lost it over Adriana in front of me, but he tried to get the words out between gulps of breath. "Why, why did I come here? I could have stayed at home and been happy. You could have made all these impossible decisions without me. I hate you."

Hot tears soaked my shirt as they dropped onto it from his swollen face. I couldn't help but lean in and press my cheek to his to try to soak them up without taking my hands off his back. He struggled against me, his hands now clutched in my button-down shirt.

"Shh, catch your breath, Nico. Slow your breathing down," I murmured. I didn't want him to hyperventilate.

"Leave me alone, West. Let me go for god's sake. She's all yours now. She's all yours and"—he blew out a shaky breath—"I can finally put this all behind me."

I knew he only spoke out of anger, but the words knifed me in the chest nonetheless.

"You don't mean that," I told him. "You're pissed, and I get it. I would be too. But you're going to catch your breath and calm down, and then we're going to talk."

He finally struggled out of my grasp with a final push and began walking back to the stranger on the porch. I was desperate to know who the stranger was, but it was clear he was a safe harbor for Nico. So I tried to let it go.

Impossible.

"Who are you?" I asked before I could help it.

Nico spun and shot me a look. "None of your fucking business. Someone who loves me and doesn't lie to me. That's all you need to know."

The guy squeezed Nico's hand as he walked past but outstretched his other to me in greeting.

"Griffin Marian. You must be West."

He was adorable in a curly-haired, dimpled way. The kind of guy who looked like he kept everyone laughing in a crowd. He had a kind face, and there was sympathy behind his eyes as he studied me.

"Yeah. Weston Wilde. It's nice to meet you, Griffin."

"Please call me Griff. Would you mind giving us some time to settle in and then maybe we can give you a call to talk about Pippa?"

I felt my jaw tighten hearing the baby's name come out of this stranger's mouth. Nico still glared at me defiantly, but I knew if he truly thought he was losing Pippa, he was going to break down the minute I left.

"I'm not taking her from you, Nico. I wouldn't do that. Surely you know that even if you're pissed at me right now."

He rolled his eyes and turned to go into the house. Griff continued to study me before speaking.

"Nico's been my best friend for almost fifteen years, West. I've only seen him cry once before today."

My heart hammered as I thought of all the times Nico had cried with me since I'd met him. Was it all because of Adriana's death? Or maybe the exhaustion of caring for a newborn?

"He's lost a lot since he came back," I said lamely.

"I'm not really sure what's going on here, but I get the feeling it's about more than the baby and his sister. You're right. He's lost a lot. I'm not so sure he hasn't found something too."

We studied each other for a moment, and I realized the man named Griff had a sparkle of mischief in his eyes. There was no point in trying to decipher the stranger's thoughts. I let out a breath.

"I'll leave you guys in peace so he can calm down." I reached for my wallet to pull out a business card that had my cell number on it. After handing it over, I met his eyes again. "Will you call me if you need me?" Clearly he understood that what I'd really meant was for him to call me if *Nico* needed me.

His face softened into a kind grin. "Will do. We'll be in touch."

I slinked back to my office with a dark cloud hanging over my head—confusion over Adriana listing me as the baby's father, frustration over Nico's refusal to let me talk to him about it, and a lingering hint of nerves over who Griff Marian was to Nico besides friends. Which, of course, just led me to the depressed realization that it was none of my business.

After getting through the rest of my workday in a daze that involved brushing off nosy questions from half the town, I shuffled upstairs, intending to crawl into bed for a long nap. Lo and behold, my brother Hudson was sitting at my kitchen table again, working on his laptop.

"Hey," I said, kicking off my shoes and going to the fridge for a beer. "Want one?"

Hudson looked up before indicating to the fast-food cup sitting on the table next to his computer. "Nah. I stopped for a sweet tea on the way over here. Needed some caffeine."

A few of my siblings, including Hudson, lived a couple of hours away in Dallas. It didn't stop them from driving out to Hobie all the time to be with the family, but it usually didn't include a weekday visit like this one.

"What did you come back to town so soon for? Here to see Darci again?" I asked, twisting open the cap and sitting down next to him.

He looked up in surprise. "What? No. Well, kind of, I guess. Actually—"

I raised an eyebrow at his rambling, and he blew out a breath.

"I came Friday for the bonfire and stayed at Doc and Grandpa's all weekend. I just haven't gone back to the city yet. Darci asked if I'd stay and have lunch with her today before she had to go to work, so I did."

"Why do you sound so freaked about it?" I asked.

"I'm not freaked. I'm just… I don't know."

"Put out?" I suggested.

Hudson scrubbed his hands over his face before closing his laptop. "I guess so. I don't know what my problem is. She's so fucking sweet and cute. Honestly? I just… don't really know how I feel either way. Isn't that terrible? What the hell's my problem?"

"There's no problem, Hud. Sometimes there's just no chemistry even when you feel like there should be. There's a huge difference between someone being right for you on paper and someone feeling right for you in your heart. Sometimes you get one without the other, and that's okay."

"You sound like you speak from experience. Are you talking about Xavier?"

I laughed and shook my head. Xavier had been the closest thing I'd had to a boyfriend in the past ten years. His family had moved to town when we were seniors in high school. Everyone kept telling me how perfect we were for each other, so I'd finally caved and agreed to give it a try when we'd found ourselves in medical school together. It was odd. I'd felt like a Ken doll walking around town with another Ken doll, feeling perfect in our perfection as we smiled at each other with matching tooth sparkles. There had been no passion, no fire. And somehow I'd convinced myself that fire was too much to ask for. Maybe real relationships didn't really have that.

Things with Xavier had been fine, but just not… great.

When I'd finally told him it wasn't working, he'd been shocked. I still remembered him saying, "But we're perfect for each other—ask anyone."

He'd been so upset he'd avoided Hobie like the plague after that. He'd taken a surgical placement in Atlanta and rarely even came home long enough to visit his parents for the holidays. I hadn't seen him in ages.

"Yes, Hudson. I'm talking about Xavier," I said, even though I'd been thinking of Nico. My brother was right. Xavier was the perfect example of what I was trying to explain.

"I just feel so bad for her. She's been trying to get me to notice her forever. How do I tell her it doesn't feel right without hurting her feelings? Maybe I'm being too hasty. Maybe I should take her out again and give it another chance first."

I looked at my brother and tried to think of how to explain it.

"Don't you want to be with someone who lights you up the minute you see them? Someone you either want to throttle or kiss or... argue with or laugh with or... just fucking attack with your entire body the moment you're in their presence? Someone you can't keep your goddamned hands off of and can't stop thinking about when you're apart from them?"

Flashes of Nico fired in my brain and my body as if a Nico fireworks show had been shot off in my nervous system.

Hudson stared at me, unblinking. "Weston? Something you want to talk about?"

"No."

He snorted and laughed until the corners of his eyes were wet. "Sure, buddy. I buy that... *not*."

I rested my elbows on the table before dropping my face into my hands and groaning.

"I'm falling for the wrong guy, Hudson. What the fuck am I going to do?"

CHAPTER 27

NICO

When Griff and his mom had pulled up to the house, I'd raced out to greet them. Seeing my sweet best friend was enough to make me burst into tears like a fool. I'd just gotten the news from Honovi about West being the baby's father, and I was already on the verge of a full-blown breakdown.

Different thoughts had swirled through my head after hearing the news. West lying to me. Pippa not being mine to care for anymore. Me sleeping with my sister's... what? Boyfriend? Hookup? Baby daddy? Ugh. Just the thought of it made me sick to my stomach.

So when I'd heard the crunch of tires on gravel outside, I'd gone running. I got to Rebecca first and flew into her arms.

"Oh, baby," she cooed into my ears. "I'm so sorry. I'm so sorry about your sister, Nico." I cried in her arms and hugged her back for all I was worth. That woman had been there for me as much as she could have for at least ten years. When I'd thought I'd broken my leg one time after being clipped by a taxi on the sidewalk, it was Rebecca who'd taken me to the hospital for X-rays and stayed with me while the doctor explained it was just a deep bruise. When I'd opened my tattoo shop, it was Rebecca who'd asked to have the honor of getting the first tattoo. We'd all been floored and adamantly refused to let her get one. But the gesture had made me feel loved and supported all the same.

"Thank you for coming," I said, pulling back. "I'm so glad you're here. Wait till you see Pippa."

Rebecca was nuts about her grandbabies, and I knew she'd see Pippa as just another one of hers. She excitedly asked where the baby was, and I pointed her to the nursery and suggested she get Pippa up from her nap in her crib.

"Fair warning, she has a runny nose," I called after her. "It's gross."

She scoffed at me, making a comment under her breath about this not being her first rodeo. After Rebecca hurried into the house, I turned to Griff. Years of unspoken communication said all that needed to be said, and I felt my tears come quickly at the love shining out of Griff's face.

"I could kill you right now," he said quietly with a sweet smile that contradicted his words.

"Griff," I whispered, my voice cracking on the name.

And then he was there, holding me tightly and whispering words into my ear about how it was all going to turn out fine.

I cried into his shoulder for who knows how long before I heard another car pull up.

West.

The one man I never wanted to fucking see again. The fucking jackass who couldn't be bothered to tell me what the hell was really going on with Pippa's custody situation and parentage. The guy who had the audacity to sleep with me after sleeping with my...

I couldn't even finish the thought. If I did, I would surely lose my lunch all over the porch. So instead, I'd lashed out at him. I'd gone flying at him with all the sadness, betrayal, and anger I felt.

It wasn't until later when Griff and I were sitting at the kitchen table and Rebecca was playing on the floor in front of the sofa with the baby that I finally realized why I was being so unreasonable.

I really liked the motherfucker.

Griff was trying to ask me a question.

"Why didn't you give him a chance to explain? Don't you realize Adriana could have put him down as the father without telling him? And that it's entirely possible that this man is not actually Pippa's biological father?"

I knew he was right, but I didn't want to admit it.

He continued. "Why are you so quick to assume he is? It's almost like you *want* to believe he's the father."

"Who else would it be?" I snapped. I heard Rebecca chuckle from her spot on the ground.

Griff's eyes sparkled at me. "A one-night stand. An old boyfriend. A coworker. Any other man in the entire fucking world or even a sperm bank."

His lip turned up in a knowing grin.

"What?" I said. "Why are you looking at me like that?"

"You like this guy, and you're trying to sabotage it. What you're seeing on my face is the sweet, sweet smugness I usually only feel when Sam is wrong and I am right. Which, let's be honest, doesn't happen very often."

"True story," Rebecca murmured.

Griff's eyes cut to his mom. "Really, Mom? Loyalty—ever heard of it?"

"Just speaking the truth, kiddo."

"I'm not trying to sabotage it," I insisted.

"Ah, so you don't deny you like the guy," he said with a cheeky grin.

I huffed in annoyance. "Fine. I like the guy. But does it really matter? I'm flying home in a few days anyway."

Griff's face turned from teasing to serious. "You haven't liked someone like this since that jackass when we were kids."

We didn't say the guy's name. I knew exactly who he meant. The guy I'd thought I'd loved who'd crushed my spirit and taught me never to give a fuck like that about someone else again.

"Don't compare West to that asshole," I muttered.

Griff's hand came down warm and assuring on my arm where it

rested on the table. "Nico, don't you think it's time to consider trying again? You like this guy. It seems pretty clear he likes you too, although... a preppy cowboy? Really? Ugh." He pretended to shudder in disgust, so I smacked him on the shoulder.

"Cut it out. He's nice. And smart. And thoughtful."

Griff's eyes sparkled again in a knowing way. "Not to mention hot as sin."

"Amen," Rebecca singsonged to the baby on the floor.

"You're not allowed to call him hot, Griffin Marian. You're a married man," I chastised. "Plus he's not... for you."

"Oh-ho-ho, listen to you. Claiming the fair-haired doctor, are you? Tell me more."

I sighed. "He's... hot. Right? Like... so very hot. Texas summer hot. Fire flashover hot. Hot Tamales at the movies with no drink, hot." I rested my chin in my hands as I thought about his naked body spread out on the bed and my hands free to roam all over that fair skin.

I might have whimpered a little bit. Just a *tiny* bit.

Griff barked out a laugh. "Oh my god. Mom, we need to call this guy and get him back over here ASAP. I want to see how Nico acts around him if this is how he acts when the guy's not even here. I bet he babbles."

"I don't babble."

Rebecca chimed in helpfully. "I bet he blushes."

"I don't— Okay... I may blush a little. But it's because he's so..."

"Hot. We know." Griff's laughter was like a familiar drug, washing over me and making me feel better instantly.

"And good at what he does and dedicated to his family. And sweet as hell. Also generous... But you can't call him. He's working," I warned.

"When are you going to give him a chance to explain?" Griff asked.

"When he's not working. But for now, let me show you guys around Hobie. We can stop off at the bakery, and I can show you what I've been working on."

I felt my mood instantly lift at the prospect of showing off the cake painting to Griff and his mom. We quickly packed up the baby and loaded up in my rental car for the drive into the town square. After parking on a side street by the bakery, we popped the car seat into the stroller-frame thing Goldie had showed me how to use and made our way to Sugar Britches.

Stevie was working at the counter, and I had a brief pinch of guilt at ditching him the previous Friday night at the bonfire. I gave him an apologetic smile, which he answered with a wink.

"Well hello everyone," he said with a friendly smile. "Who do you have with you today, Nico?"

Shooting him a smile of thanks for at least temporarily letting me off the hook, I introduced him to my friend and his mom. He helped them choose a sweet treat and got them each a specialty coffee while I wandered to the freezer in the back to pull out some of the cupcakes I'd painted the previous weekend.

Rox was in the back, putting a crumb coat on a few tiers of what looked like a wedding cake. I wondered what order it was for that early in the week.

"Hey," I said to her when she looked up.

"Oh shit, Nico. I just heard the news. I'm so sorry. I had no idea."

"What news?" I asked.

"About West being Pippa's father. Did you know?" Her face was a mix of surprise and sympathy. It grated on me.

Just as I opened my mouth to dispute her assertion, I remembered I didn't know the actual story yet. I hadn't talked to West about it. And legally, he *was* Pippa's father, regardless of whether or not he shared her DNA.

"I… I don't really want to talk about it right now if you don't mind. I brought some friends in to see the bakery, and I don't want to leave them very long."

"Sure, Nico. I didn't mean to pry."

"No, it's not that. I just… can't talk about it right now."

Rox gave me an understanding look. "No problem."

I walked back out front and showed Griff and Rebecca the cupcakes with little foxes on them.

"I painted these for you," I told Griff. His last name had been Fox before he'd been adopted by the Marians, and his husband still called him Fox from time to time.

Griff's eyes lit up, and he made eye contact for a brief moment with his mom before turning to me. "Nico, these are amazing. How did you do this? They have paint that goes on frosting?"

I told him about what I'd learned from Rox and about some of the Internet research I'd done.

"It's really fun. Like tattooing but with brush strokes. You'd love it. You can come try it with me one day while you're here if you want. I have to come in tomorrow to do a big cake for a party, actually."

"I can watch the baby," Rebecca offered with a wink. As if it was a hardship.

I nodded at her. "Sounds like a plan. Thanks."

After we left the shop and wandered through the picturesque town center, I noticed curious looks from several people and wondered just how mouthy that damned postal worker had been.

It wasn't until we were coming out of the bookstore that I got my first clue.

Officer Curt Billingham stood by a vehicle with Oklahoma plates, writing what I assumed was a parking ticket for a tourist. As soon as he saw me, his mouth widened in a feral grin.

"Well, well, well. If it isn't my favorite stepbrother," Curt drawled.

I squeezed my eyes closed for a second to remind myself not to lose my cool in front of the entire town again. It was a gorgeous October day, and plenty of people were out milling around the square within earshot of us.

I tried ignoring him. After turning Griff, Rebecca, and the stroller in the opposite direction, I heard him call out again. Griff gave me a questioning look, but I ignored it.

"Nicolas Salerno," Curt called out. "Someone told me you've been holding that baby illegally. Apparently, Dr. Wilde is the custodial parent, not you. Is that correct?"

I felt all the blood drain from my face, and my knees felt like they were going to buckle at the realization Curt Billingham could turn a misunderstanding into an actual legal situation.

"You can talk to Honovi Baptiste about it, Curt. Or Dr. Wilde himself," I called back to him, trying desperately not to let my fear show. What if he challenged me right there for the baby? Did he have a right to do that?

"Just hang on a minute, Nico," he said. His voice dripped with condescension and smugness.

I closed my eyes again before turning around. "What?"

"I think we need to call West down here for a little chat, don't you?" Curt asked. "I wouldn't want you to be accused of *kidnapping*."

Was he for real? How could there be someone so ugly and mean who used a newborn baby for his cruel games?

Luckily, I heard the shuffle of footsteps behind me and the warm familiar voice of Doc Wilde.

"Well, hey there, Curtis," Doc said in a friendly greeting. "Nico, sorry it took me so long to check out. Mary was holding some books in the back for me. Think West will be upset if we're a few minutes late?"

I had no idea what he was talking about, but I hoped like hell Curt couldn't tell.

"If he is, I'm blaming it on you," I joked back lamely.

"Sorry to race off, Curtis, but West only has a quick break before he has to get back to his patients. We're watching the baby for him today while he's at work. Gotta run."

Before Curt could argue, Doc grabbed my elbow and walked with me down the street and around a corner. I noticed West's Victorian home and office up ahead and pulled to a stop.

"We're not actually going to the practice, are we?" I asked.

"God, no. I wouldn't want to be anywhere near West right now after the shit storm he's probably having to deal with at work. Every patient has likely heard the news by now, and they're probably all trying to get the scoop out of him. I just overheard that bullshit Billingham was spewing and wanted to save you. What's that man's problem anyway?"

Griff and Rebecca walked around from where they'd been trailing behind us. "Good question. Nico, who was that, and why did he call himself your stepbrother?"

I explained everything on our way back to the house. It wasn't until several hours later that I realized Pippa's runny nose had turned into something serious.

Serious enough to need a doctor.

CHAPTER 28

WEST

After having a beer with Hudson, I wandered over to lie on the couch, exhausted from the shift at the hospital followed by the crazy day at the office and the news about the birth certificate. Hudson let me doze off for an hour on the sofa before waking me and insisting on going to Grandpa and Doc's again for dinner.

"Fine." I huffed, sitting up and running my hands through my hair. "But I hope you brought your tennis shoes because I need to work out some of this stress on the court."

Hudson's eyes lit up with the mention of playing some tennis at the ranch. Out of the ten of us kids, Hudson was the one who was head over heels in love with the game. He'd take any opportunity to play.

"Let's go, brother. Gonna kick your ass out there." He snickered.

I stood up and stretched. "Fine. Let me grab my stuff."

I followed him to the ranch and noticed several familiar vehicles in the drive. I clenched my teeth and closed my eyes. I should have fucking known. After the day I'd had and that goddamned rumor about Pippa going around, I should have known my family would show up in droves.

I got out of the car, grabbing my backpack and storming toward the house. For once, I ignored the trio of yipping dogs and made a beeline for the big kitchen and family room area in the back of the old farmhouse.

Sure enough, there were about a million Wildes spread out over the large open space. Had it been any other family, I'd have thought it was an intervention. But it was the Wildes. So it was more of a love posse.

"What the hell are all of you doing here?" I asked.

Two of my sisters tutted and came at me with hugs, laying on the sympathy and mothering thick enough to make up for my own mother being overseas.

I caught Grandpa's eyes across the kitchen island, and he gave me a grimace of understanding.

"Why didn't you tell us?" my aunt Gina exclaimed, throwing her hands up in typical dramatic fashion. Her son, my cousin Max, shot me an apologetic look from where he stood behind her, mouthing the words *I'm sorry* over his mom's head.

Gina's wife, my aunt Carmen, also rolled her eyes at me apologetically. We all knew Gina was the crazy one of the group. And, honestly, it was usually a good bet the one with the Wilde blood was the crazy one in the crew.

"Why didn't I tell you what?" I mumbled into my sister MJ's full bosom where my face was mashed uncomfortably against the sunglasses hanging from the collar of her shirt. "Let me go."

"Forget it. We're here to love you through this. You know the drill."

"What if I hate the drill?" I countered grumpily.

"Too bad," Sassy said, spinning triumphantly with something in her hands held above her head. It was red and green, with fluffy pompoms flying off it at the end of long strands of yarn.

"What is that?" I asked right as the answer to my question hit me. "Oh god," I groaned. "No. *No.*"

My aunt Brenda sulked from the far end of the huge table between the kitchen and family room. "He won the damned thing fair and square. Just fucking give it to him already. Kathryn-Anne Wilde, I blame you for this," she said, glaring at my cousin Katie. "I'm not getting any younger, and you and that good-for-nothing husband of yours need to get on the baby wagon before I die. I told you one of Bill and Shelby's kids was gonna get it first. Bunch of high achievers."

"No," I said again. "Put that thing away."

Sassy continued waving it like a flag of victory. "Nuh-uh. Grandpa spent five whole years knitting this gem for his first great-grandchild, and you're the one who earned it fair and square. Take that, Aunt Brenda. Look at it. Watch me give it to my brother West."

She was such a fucking brat.

Brenda shot Sassy a look. "Don't make me call you by your real name," she warned.

Sassy gulped down her smirk and dropped the knitted monstrosity like a hot potato.

"Aww, now look what you've done," Doc said, leaning over to pick it up. He cradled the lump of knotted yarn in his arms and petted it like it was a baby. "His beautiful Christmas stocking and no one wants to claim it. It's okay, green-and-red beast. Someone will want you one day. I promise."

Grandpa walked up and yanked the lump out of Doc's arms. "Asshole," he muttered, turning around and placing it reverently back between tissue paper layers in its box.

"Guys," I said to the room in general. "It's not what you think. Pippa's not my baby."

MJ's eyes bore into mine like lasers. The lawyer in her was blazing hot for everyone to see. "Is your name on her birth certificate?"

I blinked.

"Well, yes, but—"

"Then she's yours," MJ said triumphantly before reaching across a massive puce purse to slide Grandpa's box over to me before grabbing some carrot sticks out of a bowl on the counter. Only my sister Winnie carried a purse that ugly.

"The twins drove in as well?" I shook my head. "How many of you drove in from the city for god's sake? Don't you have jobs?"

I noticed Cal and King playing chess in the corner of the room, noticeably staying quiet. But there nonetheless. It was the first time I'd been thankful Saint and Otto were deployed overseas. As it was, the room was full to the brim with my family.

When there was trouble, Wildes showed up.

I took a moment to be grateful I had so many people who loved me. My thoughts turned to Nico, and I wondered how he was faring with all this insanity.

Hallie came plowing into the room. She paused dramatically on the threshold and clasped her hands together in front of her chest. "Oh Weston," she cried. "Of course we're all here. It's not every day your brother becomes a father."

I'd had enough of the drama. "I'm not her father goddammit!"

The chatter in the room stopped, and everyone looked past me in the direction of the front door. I turned to see what they were staring at and saw Nico cradling a bundle of pink blankets in his arms. He looked stunned, and I realized he'd heard my words. I quickly tried to explain myself.

"Nico, I—"

"She's sick," he croaked. "Something's wrong with her, West. I think she's having trouble breathing."

It was then that I realized he also looked terrified. I hurried over to him and took the baby out of his arms. "Doc," I called out.

"Take her in the family room. I'll grab my bag," he said without needing any other information before springing into action.

My family all scuttled away from the area, and Aunt Carmen began whispering for everyone to leave the room and give us some space.

I got her to the sofa and noticed someone had thrown a blanket down to protect the surface of the cushion. I quickly laid Pippa on the blanket and began to peel her own blankets away to see what was going on. Her lips were blue, and my heart sped up as my mind spun through possible causes.

Doc slid to a stop next to me on the coffee table, yanking his bag open and barking orders at me so we could work as a team to assess her as quickly as possible.

"There's a neb under the sink in the master. Go get it," he said.

I jumped up and raced to my grandparents' room, ignoring Nico's shouted questions. I found the nebulizer under the sink and saw a bag next to it with various mouthpieces. I grabbed it in hopes there was a infant-sized one.

I ran back to the room, unfurling the cord and asking Grandpa for an extension cord. In the meantime, I plugged it into the nearest outlet and rifled through Doc's bag, looking for the medicine we'd need to go in it. I found a tiny mask and got to work. Once it was all set up, I met Doc's eyes.

"RSV?" I asked, knowing the diagnosis could be dangerous but also knowing it would be better than something stuck in her throat or needing surgery.

"That's my guess. I swabbed her to double-check. Hand me the mask, and I'll give her the breathing treatment."

I helped get Doc settled onto the sofa with a bundled-up Pippa in his arms. After placing the tiny dinosaur-style pediatric mask on her face, I stepped back and took a breath. Nico was standing off to the side with his hands in front of his mouth and his eyes still wide with terror.

My heart lurched, and I grabbed for him. "Come here," I murmured, pulling him into my chest. "She's going to be okay, Nico. You did the right thing bringing her."

His arms came around me, and he held on to me for dear life. I tried to reassure him it was all going to be fine, but he was trembling all over.

"Shh," I whispered into his ear. "Baby, she's okay. I promise."

"West, fuck. I don't know how to do this. I can't do this. Thank god, you're listed as her father. It'll be better that way."

"That's not true," I said with as much conviction as I could. "That's not true, and we both know it. You love that little girl. She's your family."

I felt him sigh against me. "No. I should go."

My jaw tightened, and I wanted to shake the man. "You're not going anywhere."

CHAPTER 29

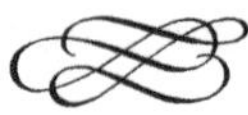

NICO

I felt like I was going to come out of my skin. When I'd noticed Pippa was having trouble breathing, I'd raced to the car and headed to Doc's house immediately. I didn't want to show up at West's house and have to admit I'd let Pippa get that sick before asking for help.

I'd panicked so badly I was halfway down the driveway before I realized I'd left Griff and Rebecca standing on the porch. I called Griff's cell and apologized, explaining I needed to get the baby help as soon as I could and would call him when I knew something.

When I'd walked in to Doc and Mr. Wilde's house and seen West standing in the middle of a roomful of people, I'd felt light-headed. He was going to know. They were all going to know how shitty I was at taking care of one particularly easy baby.

I felt like such a fool. I'd fucked up, and now Pippa was going to have to pay the price for my mistake.

And just like I knew they would, West and Doc had taken charge like the professionals they were and done what it took to treat Pippa while I'd just stood there as useless as a hood ornament.

I'd finally agreed to stay for a while and fetched the infant car seat from my car so Doc could put her to sleep sitting upright. Apparently, it helped with nasal drainage or something. What the hell did I know?

After the breathing treatment and a cuddle, Doc settled her into the car seat and took her back to his bedroom to watch over her. He seemed content to sit with her for a while despite the fact a million of his family members were present for a party. Maybe it was because so many people were there that he was happy to get some quiet time in his room.

West led me out of Doc and Grandpa's room, closing the door behind us. His warm hand was still settled on my lower back, and he used it to pull me around to face him. We stood at the end of a long hallway with no one around.

"Do you trust Doc to take good care of her for a little while so you can catch your breath?" West asked in a soft voice. It wasn't accusatory, more like sincerely concerned.

"Of course I do. Obviously, he can do a hell of a better job at it than I can," I admitted drily. "I'm not cut out for this, West."

"Stop that. You're full of shit. Do you have any idea how many new parents wouldn't have been nearly as on top of this as you were? She was perfectly healthy when I last saw her forty-eight hours ago, and Doc said he saw her just this afternoon in town. That means the virus came on quickly, Nico. Stop berating yourself. You did fine. You noticed she was sick, and you brought her to a doctor. Now cut that crap out and let's go get a drink. I think we could both use one."

"I think you might be right," I told him as a laugh of relief bubbled up.

We began walking back toward the main part of the house when West spoke again. "Nico, about the birth certificate…"

"I believe you," I said before he could say anything else. "If you say you aren't her father, I believe you. I'm sorry I doubted you. I was really upset."

West stopped and held me still by my shoulders. "I'm not her father, Nico. I promise I'm not. I never slept with your sister. I need you to know that. And I had no idea she listed me as the father on the birth certificate."

"Do you know why she would have done it?" I asked.

"I don't know. Maybe for emergencies? Maybe Honovi has a better idea. We can ask him tomorrow. Right now I want to introduce you to some of these crazies and watch you get more and more uncomfortable as the night wears on."

His words were said with deadpan humor, but he wasn't far off from the truth.

"Is this some kind of weirdo 'meet the family' ritual? Don't you think it's a little soon for all that?" I teased.

"Better now than waiting until after you've popped the question," West said with a shrug. I barked out a laugh and smacked him on the ass as he turned back toward the direction of the increasing noise from all the people who'd piled back into the kitchen and family room. I had to admit it felt good to cede control of Pippa over to an expert for a little while.

Once we entered the kitchen, I noticed Griff had arrived somehow and was talking to an older woman I didn't recognize. He was holding a glass of wine and laughing. I quirked a brow at West.

"Oh, I asked Hudson to run over and pick up Griff. I figured you wouldn't want to leave them alone, and this way I could justify keeping you here longer." He winked at me before reaching for one of the bottles of alcohol scattered across the huge kitchen island.

I greeted Griff and updated him on Pippa's situation, learning that Rebecca had chosen to stay in and rest rather than coming over to "party with all the kids."

After West brought me a stiff drink of some kind, he started introducing me around to everyone until my head spun. Someone had turned on music, and Mr. Wilde was dishing out bowls of chili. For some reason there were groans of complaints about the food choice.

"What's wrong with chili?" I asked one of the sisters quietly. I was pretty sure her name was a combination of initials, but I'd be damned if I remembered which ones.

"He's been testing chili recipes for days. He's trying to beat one of his neighbors in the upcoming cook-off, but it's never going to happen. Meanwhile, that's all poor Doc, Felix, and Hudson have eaten for days," she explained.

"Which one is Felix again?" I asked.

She gestured to a quiet guy sitting off to the side, reading what looked to be some kind of textbook. He was slender with delicate features and dark-framed glasses. Cute, in a massively geeky way. "He's the one who was raised by Doc and Grandpa. His mom, our aunt Jackie, is a famous actress. Felix hates all the attention from the paparazzi, so he begged to stay here and grow up in Hobie. He's very shy. Despises attention of any kind. Lord only knows how a woman like Jackie Wilde wound up with a kid like Felix."

"*Jacqueline Wilde* is your aunt? Holy shit. She's one of Doc and Mr. Wilde's kids? Does she come to town? Do they ever see her?"

"They refuse to now. She got to a point when she only referred to her family to score points with the media or her fans. They hated it, especially for Felix's sake. Family is everything to them, as you can see," she said with a smile, looking around the room. Suddenly I remembered the initials. Her name was MJ. "By the way, you know you can call him Grandpa, right? Everyone does. Even Doc most of the time."

"What's his actual name?" I asked out of curiosity.

"Weston," she said with a wink.

I smiled and looked around for the junior version, catching his eye from where he stood offering Griff a wine refill. West cocked his head in question, and I shook mine. My heart was doing stupid flips just at the sight of him. If I didn't leave town soon, I was going to fall even further for the guy than I already had.

"You like him, don't you?" MJ asked, leaning in so no one would hear her.

"Yep," I said on a sigh.

She chuckled. "I take it that's a bad thing?"

"Yep."

She stood straight and wrapped her arms around my neck, squeezing me into an impromptu hug.

"Cheer up, buttercup. It could be worse."

"How's that?" I asked.

"At least you're not the only kitten who's smitten."

I looked again for the man we were discussing and caught him still gazing at me. MJ removed herself from my person and wandered off chuckling while I stood there staring at the one man in the room who could ask me to strip naked right there in front of everyone and sing a Dolly Parton song, and I'd do it without a second thought.

I was so very fucked.

Perhaps I needed another drink. Or twelve.

CHAPTER 30

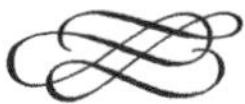

WEST

By the time the party died down, it was after midnight and most of us had had way too much to drink. My aunts had all disappeared to their rooms ages ago, and many of my siblings and cousins had stumbled across the backyard to the bunkhouse.

When Grandpa's ranch had been in full production, the bunkhouse had been just that—a dusty old bunkhouse for ranch hands. But when he'd retired and sold off the last of his stock, he and Doc had renovated the bunkhouse into guest rooms and minisuites to accommodate all the friends and family who visited regularly. With a handful of adult children and gobs of grown grandkids now, there were times the ranch hosted over forty of us at a time.

We loved it out there. As teenagers, we'd convinced Doc and Grandpa to let us get a pool table and Ping-Pong table, and we kept the common room fridge stocked with sodas and beer. Our friends always begged us to have them over to the bunkhouse for sleepovers. Little did they know Grandpa and Doc had the surveillance equivalent of a baby monitor in the common area of the bunkhouse so they could spy on us.

At one point late in the evening, Doc had pulled me aside to make me promise I wouldn't let anyone, including myself, drive home. He'd offered to keep the baby in his room and do the necessary night feedings so Nico and I could get some rest. I think he knew how much Nico needed the break from baby duty, and Doc definitely knew I had to get up and be at work by nine the next morning.

I led Griff and Nico out to the bunkhouse, laughing at the wild drunken shouts of my sisters, Winnie and Hallie. The twins were complete opposites in every way, but when they got drunk together, they turned into the bosom buddies they'd been when we were little.

"I love you, Winnipeg!" Hallie shouted into the night.

"I love you too, Halifax!" Winnie giggled, bumping Hallie's shoulder and almost sending them both into the scraggly half-dead rosebushes next to the bunkhouse door.

Nico giggled right along with them. I'd noticed at least an hour ago that he was comfortably shit-faced. I wasn't quite there, but I was heavily buzzed and couldn't stop imagining Nico naked. Just the thought of it made me suck in a breath.

"What?" he asked.

"What, what?"

"You gasped."

"So?"

Nico giggled again. "So I want to know why."

I couldn't tell him the real reason. "I can't stop imagining you naked."

Well, fuck.

More giggling. My eyes stayed riveted to the shining rings in his lower lip as we entered the bunkhouse to the big, vaulted common area.

"Kiss me," I suggested.

Nico's eyes widened, and he went from giggly to angry in a flash. He looked over at Griff, who was looking around the room in open-eyed wonder. "Don't you fucking dare," Nico told Griff.

"What?" Griff and I asked at the same time.

"Don't do it, Griffin," Nico repeated. His forehead was furrowed angrily. I had no idea what he was upset about, but it didn't really matter. It was impossible to take him seriously when he was that stinking cute.

"Do what?" Griff asked in confusion.

"Kiss him!" he shouted.

All the Wildes who'd been lounging around the common area stopped talking and turned to see what the hell was going on. Nico's words must have sunk in because within moments, a chant began somewhere, and then all those fuckers were chanting in sync. "Kiss him, kiss him, kiss him!"

Nico's eyes widened even more as he realized what he'd started. "No!" He turned to me in horror. "You can't kiss him."

He looked panicked, and I suddenly put two and two together. Nico thought I'd been referring to kissing Griff. He really was drunk.

I stepped forward and took Nico's face in my hands, leaning close until our foreheads were pressed together.

"Nicolas Salerno, there is no one within a thousand-mile radius I want to kiss besides you," I said in a low voice.

Nico whimpered and leaned into me, hooking his fingers through the belt loops on my jeans.

The chants started up again, this time louder. I was pretty sure no one in my family had ever seen me kiss another person before, but I was too far gone to care. I leaned in and kissed him like his mouth had been made for mine.

And in that moment I was pretty sure it was.

Not long after we settled into the bed in one of the rooms, Nico climbed on top of me and began seducing me with lazy kisses all over my body. The slow, tender way we touched and teased was something new and raw between us. Maybe it was the alcohol, or maybe it was the relief of knowing Pippa was okay and we could be together without worrying about her for one night. Regardless of the reason, it was a kind of lovemaking I'd never known before.

Our eyes stayed riveted on each other as we moved together, and even when we came, our eyes never strayed. Something changed between us that night, and I knew we were no longer just hooking up. Even if Nico thought what we were doing was just sex, I knew the truth.

I was falling in love with him. As his departure hurdled toward us at breakneck speed, it was only a matter of time before my heart was crushed in the wreckage.

~

I WOKE up hard as a rock in an unfamiliar room tangled with a wonderfully familiar body. Nico's legs were pretzeled with mine, and our fingers were intertwined where I held his hand on my chest. My heart immediately started its stupid flippy-floppy Nico routine, and I almost groaned at the cliché of it all.

I pulled his hand up to press it to my lips. The warmth of his skin and the smell of him hardened my cock even further. Nico shifted and leaned into me, sliding his head from the pillow onto my shoulder. The move must have woken him up because he made a small noise of complaint and winced.

"Good morning," I said, turning to run the fingers of my free hand through his purple mane.

"No."

"Yes. Any morning I wake up next to a hot, naked man is definitely a good morning," I countered.

"I'm not naked," he mumbled without moving.

"Not yet, but we can change that right this second," I said, shifting my fingers to the waistband of his underwear.

He shoved his morning wood against my thigh. "If I thought I could move without my brain or stomach exploding, I'd totally strip down and beg you for it."

"What if you just stay still and let me suck you off?"

Please, oh, please let him agree to my suggestion.

"Has anyone ever said no to that in the history of ever?" Nico asked. "Let's be real."

I carefully slid out from under him and settled his head on the pillow, pulling his hips around so he was lying flat on his back. A slice of morning sun cut through the gap between the curtains and fell across the side of his face and chest.

"Be still," I murmured as I dropped a kiss on the unmarked skin over his heart. His hands came up and held my head lightly, following my movement as I sucked on his nipples and bit marks down his abdomen to his hips.

Just before I got to the good stuff, Nico bolted upright, accidentally jamming his knee in my stomach.

"Oh fuck," I grunted, doubling over.

"The baby," he said in a rush. "We have to go check on her."

I took a few beats to mentally confirm I hadn't taken a hit to the balls. Nico must have seen my hesitation because he turned to me with an apologetic look on his face.

"I'm sorry, West. Are you okay?" He reached out and slid a hand alongside my neck, leaning in to kiss my cheek. "I'm sorry," he repeated softly into my ear.

"It's okay."

He looked around, perhaps realizing finally that we were in a strange place.

"Where are we?"

I laughed. "The bunkhouse at my grandparents' ranch. We were all too drunk to drive last night, so we stayed over."

"Griff! Oh god. Is Griff here?"

A stupid curl of jealousy tried to rear its ugly head, but I pushed it down. I knew from talking to him that Griff was loony for his husband back in California.

"I put him in the room next to ours. Don't worry. He made friends with everyone here last night, so I'm sure he's able to fend for himself."

We took turns in the tiny bathroom before getting the rest of our clothes back on and wandering out to the common area. Nico knocked on the door I indicated for Griff, but the room was empty.

We made our way over to the main house and saw most of my extended family in various stages of dress and pajamas, crazy hair sticking up, half-drunk coffee mugs on every surface, and the smell of bacon and blueberry pancakes in the air. God, I loved being at my grandparents' house with everyone on lazy mornings like this.

"Don't any of you slackers have jobs?" I called out as we walked in. It was only seven in the morning, and the fact that almost everyone was up already proved at least several of them had plans to head back to the city soon.

Griff was face down in a mug of coffee at the huge kitchen table while my aunt Gina babbled on about Napa wineries next to him. He grunted a greeting as we passed him to get to the coffee.

My cousin Felix was in an overstuffed chair in the family room, giving Pippa a bottle and making silly faces at her. The baby seemed alert and happy, smiling and squinting her eyes at Felix's antics. I squeezed Nico's hip and gestured toward Pippa so he would be reassured she was okay.

I could sense him relax the minute he laid eyes on her. He wandered over and greeted my shy cousin with a smile, causing Felix to blush and tuck his chin. Doc caught me watching them and shot a wink at me.

"She's doing much better this morning," he said. "Just gave her a second breathing treatment a few hours ago, and that might be all she needs. Fluids and rest ought to do it."

"Thanks, Doc. I really appreciate it," I said, stepping over to him and giving him a big hug. His familiar smell of Old Spice and coffee washed over me like a memory.

"You gonna explain why you're on the birth certificate?" he asked in a low voice.

"I don't know why. Honestly, I think it's just in case of emergencies or something. Health benefits maybe. I really don't know."

Doc pulled back and looked at me with his kind, blue eyes. "You going to keep her?"

The question caught me off guard. "What? No. Of course I'm not going to keep her. What the hell, Doc?"

He tilted his head and studied me. "Why so quick to answer? It's not out of the question for you to raise this child, Weston. You were there for Adriana every step of the way. You were her birth coach and her best friend. Everyone knows you'd make a wonderful parent."

I was taken aback by his assertion that I should even consider the possibility.

"Not a more wonderful parent than the Warners. Plus this is Nico's decision to make."

Nico stepped up next to me. "What's my decision to make?"

Doc and I locked eyes before I stammered, "Oh, ah, whether or not you're… ah…"

"Keeping the bakery open," Doc cut in smoothly. "Do you know yet what you're doing with Sugar Britches?"

"Well, I can't do much with it until I get the bookkeeping straightened up. I've asked Rox to stay on indefinitely and help run it for a while. Once I can get it organized, I'll reassess. Maybe find someone who wants to buy it. Right now I can't even sell it with the state it's in."

After getting some coffee down, I made a couple of plates of food and brought one to where Nico had settled next to Griff. They were occupied swapping early-morning grumbles about how so many people could be that cheerful at such an ungodly hour.

"It's unnatural," Griff complained, sipping more coffee and stealing bacon off Nico's plate. I went ahead and slid my untouched plate to Griff before getting up to fix another. He nodded in gratitude before seeming to remember he was dealing with a time difference. "Why the hell am I even awake right now?"

"Cause you have a stupid fucking baby," Nico mumbled. "They fuck up everything related to sleep. Stupid babies."

I hid my smile behind my coffee mug as I watched the two friends bitch some more from where I stood at the kitchen island. Griff's hair was a curly riot sticking up everywhere with no hope of submitting to gravity anytime soon. Likewise, Nico's Technicolor mane was somehow bobbing and weaving in giant swirls like a soft-serve ice cream cone. A pillowcase crease still marked his cheek, and there was a frowny furrow between his eyebrows that indicated he probably had a hangover headache.

MJ's teasing voice cut into my reverie. "You're staring like a lovesick puppy," she whispered on a low chuckle. "Gotta say, he's cute as hell."

"Right?" I asked with a sigh. "God. I can't handle it."

"So what are you going to do?"

"What do you mean? It's not like I have a choice, MJ. He's leaving."

"Ask him to stay."

I turned to look at her with two simultaneous but opposing reactions. On the one hand, god, how I wanted to ask him to stay. On the other, that was an absurd idea. He'd never go for it.

"You're insane," I told my sister. "He has a life, a business, friends back in San Francisco."

She reached out and grabbed my chin gently, turning my head to look at Nico before swiveling around to see all the other family members who'd gathered around him at the big table to chat with him and Griff.

My cousin Felix still held and entertained Pippa, my aunt Carmen leaned over Nico's shoulder to grab the bottle of pancake syrup, my sister Sassy pointed her finger in Nico's face to accuse him of stealing her spoon (to which he sheepishly admitted guilt), and Grandpa passed him a platter with more bacon on it.

"Looks to me like he has those things here too, West," she said gently. "Maybe he just doesn't realize it yet."

Regardless of how Nico felt about any of it, the scene filled my heart. I had half a mind to call in sick to work, but that wasn't fair to my patients and staff.

I reluctantly shoveled breakfast into my mouth before thanking Doc and Grandpa for the impromptu love-in. After running a hand over Pippa's fat cheeks, I stepped behind Nico's chair and leaned my face next to his.

"I gotta go to work," I said softly.

He turned with raised eyebrows. "Really? Already?"

"Yeah, sorry. Ah... I was wondering if maybe I could make you dinner tonight? I know Griff and Rebecca are here, but…" I let out a breath. "I'd like to talk to you about all this stuff. Pippa and everything."

"Yeah, I'd like that," Nico said with a shy smile. "See you later?"

"Count on it."

CHAPTER 31

NICO

After returning to the house and putting Pippa down for a good nap, Griff and I took turns showering and dressing for the day. Rebecca insisted on watching over Pippa while Griff and I went to the bakery.

Once we were settled in the back, painting some small cakes Rox and Stevie had prepped for us, Griff began catching me up on what was new back home. He told me about Sam teaching a wine-pairings class at his restaurant in Napa and about finally breaking ground on the house they were building on his brother's vineyard property.

I thought back to when he and Sam had moved from the city out to the vineyard to open the restaurant. It had almost been two years since then. Two years since I'd lived in the same town as my best friend.

The time had gone by fast because I'd been working my ass off at the shop. Sam had been busy with the restaurant, and Griff had been busy creating and publishing his graphic novels. They still came into town fairly often to see Griff's parents, Sam's sister, and their other friends and family. But it wasn't the same as it had been when Griff and I had lived in the same town, and since Benji had been born, they'd hardly come to the city at all.

"Do you like living at the vineyard?" I asked. "I mean, I know you do, but like... was it a hard transition when you left the noise and convenience of the city?"

Griff thought about it for a moment. "I thought it would be, but I think it was just good timing really. I'd done the single-in-the-city thing and was ready to settle down. I love walking out of our cabin and being able to see the stars, you know? And realizing that our whole lives don't have to revolve around our jobs. Now that we live at the vineyard, we spend more time outside, taking walks around the lake, hiking, even just eating out there by the lake for lunch breaks."

He spun the cake stand around until it was repositioned to his liking before dabbing paint on his brush.

"I don't know how to describe it, Nico. It's almost like... without all the distractions of the city, we're more relaxed and we can just focus on each other. Focus on Benji. I think if we were living in the city while trying to raise him, it would be a bit too chaotic for us. Plus I love the idea of raising our kids near my brother and his kids. Ella is only a year older than Benji, and if Jude and Derek ever follow through on their plans to build a house in Napa, we'll have their baby nearby too. Wolfe is just six months older than Ben. Wouldn't it be awesome raising kids around family like that?"

I wasn't sure Griff realized who he was talking to when he mentioned how awesome his big family was. I knew he didn't do it on purpose, but it still stung.

"It would be perfect, Griff. I'm really excited for you."

I remained pretty quiet the rest of the time we spent painting side by side in the bakery kitchen, and when we were done, we had each produced several painted minicakes to put out front for sale. Griff's had his version of cool superheroes on them that reminded me of some of the themes in his graphic novels. If any of our customers knew whose art they were getting on their cake, they'd flip out.

Mine were different. I'd painted recognizable scenes from around town on the cakes I'd done. One was the old cornerstone bridge over Hazlett's Creek. One featured the small peony garden in front of the gazebo in the town square. My favorite one was the green Victorian home on Dogwood Street where West lived. I'd blushed deep red when I'd realized what I was painting, but I'd gone ahead and finished it anyway, tucking it discreetly into a bakery box to sneak out of there without anyone else seeing.

Rox ushered us out after raving over our creations and calling some of our regulars over to take a look at the specialty cakes in the display case. She assured me they'd be sold before closing in a couple of hours, and I'd smiled at her enthusiasm.

"Nico, before you guys leave, do you mind watching the place while I run over to the bank?"

"No problem."

Griff decided to get a coffee and scone to take outside with him to the gazebo in the center of the square so he could call Sam and catch up. I busied myself cleaning and restocking the sugar and creamer station until the next customer came in. I recognized the woman as Mrs. Foley who had dropped off a casserole to me one of the first days after Adriana's funeral. She'd also been my fourth grade teacher and I remembered her doing fun science experiments. One had something to do with balloons and whipped cream, but I was hazy on the details.

"Hi Mrs. Foley," I said with a smile. "You in the mood for something foxy today?" I'd been thinking about the cupcakes with foxes painted on them and didn't realize how my question had sounded until Mrs. Foley stood there blinking for a minute. "Oh my… no. I meant… What I meant was, would you like to see some of the painted cupcakes we have special today?"

The older women cracked a huge smile and winked at me. "For a minute there, I thought you were offering something else, Nicolas. I remember when I had you in class and you shook your booty to the school fight song Principal Hatter played over the intercom one day."

I felt my cheeks heat at the reminder. "No, please," I said. "Erase that from your memory bank."

"Never in a million years. It was too good. I believe you chanted something along the lines of '*Go, fight, weiner*.' Am I correct?"

Her eyes sparkled with mischief, and I couldn't help but laugh. "We were the Flying Dachshunds, what did you expect?"

She giggled some more, tears appearing in the corner of her eyes. "Poor, unfortunate choice for a mascot. I think it was supposed to be Flying Dutchmen but someone messed up. The football players are still called the Hobie Hotdogs. They'll never live it down."

"It was worse for the cheerleaders. They were the Foxy Doxies."

"Still are, Nico. Still are." She gathered her hot drink and a cupcake and turned to go. Before opening the door, she turned back to me. "It's really good to see you doing so well, Nico. I was proud of Adriana, and you seem to be doing just as well. Your mom would have been proud of you. I hope you stick around."

With that, she was off. I was left with the warm feeling of acceptance I never remembered feeling in my first fifteen years there in Hobie, and I wondered if it was possible that people and places changed for the better.

By the time Rox returned, I'd had a few more friendly conversations with customers, several of whom expressed how sorry they were to lose my sister so young. They shared memories of her with me and I finally got a chance to begin thinking of her as the adult she'd been more recently, rather than the surly teen she'd been when I'd last seen her.

After we returned to the house, I noticed Doc's vehicle in the driveway next to Griff's rental. Sure enough, Doc and Grandpa were inside cooing over the baby and sharing a cup of tea with Rebecca. Her eyes seemed to be watery, as if she'd been crying about something, but I quickly realized what must have been the cause of it when I saw several boxes stacked by the front door.

"What… what's all this?" I asked.

"Oh, honey. We packed up some of Adriana's things for you. I hope that's okay," Rebecca said, getting up. I gestured for her to stay put and nodded at her.

"Okay…," I said, unsure.

Doc cut in. "Don't worry, Nico. It was just clothes and shoes and toiletries I thought you might want to donate. Nothing sentimental or important at all."

I let out a breath. "Thank you. Yeah, I guess that's good." I looked around the room to reassure myself that nothing had drastically changed. But I knew there was no point. Before I left for California, I had to go through it all in order to list the house for sale.

My gut twisted at the thought, and I felt my jaw clench. "No, that's good. Really. Thank you for getting started. I need to figure out what I'm doing with everything, and I guess I just didn't want to face it before now."

Griff reached out to squeeze my shoulder. "We can help. As much as you need."

I gave him a small smile of thanks and wandered to the kitchen to make myself a glass of ice water. I heard the rest of them chatting quietly and took a minute to ground myself with a mental reminder of what really mattered in my life.

Not stuff. People. The people I had back home. My life back home.

But who was that exactly?

Griff. But Griff had Sam and Benji and lived in Napa.

The Marians. But I wasn't really one of them.

Mike and the others who worked with me at the shop. But they were more employees than friends.

I felt the familiar coil of loneliness snake around me, which was ridiculous since I was standing in a room with four people who seemed to care about me a great deal. I looked over at Doc and Grandpa, Griff and Rebecca.

Hobie and home.

I wanted them all. I *needed* them all. Even if none of them truly needed *me*.

I wasn't so sure anymore about where home was.

It was Pippa's whimpers that woke me out of my funk. At least for a little while, someone needed me as much as I needed them.

My Pippa.

WHEN IT WAS time to head to West's place for dinner, I made sure Rebecca and Griff knew where to find the food Goldie had brought over two days before. She'd been dropping off meals for me every few days like clockwork, and I could tell that cooking was her love language. Before closing the fridge, I slid out the bakery box I'd brought home from the shop and carried it to the front door.

Rebecca called out from her spot on the floor next to Pippa on the play mat. "Nico, honey, why don't you stay over at West's tonight so you don't have to sleep on the sofa?"

I gawped at her. "Wh-what?"

She grinned and Griff rolled his eyes. "Nico, c'mon. Seriously? You're wearing cologne. You really gonna claim this is a dinner meeting and not a date? Or at the very least, a booty call."

Rebecca chuckled. "Don't listen to Griffin. Surely West has a nice *guest room* in his house where you can stay comfortably while we hold down the fort here. We'll see you in the morning." She winked at me before turning her attention back to Pippa.

I swallowed and turned to leave without saying another word. Before the door clicked behind me, I heard Griff tell his mom, "Those are his sex pants."

My face turned hot, and I looked down at what I was wearing.

Sure enough.

Sex pants.

CHAPTER 32

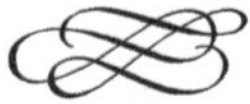

WEST

When I answered the doorbell, Nico was standing on the stoop looking very uncomfortable. He was balancing a white bakery box in one hand and a bottle of wine in another. A large document folder was wedged under one arm.

"Hey, let me help you with some of this," I said, reaching out for the box and the bottle of wine. "You didn't have to bring anything."

"I know."

He followed me upstairs to my place and set the folder on the kitchen table before shucking off his jacket. As he turned to hang it on a hook by the door, I saw his adorable round butt perfectly packaged in a tight pair of black leather pants. Dear god. I wanted to squeeze it. Or bite it. Probably squeeze it first, and *then* bite—

"What're you doing?" he asked with a flirty quirk of a brow.

"Huh?"

"You were checking out my ass."

"Well, to be fair, have you seen your ass in those pants?"

Nico turned around this way and that in an effort to catch sight of his butt. It didn't look like he was succeeding, but it sure was cute watching him try.

"C'mere," I said, reaching out for him. He grinned up at me and stepped in close so I could get my hands on him and pull him in tight. My gaze landed on the delicate hoops that always drove me crazy in his lips, and I felt my tongue come out to wet my own lip in response. "Thank you for coming over," I murmured before running the tip of my tongue along his lip.

His hands came around my waist and held on tight to the fabric of my shirt against my back. I didn't want him grabbing my shirt. I wanted him grabbing *me*. All I could think about was getting him naked beneath me again. I could hardly catch my breath from wanting him.

Our kisses turned feverish, and his leg pressed between mine until he used his hip to roll across my cock.

"Fuck," I gasped. "I hope you're not hungry."

"Not in the least bit," Nico said before nipping at my bottom lip with his teeth. "Unless, of course, you wanted me to answer with something cheesy like 'My ass is hungry for your cock,' because that is also accurate."

There was really no more need for words. I grabbed at his clothes and pulled them up, down, and off until I had a completely naked Nico Salerno panting in my kitchen. I was still fully dressed, and something about the contrast made me even hotter than I thought possible.

I spun him around until he faced my heavy wooden kitchen table, and I tilted him forward until his hands came out to support his weight on the hard surface. His bare ass jutted out, pushing into the front of my pants. I couldn't help but run my hands from his rounded shoulders down all that ink to his colorful ass cheeks.

"Bend all the way over and put your chest on the table, Nico."

My cock was leaking in my underwear, and if I didn't free it soon, it was going to choke itself to death against my fly.

Nico did as I said and laid himself face first on my kitchen table, ass presented to me like Christmas fucking morning and all mine for the taking.

I ran my hands over the rounded muscular cheeks and squeezed. A groan rumbled through me as I reached for my belt and began unbuckling.

While I worked open the front of my pants, I leaned over to run my tongue along his spine, moving wet kisses over the indentations above his ass down to the meaty flesh below. I bit gently into him with my teeth before soothing the spot with soft kisses.

Once my own cock was blessedly free, I dropped to my knees and used my hands to press him open.

"West," he breathed.

I sucked my own thumb into my mouth, coating it with spit before pressing it onto Nico's hole and rubbing firm circles into his crinkled skin.

"So sweet, Nico," I murmured. I leaned in and ran my tongue over it, taking my time now that I had him exactly where I wanted him. "So fucking good."

I teased him with my mouth and my fingers, alternating between his hole and the piercings leading to his balls. Every time I pressed my tongue against the rings, he hitched in a breath and moaned some more until his sounds became more irregular and desperate.

"Please, West," he begged.

I smiled to myself, enjoying the process of peeling away his prickly outer shell and revealing the sensual, vulnerable man inside. The one I secretly hoped he reserved just for me.

"You want to come for me, sweetheart?" I murmured against his skin while sliding a spit-slicked finger inside him again and reaching for his prostate. He cried out when I found it.

"Want you inside me first, West. Please," he croaked. "Want you with me."

My throat tightened at his words. I dropped another kiss on his sexy ass cheek before straightening back up again and lowering my pants and underwear. I reached into my pants pocket for my wallet and removed a condom and packet of lube.

Trying to get the damned things open was an exercise in futility. My hands were shaking, and all the blood was pounding in my head and cock.

Nico had begun subtly pushing his ass back into me in invitation. With every pulse toward me, his hole opened slightly, all shiny and flushed from my bites.

"Not helping," I groaned under my breath. He snickered and pressed back again. I smacked one of his ass cheeks. "Quit that."

I eventually got the condom on and the lube open, spreading it on myself before reaching for Nico's sexy-as-shit body. We both made noises of appreciation when my cock finally pressed into him.

"God, Nico." I sighed. It was tight as fuck and perfect. "Fuck. Oh god."

His hand flew back to grab for me, catching me on the hip and digging nails into my skin.

"West, wait, wait."

I froze, biting my lip and smoothing a palm up and down his spine while he adjusted. He blew out a breath and squeezed my hip more gently with his hand to let me know it was okay to move.

My hips began pressing in and pulling out as gently as I could until the clench of his hot channel was too much for me to hold back any longer. I leaned over his back and reached for both his hands, threading our fingers together and stretching them up high on the table above Nico's head.

My hips jacked into him over and over, the sounds of skin slapping and the table legs moving slightly across the floor echoed in the room. My lips came down on the tender spot behind his ear, and I pressed kisses there before murmuring in his ear how hot he was, how tight his ass felt on my cock, how absolutely stunning he looked spread out like a meal on my goddamned table.

The sex-crazed lunatic fucking Nico on my kitchen table was a stranger to me. It was a side of me that had lain dormant and unknown somewhere in the far reaches of myself, but now that Nico had awakened it, my hunger was insatiable.

I thrust into Nico's body over and over until we were both crying for release and clutching at each other's hands. It was feral and aggressive, sweaty and hot. Sex with Nico was unlike anything from even my wildest fantasies.

"Want you to come, Nico," I ground out between tight teeth.

"Fuck, fuck," he panted. He tried pulling his hands out of mine so he could grab for his own cock, but I didn't want to let him go.

I wanted him to come without touching himself.

After transferring both his wrists into one of my hands, I dropped the other hand to where my cock entered him. I slowed our rhythm down just long enough to press my thumb down on the tender skin above his hole as I slid in and out of him.

Nico made a choking sound, and then I felt it—the telltale squeeze of his body around mine that indicated his orgasm cresting.

"That's it, baby, that's it." I breathed. "Let go."

He gasped my name and threw his head back, shuddering through his release until he was spent and trembling. I wrapped my arms around him and took just a few more thrusts until my own release hit, rolling over me in delicious waves that almost forced a laugh out of me, I was so happy.

We lay there on the kitchen table—Nico buck naked and sprawled out like a sex buffet and me with all my clothes still on, lying across his back coated in sweat and panting like a dog in summer.

After a few minutes of calming down, I began to pull away from him, reaching for the condom to dispose of it before yanking my clothes back up. Nico remained fucked out on the table, and I was tempted to just stand there, taking in the view for as long as he was willing to remain like that.

Instead, I ran a hand down his damp back and leaned in to kiss the side of his face. "Come take a shower with me, okay?"

He peeled himself off the table, and I noticed the wet spots on the floor at his feet from where he'd come. Was it wrong of me to be proud of the evidence of his orgasm?

I reached for his hand and held it until we got into the bathroom. Before I had a chance to strip my clothes off, Nico reached out to do it for me, sneaking shy peeks here and there of my face as if we hadn't just been as intimate as two people could be.

I reached out a finger to lift his chin. "Thank you."

He blushed to the tips of his ears. "What for?"

"Well, first of all, the hottest sex I've ever had. Hands down," I said with a grin. "Secondly, for coming over tonight even though I know you wanted to spend time with Griff."

His tongue twisted in his mouth like he wanted to say something but was holding himself back. Finally he spoke. "I can see Griff back in California. I can't see you back in California." He crouched down to strip my pants off me before tossing them out into my bedroom and continuing. "I don't know… maybe it's selfish. But I…" More twisting of the tongue.

I brushed my hand across his cheek. "You?"

"I can't seem to stay away from you," he admitted, looking up at me with a familiar look of defiance on his face, almost like he was daring me to laugh at him.

"I sure as hell can't stay away from you, Nico. So the feeling is mutual."

His face softened. "Yeah? Well… good. I'm not the only one being stupid then." He laughed softly before rubbing his hands up and down my chest. "But… West, it's more than just sex for me. This… whatever this is here…"

He blew out a breath and looked everywhere but at my face.

I wrapped my arms around him and pulled him close before murmuring, "Is scary as shit and piss-poor timing?"

Nico just nodded silently against my chest.

"I know," I said softly. "I don't want you to go back to California. I feel hopelessly selfish."

I felt his lips turn up against my skin.

After dropping a kiss into his hair, I reached over to turn on the shower. "Fuck this. Let's shake it off and get cleaned up so we can get dirty again. What do you say?"

He nodded his agreement, and we enjoyed our shower together, soaping each other's bodies languidly while catching up on our day. I told him about the patient I'd had who got bitten by a snake in her garden, and he told me about painting cakes with Griff at the bakery.

Nico got squirrelly again a little while later, and I asked him what was going on in that colorful head of his. We were in my bedroom, and I was searching for comfortable lounge pants that might fit his smaller frame so he didn't have to spray-paint his leather pants back on.

"Would it be okay if I stayed over tonight? It's either that or sleep on the sofa at home... I mean, at Adriana's."

I couldn't hold back a laugh. "Are you kidding? Of course it's okay. You were staying here either way, but this way it's not considered felony kidnapping," I said with a wink, handing him my smallest pajama pants.

The minute the word "kidnapping" was out of my mouth, Nico's smile dropped. "Yeah, ah... we should also probably talk about Pippa."

My stomach dropped as I realized the connection he was making. Doc had told me about the run-in with Curt Billingham in town.

"I don't give a shit what the birth certificate says, Nico. You're her family. You're her uncle. I'm nothing to her," I assured him. "You know I would never let anyone accuse you of having her illegally. You *know* that. Tell me you do."

He looked up at me, insecurity plain as day in his eyes, and I wanted to scream at the injustice of it all. I'd never wanted to throttle Adriana before in my life the way I did in that moment for putting him in this situation. For fucking this up for him.

"I know you're not going to have me put in jail, West, but the fact remains that if you're listed as the father on the birth certificate, you actually have legal custody of her right now."

"That's just a paperwork issue. She's still yours," I insisted.

"No. She's not. Because this is a paperwork issue. I'm putting her up for adoption. But I can't, because she's not mine to put up. That means you'll be the one to sign the adoption paperwork."

"But I can rescind my paternal rights and—"

Nico interrupted. "Then she would become a ward of the state and the adoption process would have to begin again. Only this time she'd be in foster care. You can't transfer ownership of a baby to me like she's a vehicle I'm buying from you. I'd have to go through the entire process to qualify to adopt her. That would include home visits and background checks. Instead, you can just be the one to sign the paperwork for the Warners."

We'd slipped into more comfortable clothes and sat on the edge of my bed. I turned and took his hands in mine.

"Nico, I'll do what you want me to do. What do you want me to do?"

CHAPTER 33

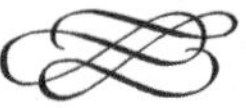

NICO

West was being so damned sweet. Didn't he know that wasn't going to help me be strong?

"I want this to be as easy on Pippa as possible," I said, feeling my throat tighten. "I think it's best if you handle it. You've been there for her all along, and you knew Adriana best."

He opened his mouth to argue with me, but I cut him off. "Don't. I've seen enough since coming back to know Adriana was different with you than how she was with me growing up. I don't know why she was the way she was when I was younger, but it seems like maybe she'd finally come into her own in the past couple of years. That's the Adriana you knew. I never knew her like that."

One of West's large, warm hands came up to cup my cheek. "I wish you had. Will you tell me why you never told her where you were all those years? Why you never contacted them?"

It felt strange to want to tell him the most shameful part of my past. For just a moment I wondered why I felt like confessing it to him. But then I laughed at myself. It was so obvious. As soon as I told him my secret shitty past, he'd know why I wasn't relationship material. It would make my leaving that much easier.

"I was a prostitute."

There was a beat of silence while I waited for the condemnation. Perfect Dr. Wilde from his perfect family wouldn't be able to wrap his head around—

"And?"

My head snapped up to stare at him. "And… I slept with men for cash and food. Sometimes just for shelter and protection."

I could see West's jaw ticking and knew he was having trouble holding in the judgment.

"Even more reason to call home and ask for help," he said slowly.

I laughed. "Yeah, right. 'Hi, Mom? It's me. Your fifteen-year-old son. I know you guys didn't want to have a gay kid or a petty criminal for a son, but let me tell you what I've been up to lately. A few blow jobs, some solicitation busts. Oh, but don't worry—there's one cop who lets me suck him off in exchange for not taking me in if I'm lucky enough to get busted by him instead of the *real* hard-asses.' West, if I thought I was an embarrassment to them before, can you even imagine how I felt once *I* learned what it was like for me on the streets?"

West's jaw was doing more than ticking at this point, but he was doing his best to keep a neutral look on his face. I wasn't fooled. He had to be disgusted. Who wouldn't be?

His silence continued, so I threw up my hands. "See? Exactly. They probably would have reacted the same way. Silence. Disgust."

I stood up, intent on finding my clothes and getting the hell out of there, but West's strong hands clamped around my waist and he spun me to face him.

"I'm not saying anything because if I open my mouth I want to scream, Nico," he admitted in a broken voice. "I can't bear the thought of you alone on the streets having to do that to survive. I can't bear it."

West pulled me in close until I stood between his feet, his face pressing into my chest. My arms wrapped around his head and neck, and I threaded my fingers in his hair. Within seconds, I felt hot wet tears soak through the worn T-shirt I had on and I realized he was crying for me. West was crying. For me. It didn't make any sense.

"Why are you crying?"

"You deserved better," he croaked. "Every kid deserves better."

I tried to push him away by his shoulders, but he held tight. "Don't feel sorry for me, dammit. That's not why I told you." My voice came out thick and mean through my teeth.

I continued to struggle against him, wanting to get away as quickly as I could so I would be able to breathe again.

"Don't," he growled. "Don't push me away for the millionth time, Nico. Just let me be here for you. I don't think that's too much to ask. And for fuck's sake—I'm not asking."

I was taken aback by his tone and managed to settle down out of sheer surprise.

"Jesus, finally," he muttered, nuzzling back into my chest. "You're like a fiery redhead but without the red."

I snorted. "Doctor Hilarious, I presume?"

"Shut it. We're having a moment here. Don't ruin it."

I ran my fingers through his thick blond waves and thought about how amazing it must be to have someone like West all the time. He was going to make some lucky bastard happy one day.

I took a moment to imagine what it would be like to be that person —to be the guy West chose to share his life with. I imagined long nights of feeling his hands on my skin, his lips on mine, his cock wedged so deep inside me that I felt full and complete. I imagined lazy Sunday afternoons watching football games on television, Friday nights eating over at Doc and Grandpa's with all the crazy Wildes. Visiting the local park and pushing our children on the swings or taking them down to the marina and teaching them how to drive a boat. I imagined being able to walk through Hobie, through the world for that matter, proudly displayed on West Wilde's arm.

It was a pipe dream—I knew that. It was a fantasy future that people like me didn't get. West needed someone more like himself—a successful professional who had his shit together and could talk about literature and symbolism, not someone like me who got a cheap-ass college degree online after six years of trying for it. He needed someone who had a pedigree, not a tattoo of a gang symbol buried deep under one of a cheesy-ass phoenix.

I realized West had snuck his hands under my shirt and lifted the hem to investigate the ink on my abdomen.

"Will you tell me about your tattoos now?" he asked, as if reading my mind.

Ah, there was another prime example of my being broken, flawed, and fucked up.

I swallowed. "I might need a drink for this story," I admitted. "Except I only just got rid of my headache from last night's drinking a few hours ago."

"What if we pulled a 'reverse dinner' and loosened your lips with whatever's in that bakery box instead?" West's grin was mischievous, and I leaned in to drop a kiss on his lips.

"Deal. Lead the way."

Once we were back in the kitchen, I removed the little cake from the box. I felt a little shy presenting him with a cake I'd painted specially for him, but his reaction took away my hesitation.

He looked at it reverently before glancing up at me with shining eyes. "Are you freaking kidding me? You did this? Oh my god, Nico. We have to take a picture of it for Doc."

West scrambled over to find his phone. After texting pictures to Doc, he looked up at me with flushed cheeks.

"We're not eating it. We can't. It's too pretty."

"Oh yes we are. I'm starving and Rox makes killer cakes."

I began searching through drawers for a knife and fork, but West tackled me to the floor before I had a chance to find them.

"What the hell?" I asked, laughing as he tried a ninja move to pin my legs between his.

"Don't touch my cake," he growled before leaning in to nibble on my neck. "Or I'll have to punish you."

His fingers were searching for ticklish spots on my ribs, and I was having trouble catching my breath. "Promise?" I gasped.

"A spanking maybe," he said in a sultry voice. "On those tender butt cheeks of yours. Hmm… do I start with the peacock or the snakes? Who's been naughtier?"

I felt my other cheeks heat at the suggestion. “If I can’t have cake, what can I have?”

West pinned me with his eyes. “What would you like, Nico?”

I felt my entire body coil in anticipation at the sound of my name on his tongue. It was one hundred percent sex. How the hell did he do that?

After quirking an eyebrow at him, I responded with, “Chili.”

He barked out a laugh. “No. No fucking way. Forget about it.”

We stood up laughing, and West moved to the fridge to pull out whatever it was he’d planned on cooking. It turned out to be steaks on the grill. He’d already fixed a salad and had a bowl of fruit cut up.

Once we had everything cooked and served, we sat next to each other at his heavy kitchen table. The one we’d fucked on just an hour or so before.

“You’re blushing,” he teased.

“Yeah? Well, your pupils are dilated, and it’s making me wonder if I have time to eat my dinner before you pounce on me once more,” I grumbled. “I’ll never look at this table the same way again.” I ran my hand lovingly over the satiny wood finish to the sound of West’s chuckles.

We ate quickly by unspoken agreement and left the dirty dishes for later. West pulled me over to the sitting area and settled us both under a quilt on the sofa.

“Tattoos,” he reminded me.

As if I’d forget.

I began to tell him about my original trip out west when I left town. How I’d spent most of my cash on a bus ticket to San Francisco with the hopes there would be resources for gay teens in the city. I couldn’t imagine where else to go that would be relatively safe for someone in my situation.

But when I’d gotten to San Francisco, I’d discovered things weren’t like I’d imagined. Obviously.

“I figured it out eventually,” I explained. “I found a group of homeless adults who banded together to look out for each other. They tried protecting me, but they couldn’t feed me or get me clothes or anything else I needed. And I got to a point where I convinced myself that I was horny enough to actually want to suck someone off, so why not at least get paid for it?"

I shifted on the sofa so I wasn't facing him. He pulled my back against his chest and lay down behind me under the blanket while I continued talking. One of his arms was wrapped around my chest, and my fingers idly trailed up and down his exposed arm hair.

"So it wasn't that bad really. I was mostly freaked about getting some nasty disease, so I was very careful with condoms and stuff. I refused anything more than oral for as long as I could, but then… well, shit happened."

I felt his body stiffen behind mine and knew he wouldn't want to hear any more details of my time on the streets. Hell, even I didn't want to hear them.

"Anyway, I met Griff and busted my ass to keep him from falling into the same line of work. There was a nice cop named Brady who was sweet on him and eventually got him into this great program at a youth shelter that was different from some of the others. That's where he met the Marians, who ended up taking him in and adopting him."

"What about you? You didn't want that too?" West asked.

"No, hell no. The idea of another set of parents or stepparents or adoptive parents having any say over my life made me crazy. No way. So I kind of fell into this limbo of having one foot in the shelter and one foot on the streets. And that's how I met this guy named Donny Jessup."

I thought back on the man and felt some of the old familiar tendrils of insecurity sneak in around the edges of my consciousness.

"Who was Donny?" West asked.

"He was this rich, older guy Griff used to call Richard Gere. Not that he was as beautiful as the actor, mind you, but he pulled the whole 'wanting to save the prostitute routine' with me. Only it didn't start off nearly as romantically as the one from the movie."

"What happened?"

"It started off with him spotting me outside a club one night with a client. The guy I was with pulled me into an alley, but before anything happened, Donny came up and told the guy to get lost. I was too overwhelmed by his audacity to react at first, and somehow he got the guy to leave. Eventually I came to my senses and barked at him about losing me money. Then I'll never forget him reaching into his wallet and pulling out a crisp hundred-dollar bill."

West made a grunt of disapproval, and I felt his arms tighten around me more.

"He started off so different from anyone I'd ever known. He told me he didn't want any sexual services from me, he just wanted me to sit with him while he had dinner at a nearby diner. I was starving—honestly, it felt like I was always starving as a teen—so I agreed easily. We sat and talked for hours. He did most of the talking, really. When he'd first approached me in the alley, he'd been wearing a fancy business suit. But once we were in the lights of the diner, I could see he was covered in ink. It peeked out from his collars and cuffs and intrigued me. It turned out, he owned a tattoo shop nearby—one I'd seen plenty of times and knew from its reputation it was successful."

I threaded my fingers through West's and brought his hand up to my mouth for a kiss. He didn't resist.

"He ended up making me an offer. If I let him use me for tattoo practice, he'd let me stay in the back storage room of the shop for a few nights and buy me some clothes and shit. I was floored. No fucking way could I be so lucky. The guy even told me I could choose where on my body the tattoo would go, even though I couldn't choose the design. Well, what the hell did I care? I'd pick a spot on my back and never see the damned thing."

I blew out a breath and tried to stay calm. Just remembering Donny made me angry.

"Little did I know it was a gang symbol. He'd been hired to ink it onto new members and was terrified of screwing it up, hence the need for a human practice session. Once I learned what it was, I demanded he cover it up with something else. He agreed. As long as I'd let him practice a few more designs on me as well.

"I went along with it. He kept offering me more and more in exchange for letting him practice on me, and once I got a certain amount of ink, I just didn't give a fuck anymore. I was fascinated with the process and wanted to learn how to do it myself. By then, we were sleeping together and he was letting me live in the back room of the shop indefinitely."

I laughed, remembering the shit hole. "I fucking loved it. My very own room all to myself. Except when he was in there, of course. Which was pretty much whenever the fuck he wanted to be. But at that point, I'd started to fall for him. He was everything I wasn't—strong, handsome, successful, rich, poised. And the fact he wanted to be with me, to take care of me, was like the greatest feeling ever even if he didn't return my feelings or want something real and committed. As humiliating as it is to admit now, I was happy with whatever bits he gave me. I felt pretty sure that was all I deserved."

West shifted again behind me and moved a hand to rest on my cheek. I nuzzled into it for a moment before continuing.

"But it weighed on me after a while, you know? Like, I didn't understand how he could be so sweet and tender to me sometimes but not want to be with me other times. It was confusing. So I finally got up the nerve to ask him about it, expecting him to say he was married or in a committed relationship or too old for me. But he said he wasn't. That wasn't it. He was having trouble coming to terms with me as his boyfriend because he was afraid of what people would think of him if anyone found out he was dating a whore. His word, not mine."

"Oh Nico, fuck," West said. "What a dick. I'm so sorry."

"That's not the worst part," I admitted.

CHAPTER 34

WEST

Listening to Nico talk about his past was excruciating. I couldn't stand thinking of him alone and vulnerable like that —taken advantage of by who knew how many men. And what were the chances no one had ever hurt him physically? God, it was too much.

I wasn't sure I wanted to know what he thought was the worst part.

"I stayed," he confessed quietly. "I stayed because he seemed to truly feel bad about it and he promised to try harder."

"Oh, baby," I murmured into his hair.

"Right?" he asked with exasperation. "I mean, who believes that bullshit?"

"Lonely teenagers who just want to be loved, Nico."

"But he at least pretended to try for a while. Took me out more, had me over to his place more and more often. Until one night we were walking back to his place from eating out at a restaurant nearby and ran into his friends. I knew it was going to be trouble because I recognized one of the guys from having… you know… slept with him, or whatever. Anyway, Donny immediately pulled away from me, and when the guy asked him when he'd started having to pay for sex,

Donny laughed right along with him. Said I was worth every penny. Said his friend should take a turn with me and see."

My heart dropped. "He didn't stand up for you?" I asked, wanting to kill the slimy motherfucker.

Nico shook his head. "Nope. I was so upset I bolted. Went straight to Griff and bawled my fucking eyes out."

"I'll bet Griff wanted to murder the bastard," I muttered.

"Yep. Wanted to rip his balls off with his bare hands. But I told him I needed him too much to let him go to jail for assault."

"You're lucky to have a friend like him," I admitted, taking a moment to be grateful Nico had Griff in his life. I wanted to send the guy fucking flowers for being there when Nico needed him most.

"Yes, I'm very lucky. Griff's the only guy besides Donny I've given a fuck about since I left here. Everyone else has just been a warm body."

As much as I assumed he didn't intend the words to include me, they still stung. I must have gone still or something because he turned around quickly in my arms, eyes wide and lips open in apology.

"Not you. I didn't mean you, West," he said before sighing. "But that's why I'm a little freaked out."

"A little?" I teased quietly, forcing myself to take a breath and relax.

"I like you more than a little. Which means I'm freaking out more than a little."

I leaned in and nuzzled his nose. "So why the bare spot over your chest?" I asked.

"Because no matter what he ever did to me with the tattoo machine, I reserved the spot over my heart for myself. One day I'll know what to put there, and it will be just for me."

Nico was wearing an old T-shirt of mine from medical school, and I ran my hand under it to find the bare patch of skin I knew was there, over his heart. His eyes locked on mine as my fingers caressed his chest.

"I'm glad you kept a part of yourself just for you," I said quietly. "You're so fucking strong."

He shook his head but didn't argue with me.

"So now I told you my shit; it's time you told me the truth."

"Truth about what?" I asked, genuinely not knowing what he meant.

"Pippa's biological father," he said. "What's the story? And how did you and Adriana end up so close?"

In light of what he'd told me about Donny, I didn't really want to tell him the truth about Adriana. It would only make him feel even more miserable. But I knew he deserved to know it anyway.

"Adriana had a thing for Reeve Billingham," I said, not surprised he tensed up at the revelation. "But they at least waited until your parents were gone to act on it."

"They were stepbrother and sister by then. Ugh."

"Yeah. Believe me, she was bothered by that but not enough to stay away."

"So what happened? He's Pippa's father? That changes everything, West."

"No, he's not. She wanted him to marry her so they could build a life together, start a family, the whole bit. But he refused. He didn't want anyone to find out they were together, especially Curt. Curt was already angry and resentful about losing their father in the accident, and Reeve knew Curt would lose his shit if he found out Reeve and Adriana were together. So they kept it a secret."

"In this town? Jesus," Nico muttered.

"Well, Reeve was in the Navy, so he wasn't around much. Most of what they had was through email and Skype calls, I guess. She thought things would be different when he was done with his four years, but he re-upped. Then he re-upped again."

"Fuck, she waited for him for that long? Jesus, West. How long were they together?"

"He went in at eighteen, right after the accident. They already had strong feelings for each other but didn't sleep together for another year and a half, which was when he finally had leave to spend time with her. She expected him to come home after those first four years, but he signed on for another four. And then another four."

"God, my poor sister," he said quietly. "So they were thirty by then. And all that time she wasn't with anyone else?"

"Nope. She'd dated around in high school, so she wasn't really this shy virgin waiting for her first love. She just knew he was the one for her and was willing to wait until he came home for her. Meanwhile, she was lonely as all hell."

"I guess so." Nico stopped for a minute to let it all sink in. "Then what happened? Didn't you say he's still in?"

"Yep. So after those twelve years, he told her he only needed to do eight more to qualify for retirement. That's when she lost it. She spilled the beans to Curt—you can imagine how that went over. Then she demanded Reeve make a commitment—get married—so they could at least start a family. She wanted a family so badly, Nico. Kids and everything, you know? But he said he wasn't ready to do that and wasn't sure he'd ever be ready."

"Fucking jackass. I always hated that guy. How could she waste all that time pining for such a selfish prick?" Nico's brows were furrowed in frustration, and I reached up to run my thumb over the creases on his skin.

"She told him to fuck off. She wanted a baby and by god, she was going to have one. After that, she threw herself into the dating scene. Matchmaking apps, blind dates, you name it. She spent as much time as she could down in Dallas with my sister MJ, trying to meet a nice man, but it just never happened. When she turned up pregnant, she wouldn't tell me anything about the father. I would have thought she'd used a sperm bank if I hadn't known her financial situation. It wasn't until the night of the embolism, when she thought she wasn't going to make it, that she told me she'd deliberately slept around with random hookups during the fertile part of her cycle until she ended up pregnant."

"Fuck," Nico breathed. "So she truly didn't know who the father was? She used some poor guy for his DNA?"

"Yeah. Once Pippa was born, the reality of it hit her hard. She'd deceived someone into becoming a father, and he'll never know about it. She had no idea who it was."

Nico seemed to be processing everything I'd told him. He leaned his face against my chest, and I ran my fingers through his colorful hair.

"I didn't want her to be alone during her pregnancy, Nico. She didn't have anyone. She'd been close to my sister, but MJ lives in the city now. And even though Adriana had made a nice life for herself here after your mom died, some people in town remembered her as the surly teen she'd been. It wasn't until her pregnancy that she truly began to shine and come into her own. I think it was her long-overdue moment of blooming into who she was without Reeve. She was calm and settled… happy. The bakery was succeeding, the pregnancy was healthy, and she finally had a future she could count on."

"Thank you for being there for her, West."

We sat in silence for a little while before he asked me another question. "What about Curt?"

"What do you mean?"

"Why is he so pissed at me? You think it's really because he is taking out his anger at my mom on me? That seems a little extreme."

"It's complicated. I think he never felt loved. His mom died when he was a preteen. Then his dad fell in love with your mom and his brother fell in love with your sister. His dad died, and then his brother went away to the Navy. After Reeve and Adriana finally ended things, Reeve got deployed to the Pacific Rim. Hasn't really been back since. So Curt's been on his own."

"Doesn't he have a girlfriend? Chloe, I think. What's that all about? Is he bi or just in denial?"

I chuckled. "Hell, Nico, that guy's still so deep in the closet he's never coming out. Every so often he'll say something that insinuates we should hook up for old time's sake. It's pathetic really. If it's his conservative upbringing that keeps him closeted, why won't the guy just move somewhere he can be comfortable in his own skin? I don't get it."

Nico shifted so he was sitting up on the sofa between my spread legs and met my eyes. His blue-green ones were steely, and the lines were back between his brows. "You ever hook up with him after that night?"

I thought about lying to him, but I didn't. "Once. In a moment of weakness."

"What happened?"

"I dated this guy named Xavier in medical school. His family lives here in Hobie, so one Christmas shortly after we broke up, he was home visiting his parents. I ran into Xavier and felt melancholy I guess. Horny too, if you want to know the truth. We were at Doc and Grandpa's big holiday party. They host practically the whole town for an eggnog and Christmas cookie thing every year, and afterward, people stick around and start a bonfire out back if the weather's right for it.

"Well, I proceeded to drown my sorrows after seeing Xavier, and later that night when Curt made his snarky little innuendos about a repeat performance from high school, I called his bluff. Took him around back of the bunkhouse and…" I trailed off, not wanting to go into detail.

"And?"

"You don't really want to hear this shit, do you, Nico?" I asked with a sigh.

"Well, no. But I want to know. Was it just oral sex, or did you fuck him?"

I saw his defiance in the familiar set of his jaw, his upturned chin, and his flinty eyes. My hands slid across his cheeks to hold him still.

"Nico," I said quietly. "It was a mistake. One I regret, and one that happened years ago."

"Figures," he ground out. "That fucking asshole."

"Now do you see the other reason he's pissed at you?" I asked with a smile.

"Because I won't fuck him behind someone's goddamned barn like some people I know?"

God, he was cute when he was pissed off. I really loved angry Nico.

"Because the whole town knows you're the one I want," I said firmly.

He rolled his eyes and scoffed. "A prime example of the slim pickings around here."

I tightened my hold on his face. "You know, Nico, you need to decide—are you going to be pissed at me or feel sorry for yourself? Which is it? Because I'm sitting here looking at the start of something pretty special, yet you seem convinced either you're not worthy or I'm not worthy. And believe it or not, both of those options make me feel pretty damned shitty."

His eyes opened wider as I spoke.

"I know you're not looking for something permanent, Nico. And I know you're leaving soon. But can we just be together for a little while without all this other crap? Even if it's just for tonight. Be with me here, Nico. Trust that I choose to have you here tonight with me because I like you and want you. And for tonight at least, let me believe I deserve it too."

He seemed to deflate before my very eyes, but then he smiled. It was soft and sweet and made my heart flip-flop. But it told me all I needed to know.

Nico was mine for the night, and it was time to take him to bed and show him how glad I was to have him there.

CHAPTER 35

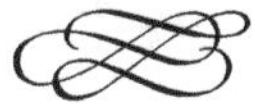

NICO

When I returned home the next day, Griff burst out laughing the minute I walked through the door.

"What?" I asked.

Rebecca turned to look at me from where she was washing some breakfast dishes at the kitchen sink.

"You look a bit postcoital, Nicolas," she teased.

"You look positively ravished," Griff said with a giant grin on his face. "Tell me everything."

I felt my cheeks ignite and tried to fan them with my hands as I snuck back to peek in on Pippa. She'd rolled onto her belly and had her big fat diaper butt in the air with her knees tucked under her tummy and her feet crossed. God, she was adorable. I watched her sleep for a few minutes before risking running a finger over the little shell of her ear. Her lips were smacking lightly in a sleepy nursing movement, and I could see the barest tip of her tongue through a small gap between her lips.

When I walked back out to the main room, Rebecca and Griff were settled on the sofa with their coffee.

"So?" Griff prompted.

"I think I need to go back to San Francisco," I confessed. "If I stay here any longer, I won't be able to leave."

Griff's eyes widened, and he shot a quick look at his mom. Rebecca leaned toward me and rested a hand on my knee.

"Is this about Pippa or West?" she asked sweetly.

"Both."

"Nico, honey, how do you think West feels about your leaving?"

I shrugged. "I think he likes me, but I can't really see him settling down with someone like me. He should be with a doctor or lawyer or something. Someone educated and put together like he is." I laughed. "I mean, can you even picture us together? What would that even be like? A businessman and the punk who's trying to pick his pocket. That's what I think of when I picture the two of us together. It's ridiculous."

"Then why does he seem to want to spend so much time with you?" Griff asked.

I gestured in the direction of town. "Have you seen how few people there are for him to choose from? I'm fresh meat."

Griff rolled his eyes. "Don't be ridiculous. He goes to Dallas all the time to hang out with his siblings. They told me so the other night. He's had plenty of opportunities. The problem isn't meeting people, Nico. Maybe the problem is meeting people who light him up inside the way you do."

"I hardly light the guy up inside," I said. "Now who's being ridiculous?"

"Still you," Griff said with a grin.

Rebecca swatted his shoulder. "Nico, you obviously don't see what the rest of us see. When he's around you, he can't keep from watching you, touching you, talking about you. How many days since you arrived here has he gone without seeing you?"

"That's different. He didn't trust me with the baby at first. He came to check up on her," I said.

Griff studied me for a moment before speaking. "I'm not going to argue with you. Clearly you're not interested in turning it into something more serious, so let's get back to your original point. It's time to go home. Let's do what it takes to make that happen. I'm sure Mike is dying for you to get back so he can take some time off from the shop. He's been working his ass off in your absence."

I felt a pang of guilt, thinking about my employees having to cover for me all these weeks. Griff was right. Regardless of what was happening, I needed to go home and handle my business.

"Right. Okay. Let's do this. I know you need to get back to Benji too, so let's come up with a plan."

We spent the rest of the morning strategizing how to rid the house of all Adriana's remaining personal items, update the bakery's financial plan and budget, and begin to pack up Pippa's things to give to the Warners or West. If the adoption couldn't go through before I needed to leave, I would have to leave Pippa in West's care until the adoption.

I refused to think too much about the adoption and swallowed down the giant lump in my throat that had seemed to move in and declare permanent residency.

That afternoon, I began sorting through Adriana's remaining belongings, creating boxes to send with Pippa and boxes to send to my place in California. I didn't dare look through the photo albums and mementos from my childhood that I'd found stored under the television cabinet, and when I came across a box of our Christmas ornaments in the attic space, I taped them up without looking at them.

Maybe one day I'd be brave enough to open the boxes, but that day was not this one.

When dinnertime rolled around, Doc and Grandpa appeared with food.

"It's chili," Doc warned. "But don't worry, it's his best one yet and it's made with chicken. Now, where's that baby?" He winked at me, and I led him over to where she was angrily batting at the hanging toys on her play mat.

"She's pissed off because I took off the crocodile toy," I told him.

He shot me a look of accusation, and I laughed. "Calm down. It had spit-up all over it and had to go in the washing machine. God, you're as bad as she is."

"Come here, princess," he cooed in a baby voice. "Come to Doc and let me make it all better. Your daddy is a meanie, isn't he? Just a mean old thing. Doc will find your crocodile for you and fix it right up."

He picked her up and carried her over to where Grandpa was chatting with Rebecca in the kitchen. I stared after him, the word "daddy" echoing in my ears. Suddenly I felt Griff's hands land on my shoulders. He met my eye with a knowing look.

"You okay?" he asked in a gentle voice. "I know this can't be easy on you. It's not too late to change your mind, you know."

"About what?"

"Giving Pippa up for adoption."

"She's not mine anymore, Griff. It's not my decision. And even if I wanted to adopt her, I probably wouldn't qualify. I'm single, gay, and live out of state for god's sake."

"You have biological ties to the baby. That counts for a lot."

"And raise her by myself over the shop? What are my options exactly?" I threw up my hands, frustrated by feeling caught in the trap of wanting something I couldn't have. "And what about her? Doesn't she deserve better than me for a parent? Doesn't she deserve to be loved by a set of parents who desperately wanted her?"

"She *is* loved by a parent who desperately wants her," he said quietly so only I could hear it. "You and I both felt unloved and unwanted by our biological families. She would never feel that with you, Nico. Ever."

My heart felt like it was going to break into a million pieces. I wanted to scream at him that everyone agreed I wasn't good enough to be that baby's father, but I knew he'd just keep arguing.

I left him standing by the sofa while I walked over to join the others in the kitchen to heat up the chili and fix dinner for everyone. Grandpa was already at the stove, telling a funny story to Rebecca, who was laughing so hard she was wiping off tears.

Doc had the baby propped on his shoulder and was swaying back and forth cooing in her ear before he seemed to remember something. "Oh, Weston, I forgot to tell you," he began. My head whipped around so fast to the front door, I almost fell over.

West wasn't there.

Everyone stared at me until I realized Doc had been talking to Grandpa. My face bloomed hot, and my heart raced. Fuck, I had it bad. Really, really bad.

"Sorry. Continue," I mumbled, turning to get a bottle of water from the fridge so I could cool off my hot cheeks.

Doc went on. "I heard from the chief of staff at the hospital that Xavier Rhodes accepted Avi's old spot as staff surgeon. He'll be here in a few days, I think. His parents are over the moon he's moving back."

Grandpa's face lit up. "Excellent. I'll bet Adrien and Margot are thrilled. I don't think they ever saw him unless they visited Atlanta. Does West know? He'll finally have someone on staff close to his own age."

As they chattered about Xavier, I realized it was the same Xavier that West had dated in med school. The realization the guy was moving to Hobie hit hard, leaving a strange calm over me. It surprised me, really. I was expecting to feel jealous and angry hearing about West's ex moving back to town. But all I felt was this weird sense of karma clicking into place. Like the universe was backing up my assertion that I wasn't the right one for West. And now Fate was serving up a better option on a silver platter just as I was leaving. How perfectly perfect for him.

Doc and Grandpa apparently thought the world of the guy. According to their inane chatter, Xavier was smart and gorgeous, clever and kind. Everyone loved him, and he probably wore a goddamned superhero costume under his scrubs. The more they described how great he was, the more I worried I'd accidentally sprained my nostrils from flaring too much.

The subject finally changed after we sat down to dinner, and Rebecca mentioned something about my tattoo shop to Grandpa.

"He's very talented," she said, beaming with pride. "It takes forever to get on his schedule. I'm sure it's been a mess for his calendar since he's been gone."

Doc smiled at me. "Actually, Nico, I wanted to ask you about a piercing—"

Grandpa's hand came up to clamp over Doc's mouth. "Are you crazy?"

Doc's eyes twinkled at his husband, almost daring him to take his hand away.

"Don't you dare say it," Grandpa warned. Doc winked at him, and holy hell, Grandpa's cheeks turned an adorable pink.

"Well, whatever you may or may not want pierced, you'll have to come see me in California. I'm heading back the day after tomorrow."

Everyone stopped laughing and looked at me with surprise.

"Really?" Griff asked. "So soon?"

I nodded. "I need to get back to work. Doc, I was hoping you could help West take care of Pippa until the adoption goes through. I can't imagine it'll take too long now that the last document is in Honovi's hands. All West has to do is sign the paperwork."

I felt like I was going to throw up.

Doc reached his hand over and placed it on mine. "Nico, are you sure about this? Why don't you take some more time to—"

"No, I'm sure. The Warners seem like wonderful people, and they'll give her a great life. It's better for her even if it's hard for me. And that's what it's all about, right?" I tried to put on a brave face even though I was dying inside.

"Well, we can certainly watch her, but—"

"Good. It's settled then. I'm going to go take a walk if you guys don't mind. Just want to stretch my legs a little bit."

Rebecca got up from her spot at the table and came around to give me a hug. "I love you, Nico Salerno. You're a good man," she whispered in my ear. "Take your time on your walk and don't worry about us. We're here for whatever you need."

I swallowed around the lump in my throat and gave the two older men a quick wave before heading out the front door and hopping down the front porch steps. Before I got to the end of the driveway, I was loping, and by the time I got to Dogwood Street, I was on a full-out run.

Before I knew what I was doing, I was banging hard on West's back door, out of breath and sweaty from the exertion.

CHAPTER 36

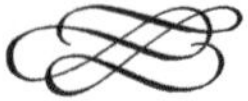

WEST

I'd been catching up on reading some articles for work when I heard the banging on my door. I wondered which of my siblings had shown up and why they were riled up enough to bang instead of using the doorbell.

I wandered down the stairs and opened the door to find a flushed and sweating Nico, but before I could register my surprise, he pounced on me. I stumbled back into the alcove at the bottom of the stairs and was barely able to kick my door closed before he began pulling my clothes off.

"What… what's happening?" I gasped against his biting teeth on my lips. "Not that I'm complaining."

"No talking," he insisted. His hands were everywhere, in my hair, on my clothes, cupping my ass. He was a whirling dervish of lust and need, and I had a hard time keeping up.

I wanted to ask him what was wrong, why he'd come, where Pippa was. But he didn't let go of my lips long enough for me to speak. I sensed his lust and need for quick release and decided to just ride the wave along with him—let it carry us through to completion before asking him what was up with him.

"Upstairs," I managed to say before he was able to drag my pants down. I grabbed his hand and yanked him upstairs, not stopping until I had him in my bedroom with the door closed.

His eyes were dark and stormy—angry sea chop instead of their usual calm waters. There was so much going on in them I wanted to get to the bottom of it. But if he needed to get off, I was fully on board with that need as well.

Nico began grabbing at me again once we were in my room. His frantic movements seemed to imply he was on the verge of losing his composure, or maybe he didn't know exactly how to control the situation to get what he needed. I decided to take over.

"Stop. Take off your clothes and lie down," I said as firmly as I could despite the heaving breaths coming out of me. My cock was throbbing, and I reached inside my track pants to adjust it.

Nico's eyes were wild, but he did as I said. Within seconds he was blessedly naked and laid out across my bed, stroking his erection between bent legs.

"Fuck," I muttered at the sight of him.

I removed my clothes slowly enough to get his attention. His face seemed to get darker the longer I took, but I did it anyway.

"Hurry the fuck up," he snapped.

I felt my grin appear and caught myself just before laughing. Angry Nico. *My* angry Nico.

"My, my, aren't we impatient tonight?" I teased, taking one step toward the bed but no more.

"I thought you agreed we weren't talking," he growled. "Less talking, more fucking."

I leaned over and reached for his ankles, yanking his legs straight and placing them firmly apart on the mattress where I wanted them. His eyes widened in surprise, and his hard cock jumped up.

"But if I can't talk to you, how am I going to tell you what to do, Nico?" I drawled.

His breathing hitched, and a small whine came out. I loved seeing his subconscious reaction to my bossing him around in bed.

I leaned over and took one of his big toes into my mouth, sucking it and nipping at it with my teeth before moving on to each smaller toe in turn. When I'd finished with one foot, I looked up at him.

"The more attitude you give me, the slower I'm going to go," I told him in a calm voice. "Test me on this, Nico. I dare you."

He shook his head without saying a word, so I rewarded him with a long lick to his hard shaft.

"Oh god, yes. Suck me off," he gasped as he arched up against my mouth. "Please."

I trailed soft kisses back down his inner thigh to the foot I hadn't paid attention to yet and began sucking each of those toes the way I'd done the others.

"Dammit," he cursed before biting his tongue to keep himself quiet.

I ran my hand back up his thigh to fiddle with his balls while I followed it with licks and nips until I took his cock into my mouth again.

His hips automatically began thrusting into my mouth, and I encouraged him with a squeeze to his ass. Just as I felt his body getting close to release, I pulled off and lurched up to slam my mouth over his. He barely had time to suck in a breath before our mouths were invading each other. Nico's hands went into my hair and held my head in place while I pressed my pelvis into his and felt the sweet, slick slide of our cocks together.

"West," he groaned. "You feel so good."

"Want you," I told him before moving down to suck on his neck. "So fucking badly."

He began whispering the word *please* over and over again, and I wasn't sure he even realized he was doing it. With every repetition of the word, my heart thundered harder and faster in my chest.

I finally grabbed what I needed from the table and began sliding lubed fingers inside him. His eyes were wide and pleading, his cock was hard and leaking, and the sounds coming out of him were stark and begging. I almost didn't last. But he was finally stretched enough that I could press into him.

I grabbed his legs under the knees and pushed back, folding him in on himself so I could see every second of his body taking me in. He threw his head to one side with a hiss as I breached his outer muscles.

"'S okay?" I murmured.

He nodded and turned back to look at me, reaching out a hand to palm the side of my face with a gentle touch.

"West," he breathed. His eyes looked glassy and full—no longer stormy but still brimming with emotion unspoken. I wanted to dive into them.

"I'm right here with you, beautiful." I leaned over him to brush a kiss across his lips before pulling out and thrusting back in again.

We locked eyes while my hips stroked in and out of his body, slowly at first and then speeding up until I was practically pummeling him. The sounds he was making went straight to my gut, and I reached for his cock between us and did my best to jack him off before losing myself to the pull of my climax.

He arched beneath me, crying out and coming as his body jerked. The sight of it ignited my own release, and I felt my cock stiffen inside his hot body.

"Nico," I gasped. His eyes widened as he watched me come, my body shaking and shuddering above him. I felt amazing, invincible, at peace.

Once we came down from our high, spent and gasping in a heap on the bed, I turned to smile at him, shocked to find tears leaking out of his eyes. He didn't look at me, rather turned his face away until he was gazing unseeing at the wall.

"Nico," I said, worried. "What's wrong? Talk to me. Did I hurt you?"

Nico's head spun back around to face me. "No! God, no. Of course not."

"Then what is it? You're clearly upset. Please tell me what's going on. Is it Pippa?"

More tears.

"I love her."

I couldn't help but smile. His declaration was said with absolute horror, as if loving that perfect child could ever be a bad thing.

"I know you do, baby," I said softly, stroking the side of his face with the back of my fingers. He turned absently to kiss them before facing me again.

"I have to leave, West."

Even though I'd already known he would be leaving, hearing it was still a punch to the gut. I felt like a big, happy balloon that had just received the sharp end of a tack.

"Yeah, I know," I said, more angrily than I'd intended. His eyes widened in surprise. "Why bring it up right now? You don't need to shove it in my face."

"Nice," he bit out.

"Fuck, Nico. What do you expect me to say? Please don't go?" I swallowed thickly when I realized that's what I truly wanted to say. I wanted to ask him to stay. But I knew it was pointless. "I'm not sure saying that would make a damned bit of difference to you."

"What are you saying?"

"Just that you're bound and determined to do what you want to do regardless of other people's feelings."

"Are you fucking kidding me right now?"

I knew I needed to stop this, whatever it was, before it got out of hand. But I couldn't seem to do it. Anger and fear bubbled up from somewhere deep and hidden, and I felt like lashing out at him.

"No, I'm not kidding. I don't want you to go. You *know* I don't want you to go. But go ahead anyway. Leaving is something you're really good at, Nico." My voice sounded foreign to my ears. It was toneless and gray, empty. I got up to head to the bathroom and stepped into the shower without another word to him.

I wasn't surprised to find him missing when I returned to the bedroom, and when I made my way to the stairs leading down to my door, I knew he was gone.

I just didn't realize at the time that he was *gone,* gone. By the time I got up my nerve to go talk to him the following day after work, there was a For Sale sign at the end of the driveway and Doc was loading what looked to be pieces of Pippa's crib into his truck. Nico's rental car was nowhere to be found.

After slamming my truck into park, I jumped out and raced to help him.

"What's going on? Where are they?" My heart was slamming in my chest, and I felt cold prickles on my skin. "Doc, where are they?"

Doc's sad eyes said it all.

"No," I said.

"Pippa's right there in her car seat," Doc said gently, pointing forward into the cab to a sleeping Pipsqueak all bundled up and rosy-cheeked in the morning chill. "Nico's gone back to California. I was headed to your place next to see what you wanted me to do with her."

"No," I said again, as if saying it could reverse what had happened. "Please tell me he didn't leave her. He didn't leave without saying goodbye to me."

Doc came around the tailgate toward me and grabbed me into a bear hug, tighter than I could ever remember him holding me. The gesture set my emotions into the stratosphere, and I couldn't hold back tears of anger.

"That motherfucker," I said. "That stupid, selfish, motherfucker. I hate him."

"You love him," Doc said with gentle firmness that brooked no argument.

"I don't," I said defiantly.

He let out a chuckle. "Oh Westie, of course you do. And he loves you too."

"Bullshit."

Doc pulled back from the embrace and gestured for me to sit on the tailgate next to him.

"It's so obvious, West. Even if you don't see it. He's used to being on his own. Clearly he's put up some big walls around his heart for whatever reason. Maybe he just doesn't believe he's worth it."

"He *is* worth it though," I insisted. "He *is*."

Doc patted my knee and smiled. "Have you told him that? Maybe you should ask him to come back and give it a try."

"He hates Hobie, Doc. Plus I already asked him to stay, and he didn't. I can't make him want it. I can't make him want to come back here for me."

"No, but you can tell him how you feel—that there's something here for him if he wants to take a chance on it. You can fight for him. Can you imagine my life if I hadn't taken the chance on your grandfather? If I hadn't told him how I felt about him?"

Just the thought of it made my heart hurt. I couldn't imagine those two without each other.

"I'm not saying it'll all turn out happily ever after for you, son. I'm only suggesting that you realize you only have this one life. If you see something you want, you owe it to yourself to at least fight for it. Stop living your life according to what you *should* do. It's okay to be a little selfish sometimes, West. You deserve happiness too. Everyone deserves to be loved."

I heard a small sound from behind me and looked back at Pippa. She was awake and staring at me with her big blue-green eyes. Her dark curls poked out from the edges of the soft cap on her head, and one of her ears had made its way out from under the cap as well. She was a tiny version of her uncle, and in that moment I was so full of emotion I thought I might drown from the weight of it.

Doc's words echoed in my head. Everyone deserved to be loved, and that included Pippa. No one could love that baby more than Nico and me. And if Nico wasn't there to love on her, then I sure as hell would be.

"Will you follow me to my place and ask Grandpa to meet us there?" I asked Doc.

"Sure. You want me to ask him to bring us something to eat?"

I felt a grin split my face. "As long as it's not chili. Tell him to bring you some work clothes and his toolbox. We have a nursery to put together."

Once I got in my truck, I picked up my phone to dial my friend Honovi.

CHAPTER 37

NICO

I'd been back three weeks by the time my employees staged their intervention. After Mike flipped the open sign to closed and locked the front door, Jax and Coco came out of the back room like they were on a mission.

"Dude, you need to tell us what the fuck is going on with you, man. This shit is not okay," Mike began.

Coco nodded her head in agreement while Jax looked on worriedly.

"What are you talking about?" I asked.

"You're in a mood, sugar. Have been for weeks," Coco scolded. "If it's about your sister, honey, we understand. Really, we do. But you can't keep being an ass to the clients."

"When was I an ass to the clients?" I challenged.

They all three looked at each other before Jax finally spoke. "Nico, you just told Shotgun Hawkins to grow a pair. Do you have a death wish? That guy could slap you in the face with his Harley."

I rolled my eyes. "Please. He was being a big baby."

Coco snorted a laugh. "You were squeezing his testicles."

"I was piercing his scrotum. There's a difference. And can someone please remind him that manscaping is a thing? The guy could use a little hedge trim if you want to know the truth. Not to mention a shower wouldn't go amiss." I shuddered. "Don't remind me. Ten bucks says he tries to ride his Harley against my orders and comes in here with more sniffles about his poor balls."

Mike's deep belly laugh echoed through the quiet shop. "Why the hell did he want a hafada anyway? You think his wife wants anything to do with his saggy nuts after all these years?"

"You never know what people do behind closed doors, Mikey. You never know. Maybe Mrs. Shotgun likes them nads bejeweled," Coco joked.

I shuddered again. "Can we please stop talking about his jewels? I'll be seeing them in my nightmares for weeks."

Jax came around the counter to give me an impromptu hug.

"What was that for?" I asked him.

"You seem like you could use a hug," he said with a shrug. There was a faint tinge of pink on his cheeks, and I was reminded about how shy and sweet the young man was.

"More likely he could use a good fuck," Mike suggested. "Want me to take you out tonight? I was going to grab a drink with a friend, but he'd probably love dragging me to Harry Dicks instead. Come on. I'll help you find someone to take your mind off your sister."

I didn't correct him by telling him it wasn't Adriana I was missing.

"You're going to go clubbing at Harry Dicks? What if I can't keep all the men off you?" I teased. Mike was straighter than an arrow, but with his big muscled biker look, he often got mistaken for a leather daddy when he wound up at gay bars with me. Guys fucking loved him and swarmed around every chance they got.

"It'll be good for my ego," he said with a wink. "My friend Ron will get a kick out of seeing me get more offers of dick than he does. Jax, you in?"

Jax's face turned even pinker. "Really? I can come with you guys? That'd be awesome. Coco, are you coming?"

"Hell no. Ain't nothing for me there but sweaty-ass dancing and candy that says look but don't touch. I think I'll head home and settle for a night in with my favorite vino and some binge-watching on

Netflix. You guys have fun though. And feel free to text me pictures of your conquests."

I thought about begging off, but I was actually horny as hell. Maybe a random fuck would replace my memories of West Wilde in bed. I could just go out to the clubs, find someone to fuck, and come home unencumbered by all the feelings bullshit. Remind myself why it was nice not feeling emotionally obligated to another person.

By the time I met up with Mike and Jax at Harry Dicks, I had a pocket full of condoms and a goal of finding some cute twinkie ass to get into. It was time to get back on the horse.

SEVERAL HOURS LATER, I caught an Uber home in a foul mood. I'd been pawed at, dry-humped, and propositioned by any number of cute men and was so pissed off at my dick for its blatant disregard for my feelings that I had half a mind to thump it with my finger in disgust.

"Lame-ass bastard. Don't tell me you're too old to get it up for hot guys anymore," I muttered at my crotch. "Traitor."

I knew the truth, of course. That fucker had been spending too much time chitchatting with my heart. Probably listening to silly notions about how there should be *feelings* involved before getting it up for someone.

Stupid, stupid heart.

After thanking the driver, I made my way into the shop and up the back stairs to my apartment. It was lonelier than it had ever been, and I fell into a massive pity party.

I thought about what my friends had said earlier in the shop, that I'd been in a funk since getting back from Hobie. It was true. I felt like I was missing something. Some*things*.

Of course, I missed West terribly. His calm demeanor, his tender touch, his take-charge attitude. I missed Pippa with her chubby cheeks and chirpy waking-up sounds. I missed the crazy cowlick in the back of her hair that was going to drive her to drink when she grew up and tried to get it to stand down. I missed middle-of-the-night feedings when it was just us in the quiet house, rocking in her nursery and singing to her under my breath as she stared up at me dreamily.

I even missed the bakery. Painting cakes and brainstorming new ideas for designs the local customers and summer lake tourists would like. I'd gotten an email the day before from Rox with an update that things were running smoother now that we had a better bookkeeping system in place. She was happy managing it but said everyone had been asking about me since I'd left. It had taken all my self-control not to ask if she'd seen Pippa with the Warners.

As I fell asleep that night, I couldn't help but imagine what it would be like if I had everything I wanted. What would that look like? West would be there for sure. And Pippa. But picturing them here in the city with me didn't feel right. They belonged in Hobie. And I knew deep down there was a part of me that belonged in Hobie too. After those weeks I'd spent back in my hometown, the only person who still gave me hell by the end of it was Curt, and he was never going to change. Most everyone else had been friendly and welcoming after the initial shock of my reappearance had worn off.

I finally fell asleep in the wee hours of the morning only to have to get up for a client appointment a few hours later. I mainlined caffeine and grabbed a quick protein bar breakfast before making my way downstairs to open the shop.

The first client was a repeat visit to add to a sleeve I'd been working on for him for a while. He was happy with the addition and walked up front to pay Coco on his way out. I took a chance to refill my coffee in the back room before coming up to the reception counter to see who I had next on the schedule.

Mike, Jax, and Coco were all standing by the front counter peering out through the glass door of the shop.

"What is it?" I asked, stretching my neck to see what they were looking at.

"Cute guy with a stroller," Coco said. "Check it out."

Just then, the bell dinged over the door and the cute guy walked into the shop.

Dr. Weston Wilde. With Pippa.

My heart leaped in my chest. He looked so handsome and strong. The beautiful man I'd resisted opening up to for so long. Just seeing him there took my breath away and did stupid things to my stomach. But he looked tired too. Most likely from trying to juggle his jobs along with a newborn. I'd been so selfish leaving her with him like I had.

"What are you doing here?" I asked, hurrying over to where he stood by the door and peeking down at her in the stroller. She looked happy as a clam, and I reached out to cup my hand over her little fuzzy head. "Is she okay? Why isn't she with the Warners? What happened? It's been three weeks, West. Did something happen? Did the adoption fall through?"

I couldn't stop babbling out of fear something had gone wrong after I left. I'd been so selfish, leaving without saying a proper goodbye to him. But I'd thought he'd only have to have her a few days until the adoption went through. Maybe it was a sign. Maybe if the Warners hadn't adopted her, it was a sign she was meant to be mine.

West opened his mouth, but before he had a chance to speak, I blurted, "I'll take her. I'll adopt her, West. Please tell me it's not too late."

"It's not too late." His face split into a grin as he stepped closer, arms reaching out to pull me in for a hug. How could that be? How could he possibly want to hug me after I'd been so awful to him?

Rather than looking a gift horse in the mouth, I stepped into his embrace and wrapped my arms around him to hold on tight. His arms came around me and pulled me in close. Good god, how I'd missed the two of them.

I inhaled his familiar smell and wanted to cry from the comfort of it. My face found his neck, and I reached out my lips to taste the skin there.

"I missed you so much." I breathed. "I'm sorry for the way I left."

"Nico." He sighed. "I'm sorry too. You have no idea how much I missed you, sweetheart."

My heart did a double take at the endearment, and my arms squeezed him even tighter. I wouldn't let him go again. I just couldn't.

I pulled back just enough to meet his eyes.

"I love you," I said, expecting to feel abject terror at the words. Or embarrassment about saying something so personal in front of my employees. But I didn't. I felt relief. It bubbled up, pushing a laugh out of me. "I love you, you big dumb jerk. Why are you here?"

West's face had morphed from shock to happiness, and his smile was like the sun on a hot, Texas day.

"I'm here because I love you too. I came to bring you home with me. With us."

I felt my throat constrict as I realized what he was saying. "Really? You came to get me?"

"I couldn't do it. I couldn't give Pippa up when she was my last link to you. You and I can love her more than anyone else in the world. Come home."

"You came to get me?" I asked again, feeling light-headed. "To bring me home?"

"Someone should have done it a long time ago, Nico," West said gently. "I came to get you, and I'm not leaving here without you. If you're not ready to go or if you don't see yourself in Hobie, we'll move here."

"But what about your practice? Your big Wilde family? Xavier?" I asked without thinking.

"I can practice medicine anywhere. My big Wilde family knows how to use the airport. And why the hell are you asking me about my ex-boyfriend?"

"He moved back. Everyone knows you two would be perfect together," I said stupidly, sounding like a petulant child. Apparently, I couldn't stop myself.

West's eyes sparkled. "Nicolas Salerno, has anyone ever told you that opposites attract? Plus, been there, done that with Xavier. He has no fire or passion. I don't want perfect. I want *you*. And you have to admit, you're about as fiery and passionate as they come." He winked at me before leaning down to seal my mouth with his.

The kiss was possessive and meaningful, rife with promises and beginnings. I didn't want it to end, but the catcalls from my employees seeped into my awareness, causing me to pull back, cheeks flaming at the realization all that shit had happened in front of their noses.

Coco jutted out a hip. I noticed Jax had snuck Pippa out of her stroller and was making faces at her.

"You gonna introduce us to your new sugar daddy or just put us on a show?" Coco teased. "Not that I'm complaining."

I sighed, feeling myself begin to let go of the weight I'd been carrying around for so long. My hand reached out for West's, threading our fingers together with a gentle squeeze.

"Yeah, okay. Guys, this is West Wilde. West, this is Mike, Jax, Coco. They make this place run," I explained, waving to the crew and then the shop. While he shook hands, I looked around at the result of my years of hard work and dedication in that tattoo shop. The memories, the ups and downs. I'd lived and worked there for almost a decade.

But it was time to take the Nico I'd become in San Francisco and join it with the Nico I'd always been in Hobie. I wasn't all of one or the other. I was a combination of the two, and I was ready to find my new normal.

"Give me that baby," I told Jax with a grin. He handed her over reluctantly, and I pulled her in close, sniffing the baby wash smell of her and nuzzling her hair. "Did your daddy pick out your outfit today? Because, girl, we need to talk," I murmured into her ear. "From now on, I'm the one you come to for fashion, not Dr. Boring Khaki Pants over there."

"I heard that," West said. "Don't even think about putting her in leather, Nico."

I ignored him and kept talking to Pippa. "Come here and let me show you some cute little tattoos you'll like when you get a little older. Surely he'll let us give you at least one."

"Nico…," he warned.

"And piercings, just think of all the tender skin we can put holes in when you—"

West's arms came around me from behind, and he took my earlobe between his teeth. "Don't even think about it, beautiful. All your piercings do is make me hornier for you. I don't want a single piercing on her body. Everyone will want to get into her pants."

I smiled and turned to kiss him. "Which one of those three clowns should we leave in charge of Pippa for the next hour while we run upstairs?"

His eyebrows furrowed. "Why? What do you need to do?"

"You."

EPILOGUE

WEST - TWO MONTHS LATER

It was a week from Christmas, and we were heading to Doc and Grandpa's house for their big holiday party. The weather was plenty cold, and I was secretly excited about the bonfire we'd end up having later in the night.

Pippa was seven months old and teething like a son of a bitch. Several of my patients had gotten a huge kick out of seeing me finally realize how ridiculous recommending homeopathic treatments were. No amount of gumming a frozen treat made up for a good, solid dose of baby pain reliever. Her cheeks were rosy from the teething and the cold, but she was having a rare moment of giggly happiness while Nico sang a ridiculous song he'd picked up somewhere about teapots and spouts.

I couldn't help but stare at him as he held her while he drifted back and forth on the wide swing in the backyard. He'd had the wooden seat engraved with our three names, and ever since then, I'd noticed him bringing her out here more and more despite the December weather.

When I'd asked him about it, he'd blushed and admitted he wanted to start some family traditions that were all our own. Special things that were just for Pippa so that she would feel the importance of what being in a family meant. I'd noticed when he'd had the freshly carved seat put back on, he'd raised the height so my knees wouldn't be bent up by my chest anymore.

There were more and more times lately when I noticed him making little gestures of unspoken kindness for me. If I pointed them out, he'd scoff at me and deny them to his dying breath, but only minutes later, I'd see him do something else sweet like that. He was thoughtful and kind even if he was still having trouble owning that side of himself.

We'd gotten lucky when he'd decided to make the big move to Texas. Mike and Coco had gotten together and offered to buy the tattoo shop from him, and we were able to stop the sale of Adriana's house in time for Nico to move into it.

When he'd first gotten back to town, we'd had an awkward period of time when we weren't sure if we were moving way too fast. By unspoken agreement, we'd kept both our places. But I'd ended up staying at his place every single night until he finally mentioned moving my shit over and making it permanent a few weeks ago.

His little house was tight, so I'd left most of my furniture upstairs at the practice. I wondered if maybe it gave him peace of mind that one or the other of us had a place to go if things got tough between us. Neither of us were naive enough to think it was going to be easy. In fact, I'd suggested going to see a family counselor I knew from the hospital in order to help us with the transition from two single men to a couple with a baby in the span of just a few months.

To be honest, our situation was rife with possible land mines, but I was still surprised when Nico agreed. We'd been going for a few weeks, and I already noticed feeling less pressure to try to make things easy and "right" for Nico. I knew he needed to find his own way as he settled into life in Hobie. I could be there for him, but I couldn't fix his problems or face his challenges for him.

He'd gone back to painting cakes at the bakery, which he loved, and he was expanding into the space above the bakery to open a small tattoo shop. I'd introduced him to a friend I knew at the nearby military base, and he'd talked with him for a long time about the need for someplace closer than Dallas to get ink.

I had enough money to support both of us, but Nico didn't want to feel beholden to me for that kind of support. In the end we both agreed to try to figure out a way we could at least make sure Pippa had us around as much as possible.

Doc and Grandpa had offered to help. When Nico couldn't take Pippa to work with him or work from home with her, Doc or Grandpa would watch her or Nico could bring her to my office and my receptionist Morgan could play with her for a while. It wasn't foolproof, but we'd try it for a while until things settled down and we learned what might work better.

"You ready?" Nico asked with a smile as he stood up from the swing and began walking toward the front of the house. "My first Wilde holiday party, huh? Gonna be nuts?"

"Yep. It's a shame you missed Halloween. That's the best one they do." I shifted Pippa's backpack on my shoulder before reaching for Nico's free hand.

"I've heard. Next year, huh?"

I looked over at him and grinned. "Yeah, next year. We'll have to come up with a costume. This year I just took her as a sleeping baby because I was too sleep-deprived to think of anything else."

After arriving at Doc and Grandpa's, we made our way into the house amid shouts of greeting from friends and family. Predictably, Doc stole the baby right out from Nico's arms and took off with her. I was sure he was planning on showing her off to anyone and everyone, as if they hadn't seen her a million times. She seemed to love the attention though, smiling and giggling whenever someone made silly faces at her.

"You sure we didn't need the Pack 'n Play?" Nico asked in a whisper.

"They have one of their own, remember? It lives in the guest room although I'm surprised they haven't turned it into a nursery yet for how often she's over here."

"We have," a voice chuckled behind us. I turned to see Grandpa and gave him a kiss on the cheek. "The nursery is finally done. Check it out. You'd better be leaving her with us tonight, boys. Doc'll flip if you don't."

"Oh, please, twist our arm," Nico responded deadpan.

Grandpa laughed and led us back to the room beside theirs. The walls were a sunny yellow, and there was a brand-new crib set up against one wall. An old rocking chair I recognized sat in the corner with new cushions that matched the curtains and crib sheets. A small bookcase sat next to the rocker and held stacks of picture books, some ancient-looking and some obviously brand-new.

Before we had a chance to gush to Grandpa, someone asked for his help down the hall.

Nico turned to me with wet eyes. He'd been doing that a lot lately. I wondered if, now that the floodgates were open, he was having trouble getting back into the habit of shoving his emotions aside. Whatever the reason was, I was glad to see him letting his feelings out.

I pulled him in for a hug and cupped his cheeks. "You okay, tough guy?" I teased quietly.

"Why would they go to all this trouble?" he asked.

"Because they love her. They're her family, *our* family. That's what families do," I said without thinking. The word "family" seemed to hit him like a barb. "Shit, Nico. I'm sor—"

He closed my lips with his fingers and smiled up at me. "Nope, don't be sorry. You're right. I'm just not used to it."

"Are you okay with it all? I know going from little to no family to this insanity is a bit much."

"It's amazing, West. Truly. I always envied Griff his huge crazy adopted family, and now I have my own. And so does Pippa."

I leaned down to brush my lips against his. He tasted like the peppermint candy cane he'd eaten in the car on the way over here.

"Always. I love you, Nico."

"I love you too. You're the best thing that's ever happened to me." His face bloomed dark pink, and I thought about what a difference it was, seeing him now compared to when he'd first arrived after Adriana's funeral. He'd gone from being a defensive prickly pear to an expressive, loving partner. Granted, he was still a work in progress—we both were—but he didn't seem to second-guess my commitment and love for him anymore.

When we made our way out to the family room area, the room was full of people talking and laughing. Holiday music played in the background, and bowls of eggnog and punch covered the kitchen island counter. All kinds of cookies and cakes from the bakery were displayed on the big kitchen table along with big pots of chili and soup Grandpa had made. Unfortunately, there wasn't an award-winning chili in the bunch, but everyone seemed okay settling for second best.

As the night wore on, many of us bundled up and made our way out to the bonfire. Everyone seemed to have gotten a buzz on, and Nico was happily chatting with my sister Hallie until Mrs. Parnell walked up with a big grin.

"Hi, Nico! I'm so glad to see you. George is desperate for me to book you for a cake like the one you did for Clyde. Please tell me you can squeeze us in the first week in January."

Nico smiled. "You'll have to call Rox and ask her. She keeps the schedule. I know we're booked through New Year's for painted cakes though, so call her soon."

"Will do, will do. Say…" She looked around as if to make sure no one could hear her even though everyone could. "How are you feeling now that ole Curt is gone, huh? You know, after the thing with Daniel Warner came to light? Can you even believe it?"

Her grin was downright shit-eating, and I reached out a hand to Nico's back before realizing what I was doing. He leaned his weight back into me slightly before responding.

"I'm not sure exactly what happened, but I hope Curt finds a nice man one day who's not actually married. How about that?" Nico gave her a polite smile, and I wondered if I was the only person who realized how deliberately he'd snuck in the fact that Curt would wind up with another *man* one day. If only his and Daniel's coupling hadn't been so destructive to poor Jenn's life as well as that of their young son. Lucky for Pippa, my brother Cal had told me about the affair the minute he'd realized the man he'd seen on the boat was the same man trying to adopt Pippa.

Mrs. Parnell continued, barely taking a breath. "Well, I also heard the new police officer hired to take Curt's place is a nice homosexual man like yourself. So what do you think about that?"

Nico snuck me a look of incredulity, and I shrugged. I wished I could tell Nico her rudeness came from too much drink, but she was this way stone cold sober too.

"Well, Mrs. Parnell," he said, reaching for my hand. "I believe I have my hands full with Dr. Wilde right now, but I'll see if maybe Stevie wants to take our new officer some of his special nut clusters."

I choked on my beer and yanked my hand out of his grip to cover my dripping face.

Nico gave her a serene smile until she tittered and tottered away to find someone else to gossip with. Meanwhile, I noticed my cousin Felix standing nearby, swaying precariously on his feet. I reached out a hand to steady him, and he turned a drunken grin on me.

"Hey there, Westerley," he said with a giggle. "Having fun?"

"I am indeed. Looks like you are too. What's gotten into you? You normally don't drink. Just feeling the holiday spirit?" I teased.

"Nope," he said, popping the end of the word with his lips. "Mommie Dearest is at it again. The big movie, you know? The one about that woman… that woman… the woman with the thing?"

His eyebrows came together as his brain fought to find the right words.

"Doesn't she play the head of the CIA in that big spy thriller coming out Christmas Day?"

"That's the one," he said miserably. "It's going to kill at the box office."

"Sorry," I said, unsure of what would make him feel better. "Are you going to do your usual and just try to lie low until the media dies down?"

His face lit up, and he swayed again, reaching for my elbow to right himself. "Nope. Not this time. Doc and Grandpa are sending me on a sebat… sebat… a research trip," he said with a hiccup.

"It's probably a good idea to get out of Dodge. Although I'll miss you if you're not here for Christmas, Felix. What are you researching for?"

"Thesis stuff. Going to a castle-type place. They have good stained glass there for me to do. I mean study. I mean write about. Research, you know? Overseas. In Europe."

He emphasized Europe, pronouncing it like *your rope,* and I couldn't help but laugh. "Sounds good, buddy. You ever been there?"

"Barely been out of Texas. What about you, Westlake? You gonna take Nicopotamus somewhere sometime? You should come see me at the cattle… The cattle… The *castle.*" His tongue seemed too big for his mouth and he stuck it out a little to make room.

I bit my own tongue to keep from laughing. I had seriously never seen my shy little cousin this chatty. It was adorable.

Nico leaned in from the other side to whisper in my ear. "What's wrong with him?"

I turned and put my mouth against Nico's ear, running my tongue across the array of earrings there before answering him. He shivered. "He's adorably shit-faced. Gonna be feeling it tomorrow."

Nico leaned around me to smile at my cousin. "Hey Felix, buddy. How ya feeling?"

"Your hair used to be purple," he said.

I thought Nico was going to bust something from holding back his laugh.

"Yes. Indeed it did," he said through a smile.

"And now it's like… rainbowy more. Or something." His eyebrows furrowed in confusion.

"Exactly. All the colors of the rainbow," Nico said, running his slender fingers through his mane and letting the colors peek out in the firelight. I fixated on those fingers, thinking back a few hours to where they'd last been. We'd played a rousing game of Doctor, and I'd been the lucky recipient of the prostate exam.

My dick stirred in my jeans, and I swore under my breath when Nico gave me a knowing look.

"West, are you feeling okay?" he asked all fake innocence. "Did you need a doctor?"

I groaned and turned my face into his neck. "Don't tease me, jackass," I mumbled quietly.

Nico leaned back around me to smile at Felix again. "Sorry, Felix. West isn't feeling well. I think I need to take his temperature really quickly. Be right back, okay?"

Felix swayed a little more, and I motioned to my brother Cal to come stand with him.

Nico grabbed me and pulled me toward the bunkhouse. *Oh goody, bedtime,* I thought with a grin.

Only, before opening the door to the bunkhouse, he veered sideways and dragged me around the back of the building until stopping abruptly and throwing me against the outer wall.

"What—" I began before I realized what he was doing. His hands reached for my belt buckle, and I heard the light clink of metal as he pulled it open. Cold hands reached into my underwear, and I hissed. "Jesus, baby, you're gonna shrink everything until there's nothing good left in there."

"I'll warm it back up with my mouth," he promised, lowering himself to his knees with a feral grin.

"Fuck," I gasped as his cold hands were replaced by his hot mouth. My hands came up to comb into his hair, and I looked around to make sure none of my family members were nearby.

"Someone might hear us," I choked out.

"Who the fuck cares? It's not like everyone doesn't know we're together."

I smiled down at him as he returned to his task. My fingers reached into his long locks and caressed his head.

Nico wasn't holding back. He licked and sucked and pulled as if his life depended on it, and within moments, I was coming down his throat, my teeth biting the jacket sleeve over my arm to muffle my shout.

As soon as I caught my breath, I reached into my wallet for the condom and lube and pressed it into his hand. He looked up at me with wide eyes.

"Please, Nico?" I asked. I turned around and faced the wall of the building, putting my hands out in front of me on the rough boards after shucking my pants and boxer briefs down to my thighs. My ass was hanging out in the cold night air, but I didn't care. I wanted my partner to use me for his pleasure. I wanted him to feel good.

"God, you're so fucking hot like that. I want to take a photo for our family album," he said with a laugh. His hands fumbled with the supplies until I heard the snap of latex and felt freezing cold digits brush my hole.

"Jesus fuck, that's cold. Dammit, Nico," I growled.

"You should have brought that useless baby wipes warmer piece of crap. The only thing it's good for is keeping our lube warm," he said as he pushed farther in.

I hissed and pushed back on him, wanting this part of it over as fast as possible. Once his fingers were warm inside me, they felt amazing. I loved it when Nico stretched me. He was so sweet and gentle, and he got the cutest little worry furrows over his eyes whenever he did it.

I reached a hand back for his wrist and pulled it around my front. "Enough of that shit. Get on with it."

He brought his lips to the back of my neck and laughed. "Bossy, bossy," he scolded. "I'm going to go in slow motion as long as you're giving me attitude like that."

The fat head of his cock brushed lightly against the sensitive skin of my hole, and I thought I was going to scream with impatience.

"Now you're using my words against me." I sighed. "Cruel bastard."

"What comes around, goes around, Dr. Wilde," he cooed. "Bend your knees, you big goof. You're like ten feet tall. My damned dick doesn't reach."

I did as he asked. The tip pushed farther in, and we both groaned.

"Shhh." Nico purred. "We don't want any witnesses while I make you whimper like a baby, do we?"

I let out a sound that absolutely was not a whimper.

"That's it," Nico teased in my ear. Gooseflesh was up over every inch of my skin at the sound. "That's it, West. God, you're so tight. I love running my hands over this fine ass and knowing it's mine."

His hands squeezed my ass cheeks, and I clenched around him in response, making him groan again. The first time he'd asked to top me, I'd hesitated. I was unsure whether or not I'd be okay letting go of control. But fuck if it didn't blow my damned mind. Feeling Nico's cock inside me and ceding control of my body to him was one of the most exciting milestones of our sex life so far. He knew I loved it. And there had already been nights we'd argued over who got to bottom.

But we both loved to top too, so I knew we had plenty of fun ahead of us.

My cock jumped as Nico's thrusting hit my spot, and I grabbed for the wall again.

"Fuck, baby. Right there. Gonna come." I gasped.

His inked hand came around to clamp over my mouth just as I opened it to shout his name. I felt his teeth grab into the skin at the base of my neck, and I sucked in a breath at the slight jab of pain. For some reason the sensation caused my dick to jump again and more come spilled out.

Nico's cock twitched inside me as he finished releasing, and his warm arms came around me strong and tight.

"I love you so much," he said quietly as he caught his breath.

"Does that mean you might agree to marry me some day?" I asked, knowing what his answer would be. I'd already brought it up before and noticed him blush deep red every time I did it.

"No," he said.

"Liar." I snorted, knowing with one hundred percent certainty we would be together forever.

I turned around to face him while he removed the condom, tied it off, and stuck it in a pocket. Instead of putting my arms around him, I reached under the hem of his shirt to warm my cold hands on his warm belly.

Nico sucked in a breath. "God, we should go inside. Your fingers are fucking freezing."

I ignored him and ran my hands up his chest to take advantage of his warmth. "That's what I have you for. To warm up my cold skin."

Nico's lips widened into a grin as his sparkling blue-green eyes met mine. "Speaking of your skin… I was wondering if you'd let me give you some ink."

My heart kicked up with excitement. I'd never gotten a tattoo before, but I'd known being with Nico meant it was only a matter of time.

"What exactly did you have in mind, Nicopotamus?" I teased.

"That's not a thing. Just because Felix got drunk and stupid, doesn't make that a thing now," he said with an adorable pout.

"Hmm, I'll take that into consideration. Back to the ink. Continue."

His grin returned. "The design I have in mind is circular in nature. It goes around some very delicate skin and might hurt like a bitch. But I know a doctor who can get his hands on some decent painkillers if you really need them."

Fuck. He wanted to tattoo my dick. No way.

"Nico, if you think I'm going to let you put needle near my—"

He was laughing before I could get the word out. "No, West. God. Not that. Not your precious tongue depressor. I was thinking more about one of those talented doctor fingers I like so much."

"You want to tattoo my fingers?" I pictured knuckle sets and wondered what mine would be.

L-I-V-E L-O-N-G
S-T-A-Y W-E-L-L
B-I-T-E D-O-W-N
P-L-S C-O-U-G-H
F-L-U-E S-H-O-T
L-O-L-L-I-P-O-P

"What are you doing?" Nico asked.

"Wondering what knuckle tatts I should get. Any ideas?" I asked.

"Um, West, babe… I was not picturing you with a knuckle set. I was thinking more along the lines of a simple band of ink around the third finger of your left hand."

I blinked at him.

"I mean, not… It doesn't have to be anytime soon or whatever. Just maybe someday. If you want…" He blew out a loud breath, his exhale clouding in the cold air. "Never mind."

"Oh thank god," I said with a giant sigh of relief. "For a minute there I thought you wanted me to get something epic that would require, like, a serious commitment. But a slim band on one little old finger? Pfft. No problem."

I smirked at the cutie, waiting for him to realize what I was saying.

"Really?"

"Is there room for you to get one too so we can be twinsies?" I teased.

"Shut up, jackass. I'm being serious."

I leaned down until our foreheads were pressed together. "Nico Salerno, that permanent ink has been in my skin already for weeks. If you'd like to make it visible to everyone else, I'd be more than happy to do that as soon as we wake up tomorrow. Just say the word, and I'm there. I love you. And you're the sweetest fucking thing in the entire world. The minute I can show you off as mine forever, I'll be the happiest man alive."

Nico's face widened into a grin. "Sweet talker. Have you been sipping from Felix's cup?"

"No, but I *do* like how your hair is rainbowy more," I said, running my fingers through it.

"Thank you for loving me the way I am, West."

"Thank you for coming home with me where you belong, Nico." I leaned in to kiss his beautiful face before pulling him behind me toward the door of the bunkhouse to get warm.

Felix's slur cut through the night as he approached us from the direction of the bonfire. "Yo! Wait up, guys. Nicopotamus, where'd you go?"

"Goddammit, tell him that's not a thing," Nico muttered, holding my hand.

"Face it, babe," I said with a laugh. "It's a sign you've become an official Wilde child. Whether you like it or not."

UP NEXT, follow West's cousin Felix Wilde as he travels overseas to the mysterious Gadleigh Castle in pursuit of the world's most beautiful stained glass… and an unexpected hidden royal…

Felix and the Prince, Book Two in the Forever Wilde Series

LETTER FROM LUCY

Dear Reader,

Thank you so much for reading *Facing West,* the first book in the Forever Wilde series!

Up next is *Felix and the Prince*. Follow West's cousin Felix as he goes on an adventure to a cattle... cattle... castle-type place and meets a special someone who's hiding a big secret from him.

Be sure to follow me on Amazon to be notified of new releases, and look for me on Facebook for sneak peeks of upcoming stories.

Please take a moment to write a review of Facing West on Amazon and Goodreads. Reviews can make all the difference in helping a book show up in Amazon searches.

Feel free to sign up for my newsletter, stop by www.LucyLennox.com or visit me on social media to stay in touch.

To see fun inspiration photos for all of my novels, visit my Pinterest boards.

Finally, all Lucy Lennox titles are available on audio within a month of release and are narrated by the fabulous Michael Pauley.

Happy reading!

Lucy

ABOUT THE AUTHOR

Lucy Lennox is the creator of the bestselling Made Marian series as well as the creator of three sarcastic kids. Born and raised in the southeast, she is finally putting good use to that English Lit degree.

Lucy enjoys naps, pizza, and procrastinating. She is married to someone who is better at math than romance but who makes her laugh every single day and is the best dancer in the history of ever.

She stays up way too late each night reading M/M romance because that stuff is impossible to put down.

For more information and to stay updated about future releases, please sign up for Lucy's author newsletter on her website.

For other Lucy Lennox books, please turn the page.

Connect with Lucy on social media:
www.LucyLennox.com
Lucy@LucyLennox.com

WANT MORE?

Join Lucy's Lair

Get Lucy's New Release Alerts

Like Lucy on Facebook

Follow Lucy on BookBub

Follow Lucy on Amazon

Follow Lucy on Instagram

Follow Lucy on Pinterest

Other books by Lucy:

Made Marian Series

Forever Wilde Series

Aster Valley Series

Twist of Fate Series with Sloane Kennedy

After Oscar Series with Molly Maddox

Licking Thicket Series with May Archer

Virgin Flyer

Say You'll Be Nine

Visit Lucy's website at www.LucyLennox.com for a comprehensive list of titles, audio samples, freebies, suggested reading order, and more!

CPSIA information can be obtained
at www.ICGtesting.com
Printed in the USA
LVHW050827110222
710661LV00001B/80